T0365932

Scarlett Berg

WESTBOW®
PRESS
A DIVISION OF THOMAS NELSON
& ZONDERVAN

Cover illustration by Robyn Neild.
Cover photography by MollyAnn Wymer.

WestBow Press books may be ordered through booksellers or by contacting:

WestBow Press
A Division of Thomas Nelson & Zondervan
1663 Liberty Drive
Bloomington, IN 47403
www.westbowpress.com
1 (866) 928-1240

ISBN: 978-1-4908-3837-3 (sc)
ISBN: 978-1-4908-3838-0 (hc)
ISBN: 978-1-4908-3836-6 (e)

Library of Congress Control Number: 2014909361

Printed in the United States of America.

WestBow Press rev. date: 9/18/2014

To Gary,
My husband, dearest friend,
and biggest fan; I love you.

❀   ❀   ❀

"Your adornment must not be merely external—
braiding the hair, and wearing gold jewelry, or putting
on dresses; but let it be the hidden person of the heart,
with the imperishable quality of a gentle and quiet
spirit, which is precious in the sight of God."

1 Peter 3:3-4 (NASB)

"I think playing dress-up begins at age five and
never truly ends."

–Kate Spade

Chapter 1

"Did you want whipped cream with that, miss?" the new guy behind the counter asks me for the gazillionth time. The frothy percussion of latte magic echoing from behind the counter muffles his voice.

"Oh, yes, please," I say graciously, and I give a meager smile in an effort to mask the impatient lack-of-caffeine look in my eyes.

I really can't complain. The line is moving rather quickly despite the lengthy trail of customers rapidly wrapping around the outside of the Corner Street Coffee Shop. It's controlled coffee chaos—a small taste of New York City life in motion.

"Yes for whip on that macchiato, Shelly," the new guy calls out to the other girl working frantically behind the counter. He squirts some sort of chocolate sauce on top of another drink order. Pavlov's law in action, my mouth begins to water.

I have to say, the new guy is handling the morning rush quite well. He seems only lightly frazzled yet surprisingly in control. Now, I, on the other hand, would be a complete basket case if people were barking narrative-long drink titles at me all day. Take, for instance, the blonde girl behind me, with her trendy running clothes and toned quadriceps. She orders an organic, nonfat soy blah, blah, blah. A faithful coffee shop patron, I don't even get it all myself. I wouldn't expect the new guy to either.

I wait without complaint as the welcome bell rings and another patron takes his place in line. The light breeze from outside stirs a new wave of the scent of coffee beans throughout the air. There's something energizing about this place that gets me going in the morning—I'm not sure if it's the caffeine jolt, the smell of freshly baked cinnamon rolls, or the vibrant energy of the hustle and bustle in general. I love how the cozy atmosphere here takes me back to memories of my grandmother's kitchen: cheery and inviting, with dark maple floors and sunny yellow walls. Even down to the whimsical blue-and-green paisley curtains, this place makes me feel right at home. However, Corner Street still maintains a modern vibe with stainless-steel countertops, contemporary art displayed along the walls, and art deco lighting. The style is like Giada De Laurentiis meets Paula Deen.

"Here you go—a grande extrahot macchiato with whipped cream," the new guy says, and he tightly snaps the black lid onto the yellow paper cup.

I step up to the counter, and the new guy hands me my daily contribution to the obesity epidemic. I squint to make out the small white print on his black name tag. He shifts his tall frame before I can focus. It's not the greatest day to have forgotten my contacts. I'm like a walking bad eye exam.

"Busy morning, huh?" I ask with a hint more enthusiasm.

I hate to admit it, but I definitely fall into the not-a-morning-person category. Normally, it's best not to speak to me before at least ten o'clock. I tend to be rather nonfunctioning as a human being until then. Morning coffee with a big dose of sugar mixed in has become essential to my daily survival.

"I'll say. It's pretty crazy," the new guy replies. He is slightly out of breath, yet his smooth, melodic voice resonates a sense of calm collectedness under pressure.

"You're new, right?" I ask. *Duh, like that isn't obvious.*

"Let's just say I'm a barista in progress," he replies confidently but with a modest smile. I immediately notice his striking grin, like one of those pretty people on the teeth-whitening commercials.

"If it's any consolation, I think you're doing a superb job for your first few days." I bashfully grin and push a strand of overhighlighted brown hair behind my ear.

"Thanks," the new guy says graciously, arching his eyebrows underneath his cap.

"I mean, you almost need a degree in rapid cognitive memory to work here. I would never remember who wanted whipped cream. Uh, not that your memory isn't excellent." I continue babbling when I really should be quiet. I have this nervous habit of talking just to fill up empty space.

The new guy chuckles as he looks down at me over the low glass barricade. I feel as if I should look away, but I can't help myself. Even without my contacts, I can see well enough to know he's completely adorable.

"My name's Katelyn, by the way. I come here almost every day— gotta have my caffeine fix, ya know." I giggle sheepishly.

He smiles warmly and tips the front of his tan-colored coffee-shop cap; a dark brown ringlet escapes and falls in front of his eye.

"I look forward to seeing you, Katelyn—grande extrahot macchiato with whipped cream."

I point in his direction as if he's just answered the million-dollar question. "You got it," I say. "See? You're a pro already."

Pivoting on the heel of my slightly used black-leather pumps, I give the new guy a friendly wave good-bye and turn to leave.

"I'll see ya around," I say cheerfully.

"See ya," he replies, kindly raising his hand to return the gesture. *Boy, new guy has his hands full. I do hope to see him tomorrow. He's easy on the eyes, and he'll certainly be a nice accompaniment to my daily coffee ritual.* Unfortunately, I've noticed that the turnover rate at the coffee shop seems to be pretty high. There are new guys and girls every other week, it seems. *No wonder—look at that line; I wouldn't last an hour.*

I carefully maneuver myself around the growing line of coffee drinkers waiting their turn. "Excuse me," I say politely to the old guy standing near the entrance; he's holding a copy of the latest *New York Times*.

The old guy is also a regular. He reminds me of Gandalf from the Lord of the Rings movies, except he has a shorter beard and doesn't have the long, billowing robe and wizardly powers. He likes to sit at the same corner table, sip his coffee, and intently read the paper. Then there's the goth girl; she's claimed the small booth in the opposite corner from the old guy. She's constantly pushing her unnaturally jet-black hair behind her ears, away from numerous silver body piercings. She seems a bit angry as she vigorously writes in some sort of daily journal. And of course, there's me, rushing in to grab my caffeine jolt before heading to the most boring job of all time.

"Excuse me," I repeat more firmly to the old guy. He seemingly does not want to budge, or else his hearing is bad.

Judging by his extraloud grunt, I think he has a case of selective hearing, as he moves reluctantly away from the door.

"Thank you," I begrudgingly offer, and I carefully try to squeeze my way out the front door.

I push up the sleeve around my coffee cup and readjust the strap of my one and only designer handbag—a guacamole-green and purple plaid Burberry classic. When it comes to apparel, I tend to lean toward the more "frugalista" shopping style, mostly because I have to. My measly salary will not allow otherwise. So this handbag is the exception, a splurge from when I first moved to the city. I couldn't resist its prettiness or its functionality—it was a true investment. I do live in the fashion capital of the world, and New York City has a certain way of pulling you under its hypnotic spell.

Making my way onto the busy Manhattan sidewalk, instantly, I feel the late-summer sun warm on my face, with a cool hint of fall around the corner. A light breeze flutters through my hair as I prepare to embrace what has come to be my favorite part of the morning. I open my grande cup of goodness, and the smell of heaven on earth dances through my nose. Closing my eyes, I deeply breathe in the fresh, adrenaline-boosting aroma. It sends my senses swirling.

Transfixed by the momentary indulgence, I continue to inhale the sweet, heavenly scent and begin to tip the cup upward toward my lips. A quick, jolting motion against my shoulder abruptly interrupts my first sip. Quickly opening my eyes, I see the backside of a short, robust man dressed in a gray suit. He's briskly walking away down the sidewalk and speaking forcefully on his cell phone. His large bald spot is bouncing like a moving target. The force of the bump has jostled me just enough to cause a drizzle of coffee to splash out of my cup. I watch helplessly as it splatters onto my white button-down dress shirt, and a few dribbles make their landing upon my freshly dry-cleaned pencil skirt. The mocha-colored spot unfolds noticeably darker against the lighter stone hue.

I shoot a look at him angrily. Not very Christlike of me, as my mother would say, but this guy might have ruined my best work outfit. It's obvious he doesn't care. *Look at him, still walking and talking away on his phone.* He doesn't even look back, and he certainly doesn't offer any kind of apology. *How rude!* These are the times I miss my southern roots.

I start to yell back at him just to satisfy my anger, but I realize that it won't do any good, when he's already a full block away. Disgusted, I look down at my fresh coffee stains, not sure what to do about them. Unfortunately, the coffee-splatter look is not in this season. And I'm too far from home to go change. I stand there stunned for a minute and begin to rack my brain to come up with a solution. I think I might have it as I spot a woman walking by with a bright red silk scarf wrapped around her neck. Why didn't I think of that before? A scarf is perfect. It's an added plus to most any outfit, and I wouldn't be wastefully spending. And of course, this is a true emergency. I guess you could say I have a knack for buying things I don't need. I'll consider a scarf purchase as an exception. Pondering the idea, I tap my finger against the side of my coffee cup. Goodness, it sounds tempting, but I'm already late for work, so there really isn't time for scarf buying, no matter the purpose. Besides, I don't think Louise, my meticulous boss, will appreciate another last-minute

5

shopping spree. Okay, so I'm not proud of it, but I've done that once before—but only because there was a fabulous two-hour sale at Macy's that I just couldn't pass up. Not to mention I waited an hour before sunrise for the door busters.

A few minutes pass, and I realize I can't just stand here all day thinking this spot will magically disappear. I need to start carrying one of those spot-remover pens around with me to avoid dilemmas such as these. I take one more sweeping glance at my surroundings, growing more frustrated by my current predicament. By now, I'm definitely late for work and, alas, with no miracle pen in hand. Stain or no stain, I must get on my way. I take a step forward and quickly notice another slight problem: my left foot seems to be immobile.

Perplexed by this sudden inability to move, I look down and realize that somehow my two-inch heel is carefully wedged in a deep crack in the sidewalk. I suppress the urge to moan aloud in frustration, and I hold tightly to my coffee cup. Casually, I try to move once again; the heel is still not budging—no luck. *Oh, this can't be good.* Funny, did I mention that I'm not one for drama? I'm guessing this has to be a bad dream, and I look around, wondering if an ugly monster is looming in a nearby dark alley. Where is a superhero when you need one? *Okay, don't panic, Kate,* I say to myself. *Just relax and slowly work it out. You can do this—it's just a shoe, for goodness sake.* I really don't know why these situations find me, but somehow they do, like the time in college when I walked right into a glass door, thinking it was open. I had a black-and-blue bump on my head for an entire week.

I guess the best thing here is to try to remain positive. So I calmly attempt again to wiggle the heel by rocking my foot back and forth. A good ten wiggles go by, and still no luck—it's as if I've stepped in superglue. I'm still wiggling a good five minutes later, and I'm sure that by this time, I look like a complete idiot. Not only am I not a good dancer, but now I look like a fool standing here jiggling in place with no music. Two women walk by and look at me as if I've lost my mind, neither one of them noticing that I could use a little help. And I feel like the poor Samaritan guy in the Bible story as more people stare and keep walking past me.

This is ridiculous; I have to do something. I can't stand here wiggling in place all day. The idea that I might have to abandon this shoe is not one I welcome, but at this point, I might have no other choice. I mean, these shoes are practically brand new, a classic black pump with a small heel—a great choice for any career-minded young female. The truth of matter is that it's not as if my discretionary income is bubbling over in wealth lately. I need these shoes.

I softly grin at another passerby and stop my foot from wiggling and jiggling. The young businessman glances my way, giving me a wary smile. Yes, I know I look foolish, but it's not nice to stare. I ignore him. The longer I stand here, the harder it is to try to maintain some optimism. I find this difficult as I imagine Louise at the office, standing by my cubicle like a prison guard, tirelessly watching the second hand on her wristwatch. A blaring car horn sets my heart racing, and I realize that I have to try one more last-ditch effort to dislodge this shoe. So I carefully bend down and reluctantly set my coffee on the sidewalk next to me—the thought completely disgusts me. I already want to pull out the hand sanitizer and spray at will as if a swarm of invisible bugs is attacking me. I might lose this shoe, but I will not go down without a fight, and I'm certainly not wasting my coffee.

With another deep sigh, I stand back up and slip my bare foot out of the stuck shoe. *Maybe next time I'll reconsider wearing hose,* I think as I hold my shoeless foot off the ground. *Okay, this is totally gross. Kate, please don't touch your foot on the sidewalk. I repeat: please don't touch your foot on the sidewalk.* I cringe to think of the magnitude of the bacteria infestation going on down there. I tighten my core like they tell me to do in Pilates class and then rest my bare foot against my opposite knee, as if I'm practicing my best yoga pose. Steadying myself, I begin to pull on the shoe. I have no luck at first, so I keep pulling. Unfortunately, the pulling soon proves to be futile and quickly turns to intense wiggling and yanking, all in one chaotic combined motion. I'm utterly amazed at how my mini circus act hasn't sent me falling to the ground below. I'm never this coordinated. Maybe it's some subconscious adrenaline effect as a result of intense and dire circumstances—sort of like when a hundred-pound person can lift a car off of someone trapped underneath. This is my moment. Of course I would have a moment with no one here to witness it.

Determined not to let half a pair of eighty-dollar shoes defeat me, I continue to pull with all my might. Then, suddenly, after a few more desperate yanks and a loud cracking sound, I manage to jerk the lodged shoe out of the gaping crevice. *My goodness, that was more difficult than I thought it would be.* I push my now tousled hair back from my face and attempt to regain some composure. The victory feels sweet, and I can almost hear thunderous applause in the background. So like that incredible plane landing on the Hudson, I'm immediately convinced this is a miracle of vast proportions. Okay, maybe it's not comparable, but for me, this moment is a big deal.

Letting out a huge sigh of relief, I wipe away a bead of sweat from my brow. I hesitate, however, to feel triumphant over my feat of victory when I notice the unthinkable scenario flashing before my eyes: my greatest of efforts has left me partially satisfied as I stare helplessly at only half of my shoe. I look down at the sidewalk and shake my head in disbelief. Taunting me like an unruly child, the remaining part of the black heel is still stuck in the crack.

My previously suppressed moan escapes out of my body like a rush of wind. Glancing at my partial shoe, I conclude that I should've ordered extra whip on that macchiato, with a double shot of espresso. *Looks like I'm going to need it to get through this day.* I shake my head again in frustration when a string of melodic beeps resonates upward from my purse, notifying me of an incoming text. I exhale another more muted moan and read my message: "FYI, Louise on the hunt. Where are you?"

Chapter 2

I started at *Fancy Feline* magazine almost five years ago. I know it seems stifling for a girl of my potential. I can hardly believe it myself sometimes. I'm not even that fond of cats. The small magazine—insignificant to most, if not all, dog lovers—has been my first and only job out of college. I'd had other offers, of course, but none in New York City, and there were no second or third options. For this southern girl, it was New York or bust. Ever since I was a little girl, the Big Apple always seemed glamorous to me, with its massive skyscrapers, Times Square, and the endless parade of celebrities—and who can forget about the Macy's Thanksgiving Day parade? The thrill of a massive-sized Snoopy balloon floating by on Thanksgiving Day kept me glued to my window. I just couldn't bring myself to try any alternative, even though I'd had an excellent opportunity at my small hometown *Courier Tribune*. With a deep need for some adventure, I decided to pass on the Appalachian Mountain views and head for the gray skyscrapers.

So of course, when Louise called to offer me a job, I jumped at the chance to come immerse myself in my own New York fantasy. My parents thought this to be a bit indulgent, but I had to explore the dream and live it out for myself. The grandiose ideas of star journalism, however, have quickly faded as I find myself in a job rut. I thought *Fancy Feline* would be my foot in the door of opportunity, opening to a greater world of possibility. Sadly, the foot in the door has become more like a foot stuck in the mud. I had planned to be here for only one year, gain valuable experience, and move on to bigger and better things. Somehow the one year has turned into five years, four months, two weeks, and four days of uninterrupted misery.

"Katelyn, you're late," my boss, Louise, says as I hurriedly walk through the main door, tapping her finger on her wristwatch.

"Sorry, the line at the coffee shop was out the door today," I say casually, and I quickly breeze past her. My disproportionate gait, however, slows me down a bit.

I'm late often. Some days, I can slip in without her noticing, and other days, I'm not so lucky. It's not a habit I'm proud of, and I'm working to change.

Louise peers at me through her large, round gold-rimmed glasses. "Make sure you mark it as paid time off," she says sternly, her voice slow and shaky like my eighty-one-year-old grandmother. Louise isn't eighty years old—more like in her fifties—but she sounds, moves, and dresses as if she's decades past retirement.

"Yes, Louise, I will," I say in my best subordinate manner, and I scoot into my closet of a cubicle.

My paid time off is dwindling down to nothing at this point. As I said, I really do need to work on my punctuality, or I'll be stuck here all summer with no vacation days. This year, I had my heart set on a Bahamas getaway. I've been saving all my change. My two-gallon container, which has a picture of the Atlantis Resort taped to the front, is currently a quarter of the way full. Between my tardiness and the slow progress my stash of change is making, I might be looking at a Saturday picnic in Central Park.

It's apparent right away, from the immaculately clean foyer with the cat magazines stacked precisely one on top of the other, that here at *Fancy Feline*, Louise Fletcher likes to maintain all sense of order with little deviation. She goes strictly by every word of every rule of every policy ever written in the employee manual. Louise is one of those people who can't veer away from a set standard no matter how ridiculous it might be. She likes the black and white. I tend to stray near the undefined areas. I never break the rules; I just bend and twist them a bit—you know, navigating the gray. Although my father still calls this disobedience, I call it creativity.

"Psst! Katelyn."

I glance up and see Sara Beth, fellow staff writer, peeking at me from around her adjacent cube, her grown-up blonde pigtails whipping around like propellers.

"You know we have a staff meeting in five minutes," she whispers as if she's afraid to get caught passing along top-secret information.

"Right, staff meeting in five. Sure, I remember," I say, fumbling around in my purse for my pink lipstick, as the first coat is now covering the lid of my coffee cup.

That wasn't completely true about the meeting; I did forget—intentional occupational hazard, I'm afraid. Staff meetings around here are like conferences of the living dead.

"Hey, thanks for the warning text, by the way," I call out into the cubicle wall separating me from Sara Beth. In seconds, she's slowly walking by my desk with pen and paper in hand, looking ultraprepared.

"No problem," she says. "She was asking for you, and I didn't know what to say. I would want someone to warn me."

"I really do appreciate it. Thanks."

"Anytime." Sara Beth smiles cheerily and bounces off down the hall toward the meeting room, her pigtails bobbing along beside her head.

Our small office space is located conveniently over a tiny pet shop. We can hear the barking of dogs and chirping of birds through the old, musty building's ventilation system. I'm sure I'm breathing in asbestos every day. I've thought about wearing a mask, but I don't think it would go well with my wardrobe, not to mention that it might frighten someone—well, mostly Sara Beth. She thinks she's had the bird flu twice this year.

I'm the last of the staff to walk into the conference room, still hobbling on my broken shoe. I think about breaking the other heel off for even walking, but I'm holding out hope that with some superglue, the shoe might still be salvageable. Luckily, I finally was able to knock the remaining part of my heel out of the sidewalk crack with a nearby rock. The heel is now located somewhere in the depths of my purse. Walking normally with lopsided heels is not as easy as one might think; however, I'm attempting to act as if nothing's wrong, in hopes of not drawing any unnecessary attention. I think I've almost accomplished my mission, when I hear an annoying hyena-like snort coming from the far end of the large, rectangular meeting table.

"Well, look at what the cat drug in, everybody," someone drawls.

For the second time in one day, I am inches away from dropping my coffee. Clive Peters is smirking at me from across the room. He's sitting slumped back, swaying his chair side to side with his long, lanky legs crossed over one another. Clive thinks he's important because he's our staff veterinarian—nonpracticing veterinarian, I should say. I wouldn't trust him with my stuffed bear, let alone my animal.

"Funny, Clive—very funny," I say sarcastically. "Obviously, you're not up on the latest fashion trends. I'm wearing what they call half shoes. It's on all the runways."

"Really?" says Sara Beth, her eyes wide with curiosity.

"Absolutely! It's a new take on urban wear. Pair them with a semistained blouse and skirt, and there you are—you have the perfect outfit. It's more for us organically minded," I say confidently, flinging my hair behind my shoulder and taking a seat in the back corner.

Everyone seems sort of confused and not quite sure what to make of my interpretation of urban wear. I hear whispers about the room: "Half shoes? I've never heard of them—have you?"

"That's the silliest thing I've ever heard," Clive snidely remarks with a look of bewilderment. He rubs his scrubby chin, noticeably missing his morning shave.

"I'm not sure this level of style suits you, Clive. It takes someone with, shall we say, a bit more pizzazz and sophistication," I retort.

He smirks but doesn't respond as Louise walks into the conference room. She takes her post at the front of the large cherry-wood conference table, and the room goes silent, filled with glassy, robotic stares. I open my notebook and pretend to take notes. An hour into boredom, I'm sitting in my back-row seat, jotting down a few items to get an early start on my Christmas wish list. I'm sipping the last of my grande goodness as Louise presents the latest findings on cat-toy recalls. She says she wants an article concerning the subject in next month's edition. *Yippee, I'm just dying to volunteer for that one.* As she mutters on, I can feel my head beginning to throb due to the accumulation of dying brain cells. Listening to Louise is like listening to the teacher in the old Charlie Brown cartoons—"Whah, whah, whah, whah, whah." Her voice is like a sonic tranquilizer aimed at putting us all to sleep.

"Katelyn?"

My head jerks up suddenly. Louise is looking directly at me, her eyes eager with anticipation. "Anything new?"

"Excuse me," I say, startled. My eyes widen like those of a deer caught in headlights.

"Anything new on your end?" Louise fervently repeats her question.

As a matter of fact, I did notice this darling new boutique across the street yesterday. Oh, right, that's not what's she talking about. She means with my actual job.

"Yes. Actually, I'm working on a weight-loss piece," I say, attempting to appease her interest.

"A weight-loss piece, hmmm," Louise says, and she tilts her head as if she's confused.

"You know—for your feline, of course. Well, not necessarily for *your* feline, Louise. I'm sure all of your precious kitties are in perfect health."

I'm the nutritional writer for the magazine. I still don't know how I managed to get this assignment. I know nothing about nutrition, with the exception that I know I need to eat more fruits and vegetables and that a slice of pepperoni pizza is not the best example of a balanced meal. The reality is that there is only so much one can write about when it comes to cat food.

"Weight loss for your feline," Louise says, staring blankly out one of the three windows in the office.

I can't tell if she's pleased or if she hates the idea. With Louise, it's hard to tell what emotion she's registering. Sometimes I think I have an automated machine for a supervisor.

"As responsible cat owners, individuals must recognize when their cats are overweight," I reply in my peppiest voice.

Louise continues to stare and lightly nod her head at me.

"I'm thinking of titling it 'Do You Have a Fat Cat?'" I say, tapping my pen on my flower-doodle art. Sara Beth giggles quietly in the opposite corner, and Clive coughs loudly.

Louise gives another long, silent pause before she speaks. "Interesting, Miss Turner. I look forward to reading it," she says. There is no change in her stoic expression.

"Great, me too," I say with a mustered smile. Not really—I would rather read a copy of *Science Daily*. That's saying a lot, considering I once failed chemistry in college and am horrible at math.

The meeting goes on well into the morning. My stomach keeps growling with hunger pains, and the temporarily induced attention deficit disorder is beginning to overwhelm me. As my attention drifts, my leg begins to shake, and I can't keep still in my seat; the whah, whah, whahing is ringing like a broken record in my ear. Worse, the recently consumed twenty-ounce vat of caffeinated liquid is now making its way to my bladder, increasing it to twice its size.

My squirming becomes more intense as the talk of feline issues continues for what seems like an eternity. Louise starts to review the budget as another sharp pain hits my bladder. I grimace in my seat. I look around at everyone intently listening to Louise—everyone but me. It sounds like a simple thing, just going to the restroom. Louise, however, dislikes for us to leave one of her meetings. She hates for anyone to interrupt her incredibly detailed agenda. Once Louise is thrown out of sync, it's difficult for her to find her rhythm. I do understand, but this isn't astrophysics were discussing here. I wiggle in my seat again, and I know I have to do something quickly. I'm afraid that this time, I might have to break the rule—or else things could get messy. I really don't want to be known as the employee who once tinkled in her pants in a staff meeting. Clive alone would torture me daily.

So it seems I need to make a game-time decision here. Do I become the laughingstock of *Fancy Feline* or risk the disapproving eyes of the chief kitty herself? Another searing pain in my bladder gives my answer, sending me straight up and out of my chair. Like many pleasures in life, the grande goodness has its consequences. I run—or, should I say, hobble—as if my pants are on fire to the nearest little girls' room.

Chapter 3

My brain is slowly turning to mush the longer I linger at *Fancy Feline*. It's like when you haven't used certain muscles, and they begin to atrophy. I wonder, at times, what ever happened to my passion for writing. It's seems forever buried under meaningless words about cat chow. Quietly, I walk into my small apartment. I should clarify—extrasmall; this place is smaller than some people's bathrooms in the South. Then again, this is New York City, and I'm happy with my miniscule closet apartment. I live in what was once an industrialized part of the city, now transformed into an artsier residential area referred to as DUMBO. Cute, I know, but often mistaken for the sweet little Disney elephant with extralarge ears. *DUMBO* is actually short for "down under the Manhattan Bridge overpass." So basically, I live in Brooklyn.

As expected, I find my roommate, Josie, glued to the tube in anticipation of our evening ritual, *Wake Up with Rob and Mya*. I know it's a morning show, but thank goodness for DVR. Mya Sasser, actress and talk-show host extraordinaire, recently returned after giving birth to her third child. She still looks nauseatingly gorgeous. Mya has that oh-so-cute petite frame that I'll only have in my dreams. At five nine and a half, I generally tower over most everyone. I consider myself more giant than tall, and the small frame? Forget about it. The last time I checked, I believe I was within normal limits of that body-mass-index thing. Okay, maybe I'm barely within normal limits, but who's counting anyway? The fact of the matter is that I'm not Sasser, and no matter how I wish I could squish myself down four or five inches, I never will be.

"How was the fiend feline?" Josie asks amusingly, still staring at the TV.

I grab my medicating bag of peanut M&Ms off the kitchen counter and plop down on the sofa next to her.

"Dreadful as always, not to mention I almost had a bladder meltdown near the end of our staff meeting. I excused myself without permission. Louise was in midsentence," I say, and I pop a red M&M into my mouth.

"That's never good."

"Yeah, no kidding. She called me into her office afterward and gave me the diatribe about work preparedness."

"Sounds painful," Josie says sympathetically.

"You have no idea. And all I could do was stare helplessly at her tattered red sweater and brown pants from 1985."

Josie lightly gasps. "You know, she'd be the perfect fashion victim for that show." Josie turns to me, smiling mischievously, eyebrows raised, twirling a red ringlet of hair with her finger.

I sigh. "I've thought of that before," I say, "but unfortunately, I think I need my paycheck more than Louise needs a visit from *What Not to Wear.*"

Sadly, Stacy London and Clinton Kelly probably would want to do a fashion overhaul on me as well. I do believe that I'm a few steps above Louise, but I don't think I totally have it together. I sort of buy things in pieces instead of outfits and hope they coordinate. And I highly doubt my favorite screened T-shirts and sweatpants would qualify as couture.

"Yeah, that reminds me," Josie says, looking away from Rob and Mya's opening chitchat session. "The lady from MasterCard called again."

I groan. "Seriously, why can't they just leave me alone?"

"Oh, I don't know—maybe because you owe them money," Josie answers with her usual charming sarcasm.

"Right," I say, annoyed. Like I don't know that already.

"Why don't you get a second job? You know, something temporary until you can pay off a few bills. They can always use extra help at the university," Josie offers cheerfully.

Josie's an art professor at Columbia University. She loves her job. I hate mine. She also makes more money than I do. It's hard not to be jealous.

"Sure, maybe they have something open for me at the student café. Can't you see me now in my hairnet, standing in a tray line, asking a student if they want a hot dog?" I reply.

"Okay, then think of all the money you'll save by wearing a uniform."

"Absolutely not! It gives me nightmares just thinking about it."

"Yeah, well, I don't think you'd do so well in the café anyway. I mean, look at your mac and cheese." Josie scrunches up her nose in a disgusted manor.

"What's wrong with my mac and cheese?" I ask defensively.

"Sorry, Kate. I never liked my mac burnt on the top and soggy on the bottom."

"Hey, that's a special cooking technique. It took me years to perfect it."

"You perfected it all right," she says, smirking.

Josie's right, though—I could use a second job. My credit card balance is a tad out of control. I mean, it's not quite as bad as that girl in the shopaholic movie. I can honestly say I'm not in denial. I don't have a secret credit card frozen in the back of my freezer. I check my statements each month, and they seem correct. The problem is that I'm not sure how to go about managing it—that's all. Honestly, the amount of my debt has snuck up on me. Between the daily macchiato, a couple of Broadway plays, and my favorite Burberry handbag (it was on sale), I have nearly reached the max allowable limit. Granted, it wasn't a big limit anyway, but still, I'm completely embarrassed about it—not to mention I somehow missed a payment last month. I'm not sure how that happened. I've never missed a payment. So now this strange woman, who I'm sure is calling me from a New Delhi call center, wants to chat with me about my finances. Yeah, I don't think so.

"Maybe Sasser needs a weekend babysitter? She has her hands full with three children," I say cheerfully. "Do you think she'd let me borrow her clothes?"

"First of all, if she let you borrow her clothes, you'd have to add about four inches of fabric to them. They would fit me much better. Secondly, I hate to burst your bubble, my dear friend, but I'm pretty sure that the Mya Sasser nanny job is already taken."

"Yeah, you're right. But come on, Josie—what an awesome job that would be," I say fawningly.

"I totally agree."

The commercial ends, and with a synchronized turn, we focus our gazes on the TV as if we're hypnotized, imagining for a moment what it would be like to be Sasser. Josie and I both sort of stand out in a crowd. I'm the Amazon brunette, and she has the slightly out-of-control, curly carrot-top hair. We're easily spotted in a group picture.

Josie and I finish watching *Wake Up with Rob and Mya* and finish off the large bag of M&Ms. I'm completely bloated, and it's likely my indulgence is the reason I'm having a hard time fastening the button on my jeans. I throw my coffee-stained work clothes in the laundry and decide to wear my favorite pair of tattered blue jeans and a pink Care Bear T-shirt. It's not the most grown-up outfit, I guess, but I like it.

Tonight I'm attending the young-adult group at church. I haven't gone in several months, mostly because of a bad date situation last spring. I'm not sure what it is, but I have this knack for attracting guys with varying emotional problems. My last date was no exception. For most of the summer, I've been avoiding any contact with this slightly neurotic person. I miss the fellowship of my friends, though, so it's time I face the potential awkwardness. I do have a bottle of mace in my purse just in case.

I arrive at New Garden Church a few minutes early so that I can hit the free coffee bar. Sadly, I think my day revolves around where and when I fill up on this hot caffeinated beverage. What coffee lover can resist free coffee? Okay, seriously, that's not why I come to church here; it's just an added bonus. Some might say it was an accident that I found this place. I believe it was more than a coincidence. I've noticed, even in my short lifetime, that God has a funny way of colliding our paths with others at exactly the right time. If we look for it, we can see this pattern repeat itself time and time again. The problem is that I'm usually so busy with myself that I often fail to notice what He's doing around me.

The story goes that it was a chilly Sunday morning about five years ago; I stumbled by the inconspicuous church building on my way home from Corner Street Coffee Shop. It's quite an odd structure for a church when you think of what most churches look like, with their grandiose steeples and stained-glass windows. This building doesn't look like a church at all. It's actually an old warehouse where they used to make Brillo soap pads. It's been converted into a modern sanctuary. I would've walked right by if it weren't for the refreshing worship music pouring out into the street.

This young-adult group is a varied mix of bright-eyed singles and bubbly young married couples; many of the marriages actually resulted from relationships sparked in this group. As for me, well, I've yet to have an enduring spark with anyone. I guess you could say that my Prince Charming hasn't ridden in on his white horse just yet. At this point, though, I would settle for any mode of transportation—a white horse is not particularly necessary.

"Katelyn, it's so good to see you."

I turn to the left as I stir in my second pack of sugar. Julie Parker is waving and walking toward me, her soft blonde hair bouncing on her shoulders.

"Julie, hey, it's good to be back," I say cheerfully, and I toss my stir stick into the trash can beside the table.

"We've missed you. Philip was just asking about you yesterday," she replies sweetly, and she reaches out to give me a hug.

Julie and Philip Parker are the young-adult group leaders. They're like my surrogate big brother and sister. They took care of me when I first moved to the city, introducing me to everything and showing me around. I would've been lost without them.

"I guess things were a bit awkward after my date with Carter," I whisper, looking around cautiously.

"Ah, yes, the infamous date with Carter—I had forgotten about that."

"Yes, definitely not my best date ever. Does he still come here?" I ask, still whispering.

"On occasion, I suppose. I'll see him sitting in the back. I haven't seen him yet tonight, though," Julie says reassuringly, and she takes a quick glance around the large, open room. "I think you're safe, Kate."

I sigh. "Good," I say, relieved, and I take a sip of coffee.

"I know you guys didn't necessarily hit it off, but Carter's really a good guy," Julie says as her four-year-old daughter, Chloe, suddenly comes barreling over, grips her leg, and knocks Julie slightly off balance.

"Mommy, Emma took Charlie and want give him back," Chloe says adamantly, her face bright red, one large tear rolling down her cheek.

Julie softly reaches down and gently touches the little girl's matching blonde waves. "Honey, was there a reason Emma took your horse?"

I love how mothers always search for the deeper meaning behind the action. I could never get away with anything with my two sisters.

"No! Emma's mean to me," Chloe says angrily. She crosses her arms in front of her chest.

"Chloe, did you do something to Emma? She only takes things from you when you've done something too."

"No!" Chloe's face is growing increasingly angry.

"Are you sure, sweetie?" Julie says softly, maintaining her composure.

"Emma said I was more little'wer than her. She said I couldn't sit at the big-girl table," Chloe says, gazing up at her mother, her blue eyes shining.

"Oh, I see," Julie continues patiently, still gently stroking Chloe's hair.

"I pinched her arm," Chloe says proudly, fervently placing her hands on her tiny waist.

I want to laugh, but for Julie's sake, I maintain my composure.

Julie calmly squats down until she's eye level with Chloe, her voice still soft and calm.

"Chloe, that wasn't very nice. I know Emma hurt your feelings, but we don't pinch each other, okay? Would Jesus want you to hurt Emma?" Julie asks with probing care.

Ouch, Julie's good. I hated it when my mother would toss out the "What would Jesus do?" card.

Chloe's little bottom lip pushes out in front of the upper one. "No, ma'am, Jesus would be sad," she says quietly, and she humbly hangs her head.

"Yes, sweetie, Jesus would be sad. Chloe, honey, why don't you tell Emma you're sorry and tell her Mommy said for her to give Charlie back? Now run along and play, and tell Emma that I said you can sit at the big-girl table."

"Okay." Chloe's smile returns, and she blissfully runs off as quickly as she made her way over.

"Shoo! Drama averted," Julie says cheerfully as she stands back up.

"Wow, I don't know how you do it."

"Sometimes I don't know how I do it either. It takes practice, with lots of love and prayer. I'm sorry for the interruption."

"Not a problem."

Actually, I am happy about it. I'm not interested in rehashing the Carter Stinson date.

"Katelyn, what I was saying is that I think Carter didn't mean to be so forward."

No such luck—it looks as if we're going to talk about it.

"Forward—is that what you call that? I was thinking more along the lines of crazy. You know, I did recommend a good counselor to him," I say rather proudly, twirling my finger around the side of my head.

"Kate"—Julie shakes her head—"I think you may have misjudged Carter. That's all I'm saying."

"I don't think so, Julie. One minute, Carter was acting like I was the One, and the next, he was referring to me by his ex-girlfriend's name. Then he acted like a spoiled child when I said I didn't want to go out again. There were red flags flying all over the place. Gosh, Julie, he had me thinking I was going to be in the morning headlines for another young woman gone missing. It wasn't normal."

"No, you're right. That wasn't normal. He was wrong. But I've seen Carter interact here at church, and I think he's genuinely a good guy. Maybe he's not so good with expressing his feelings with girls," she says considerately in Carter's defense.

I shake my head. "I don't know, but it was obvious that there was something missing. He's not the guy for me—that's all," I say amiably.

"That's understandable. But just remember, no guy is going to do everything the way you think he should," she says, sounding like my mother giving advice.

"I know. I just thought I would find the right guy at church." I look around at all the single men in this room and let out a small, frustrated moan.

"And maybe you will. However, don't forget that church is full of imperfect people," Julie says reassuringly, and she puts her arm around me.

I smile in response and lightly place my head on her shoulder. She squeezes me tightly and turns to walk up toward the front of the room. Julie joins Philip near the worship team. I watch her as she says something in his ear. Philip darts around, quickly spots me, and offers up a big smile and a boisterous wave, his bald head shining like a slick bowling ball underneath the stage lights. They always know how to make me feel welcome. I smile and cheerfully wave back. I take a seat somewhere in the middle of the rows of black metal chairs. Soon the worship team begins to play Chris Tomlin's "How Great Is Our God." I close my eyes, and I feel the worries of the day begin to fade away.

Chapter 4

Thursday morning, I'm walking to the Corner Street Coffee Shop, when I notice a lot of commotion going on outside the storefront. A camera crew and a few photographers hover in the background while a gray-haired beauty talks to a few reporters. She's purposely poised, taking her spot in front of a sleek black table where a brightly multicolored banner draped above her reads Runway Star.

Curiously, I glance at the commotion as I reach the front door. Honestly, I'm not surprised in the least. In fact, it's common to see a camera crew on any given day. People are always filming movies and TV shows in various parts of the city. Last week, I peeked through a barricade of cones as a crew filmed Reese Witherspoon's new romantic comedy, although I only spotted the back of her head. And last year, I participated in part of an episode of *Celebrity Apprentice*. Well, sort of—I bought a slice of pizza from the men's team. They edited me out, of course, but I think I spotted the side of my right hand paying for a slice of New York–style pepperoni pizza. The point is that you're almost immune to TV crews after a while, but they're usually not directly in front of my favorite coffee shop.

I push my way through the mass frenzy that seems to be quickly building outside. Surprisingly, the line for coffee is rather short this morning, likely due to the many people who are standing ogling out the front window. The goth girl is notably annoyed, curled up in her corner booth. I've never seen her write so quickly; she is scowling.

My eyes sweep the room, looking for the new barista guy, and to my delight, it looks as if he has survived a few more days. *This place eats people alive,* I think. I feel a slight extra beat in my heart as I walk up to the counter.

The petite girl with spiky blonde hair with blue streaks starts to take my order, when the new guy calls out to her, "Shelly, I do believe she'll have a grande extrahot macchiato with whipped cream." He winks at me and then hands a man a scrumptious-looking piece of cinnamon-and-sugar coffee cake.

Oh my goodness, how sweet is that? He remembered. I smile sort of girlishly. *Doggone it, I still can't read his nametag.* I feel sort of odd referring to my future husband as "the new guy at the coffee shop." I know that's a bit premature—my mind tends to run away from me at times.

"What's all the commotion?" I ask Shelly.

"Oh, that. Apparently, they're having a contest for the next big runway model," she answers without the least bit of enthusiasm.

"Hmm, really? I don't know—that could be fun," I tease. "It could be if you're into that sort of thing, I mean."

"I don't think so," Shelly scoffs, scrunching up her nose as if she's about to sneeze.

Maybe Shelly doesn't like models. Judging by her slightly hostile attitude, I don't think Shelly likes people in general.

"Why not?" I ask jovially.

You would have thought I had asked the magic question of the century. Shelly's eyes open wide with intensity, and she begins to answer with great urgency.

"Models contribute to the slow advancement of women's rights. Men gawk at their beautifully thin bodies, while normal women try desperately to become like them in order to turn the eyes of those men who keep them down."

"Interesting," I say less earnestly.

Wow, I do believe Shelly's a tad bitter. I bet she could use a macchiato.

"So I gather you're not trying out then?" I reply with some sarcasm.

Shelly rolls her eyes and asks if she can help the next person in line. *Oops. I didn't mean to offend her, but some people need to lighten up a bit,* I think. *How could a modeling contest hurt anybody? It could be fun. Not for me, of course. I'm not model material. I have the height but not the body. Then again, maybe Shelly has a point. Let's think about this for a moment. Average girl turns famous model, inspiring young girls around the world. It could make a fabulous story. I'd be just the person to write it. Hmmm, and just maybe this could finally be my ticket out of the cat circus.* Then I stop myself. *Kate, what are you thinking? That's crazy talk. I don't want to be in a modeling contest.*

"Grande, extrahot." A soothing male voice wakes me from my contemplation.

I look up to meet a pair of deep chocolaty-brown eyes. *Oh, it's extrahot all right,* I think to myself. He is handsome in an Orlando Bloomish, *Pirates of the Caribbean* sort of way minus the eye patch and sword.

"It's Katelyn, right?" the new guy asks as he pulls down the lever on the latte machine. I hear sounds of a frothy brew from behind the counter.

"Yes. I'm impressed you remembered," I say with a hint of surprise.

"Macchiatos are my favorite too," he replies cheerfully. "And you forgot your Corner Street Bonus Card. We kept it here behind the counter."

He pulls out a little blue-and-green plastic card from the recesses of the countertop and kindly hands it to me. My name is nicely printed across the front.

Bummer, I think. *I guess Mr. Right didn't remember my name.* My hopes slightly deflate. *Okay, so I'll at least give him some credit for remembering the drink order—much more complicated but not as personal.*

"I'm glad to see you're still around," I say with a smile.

"Thanks. What can I say? I'm a fast learner," the new guy says, reaching up for a lid to place on a coffee cup.

"I can see that. Survival of the fittest, you know—that's what I think," I reply merrily.

I start to linger longer, staring at the new guy's dreamy eyes, when I feel Gandalf's evil twin behind me, his eyes boring into the back of my head. Why are people so impatient? Can't he see I'm having a conversation here with an attractive man? This doesn't happen often.

"Are you going to try out for the model show?" the new guy asks, pointing outside at the mayhem.

I giggle sheepishly. "No, um … Oh, I don't know. I doubt I'm what they're looking for."

"You should go for it. Don't sell yourself short. I think you'd have a great shot," he says optimistically, and he raises one eyebrow, handing me my macchiato.

My face becomes hot, and I know I must be bright red with embarrassment. "Really? You think so? I'm not so sure."

The old guy grunts twice and clears his throat. I take the hint.

"I guess I better get going. Will I see you here tomorrow?" I say.

"Same time, same place, I'll be here." The new guy flashes a warm smile, his tall frame hovering above me—a rare event.

Okay, it's official. This guy is absolutely adorable. I feel my entire body want to melt. I almost begin to skip out the front door, immersed in my own daydream of the new guy riding gallantly in on that white horse. I look up just in time to avoid bumping into a pretty petite blonde woman as she makes her way into the coffee shop.

"Excuse me—I'm sorry," I say timidly as I turn her way. We make eye contact, and immediately my heart begins to race.

No. You've got to be kidding. No, it can't be. I look at her again, mouth gaping. She looks at me and smiles unassumingly. I can't believe it's really her. It's Sasser—*the* Mya Sasser.

"No problem," she softly answers. Her voice is just as sweet and angelic as it sounds on TV.

Stunned speechless, I can only nervously smile at her response. *This is your chance, Kate. Speak.* I swallow hard. A voice from inside continues to push—*Go ahead and speak. What's wrong with you?* For some reason, my mouth is open, but no words will come out. I stand there gaping at her as if she is an alien from another planet. Once again, I start to speak, trying to find the right words to say, but then it's too late. Her entourage comes barreling in behind her, followed by the camera crew, and quickly pushes me out of the way.

Unbelievable. A once-in-a-lifetime opportunity, and I mess it up royally. I'm hardly ever at a loss for words. This might have been my one and only chance to have a conversation with Sasser, and I've blown it. *Josie's going to kill me.*

I wonder what she's doing at my favorite coffee shop. I continue to stand in the doorway as people push their way around me. Starstruck, I stare at her as she orders what I think sounds like a nonfat chai latte. Mya's wearing the cutest retro-style navy polka-dot wrap dress with red patent-leather high heels that match the belt cinched tightly around her miniscule waist. It's darling. I'm dressed in the only black pantsuit I own. Actually, it's the only suit I own, and it's slightly outdated. I hate to admit it, but it was my mother's before she retired. I like it because it's the only time I can get away with wearing my Tinkerbelle T-shirt to work. When I wear the jacket all day, all others see is the yellow part of Tinkerbelle's hair and the light green tip of her fairy wings—totally work professional.

Thoroughly depressed by my cat-got-your-tongue moment, I step outside to leave. The beautiful gray-haired woman by the table is talking to a reporter. I check my cell for the time, and amazingly, thanks to the extrashort line this morning, I have a few extra minutes. So I stop to listen.

"Can anyone sign up for the contest?" the reporter asks with composed excitement.

"Yes, of course, any young woman between the ages of eighteen and twenty-eight who has a dream to be a model," the silver-haired beauty answers with a sultry, confident voice that pairs fittingly with her tall, thin frame.

"What are they competing for, Camilla?"

"These girls will be competing to win a chance to become America's next Runway Star and a two-hundred-fifty-thousand-dollar contract with my world-renowned modeling agency, Sparks International, as well as the opportunity to meet Mya Sasser and other celebrity models."

Now, that makes complete sense. Why else would Mya Sasser be at this coffee shop?

"What is Mya Sasser's involvement in the contest?" the bubbly reporter asks, as if she's just read my mind. She holds the microphone closer to Camilla. Camilla is noticeably uncomfortable with the invasion of personal space as she awkwardly takes two steps back.

"Mya has graciously agreed to host the show for us this year. We're honored to have her. She's here today to help kick off our model search."

My favorite celebrity is going to host a model search. Maybe I need to consider trying out for this thing after all. That's so silly. I mean, I probably wouldn't make it past the first round. Okay, but then again, does that really matter? I'd get to meet Mya. After my pitiful performance today, I have to redeem myself, don't I? And Lord knows I could certainly use that quarter of a million dollars. Miracles do happen.

"Tell us, Camilla—what do the model hopefuls need to do to try out?" the reporter asks eagerly.

"Kelly, we'll be having our first-round auditions starting this weekend on the campus of Columbia University. We'll be looking for the best and brightest," Camilla says with perfect poise, tilting her head upward toward the camera as if she's being photographed herself.

"Thanks, Camilla," Kelly cheerily replies, and she turns back to face the camera. "You've heard it live here first, ladies. Come on out to Columbia University this weekend for your chance to be the next Runway Star. This is Kelly Short, Channel Three News."

I may not be the next super model, but I'm most definitely going to meet Mya Sasser. Watch out America, you're about to meet Katelyn Turner. Suddenly, I start to feel an overwhelming sense of excitement. Or it could be that I've completely lost my mind. My head is spinning with ideas, like the time I decided to try out for *Annie* in our middle school theater. This time, I promise myself I will not do anything silly, such as dying my hair red with food coloring. Rust orange is not a good look, and it doesn't come out in only a few washes.

I head down the street in the opposite direction, toward *Fancy Feline*. I take a sip of coffee, almost burn my tongue, and luckily catch myself before I stumble and fall. I never said I was graceful.

❀   ❀   ❀

"You said *what?*" Josie says in shock, her amber eyes about to bulge out of her head.

"I said nothing," I answer solemnly.

"You said nothing?"

Josie is now pacing aimlessly around the apartment and biting her nails. I think she's picking up my nervous habits.

"I said nothing."

"You were practically rubbing shoulders with Mya Sasser, and you didn't say one word."

"I know—it's terrible, isn't it?" I open my hands in disbelief and drop my head in shame.

Josie walks into the kitchen, opens the old white cabinet door, and takes out a box of Cocoa Puffs cereal.

"I'm so disappointed in you, Katelyn," Josie says between bites. She's shaking her head and sounding like my father would if he ever knew about the balance on my credit card.

"I wasn't thinking. I couldn't think. It was like my mind went totally blank. Completely out of character for me, I know."

"I'll say," she says, appalled, and she crams a handful of cereal into her mouth.

31

"All these people came rushing in after her, and I got lost in the crowd. I did hear her order a nonfat chai latte, though."

"Weally? I wuff thosf," Josie says blissfully, placing her hand over her mouthful of cereal.

I rise from sitting on the couch and walk over to our small peephole of a window; the light blue paint is chipping off around the window ledge. Likely, judging by the age of this building and the layers of paint, the paint is lead based. No wonder my memory is terrible.

"It's not every day you run into Mya Sasser. You missed a golden opportunity," Josie continues, mouth momentarily free of cereal.

I turn around as Josie's giving me the stink eye.

"Don't you think I know that? You don't have to rub it in."

"Sorry, I can't help it."

"What makes you think you wouldn't have done the same thing? Everyone chokes under pressure at some time. Remember when you won Teacher of the Year and forgot to thank your parents?"

Okay, so that was low, but it's all I've got.

Josie rolls her eyes. "I guess you have a point."

"Listen, I think I may have a chance to redeem myself," I say with some assurance, opening the refrigerator door and reaching for a Coke can.

"How's that's? Did you get tickets to *Wake Up with Rob and Mya*?"

"No, but that would've been a good idea." I frown and pop the top of my soda, which makes that bubbly, effervescent sound.

"Tell me, so what's this grand idea of yours?"

"It's so much better, and I think this could be my break from *Fancy Feline*."

"Go on." Josie looks at me skeptically.

"Well, there's this show called *Runway Star*," I say excitedly.

"*Runway* what?" A look of confusion drapes Josie's face.

"It's a reality-show model contest."

"Don't they have one of those already?" Josie reaches in and pulls out another handful of chocolaty cereal balls.

"Yes, but this one's better."

"Better how?"

"Mya will be hosting the show."

"Seriouzeely?" Josie says mid–cereal crunch, her interest noticeably piqued.

"Totally serious. That's why she was at the coffee shop today. She was there promoting the auditions this weekend."

I look at her as if she already knows what I'm thinking, our minds synchronized into one idea. After four years of rooming together, we can read each other like a book.

"Katelyn, you know what this means, don't you?" Her eyes expand with excitement.

"I know. I can't pass this up, can I?"

"I'll torture you forever if you do," she says fervently, putting down the Cocoa Puffs.

"But I'm not modeling material. Look at me," I say uncertainly, and I do a whooshing motion with my hands, almost tipping over the tall white metal lamp beside the couch.

Josie shakes her head to disagree. "Kate, it's not that you're not model material. I mean, not all models look like Gisele. Some models aren't even pretty. I think all you need is some polishing. You've got the tall thing working for you, of course. All the other stuff you can learn."

I'm not sure if I should consider any of that a compliment.

"Can I learn it all by this weekend?"

"You can learn enough to get your foot in the door."

"Who's going to teach me?"

Josie exaggeratedly clears her throat.

"You?" I ask apprehensively, and I cross my arms in front of my chest.

"Yes, of course, me. I knew all those hours of watching celebrity TV would come in handy one day," Josie says as she twirls around dramatically and throws her hands in the air. "I'm going to make you a star."

I try not to laugh as she skips gleefully across the living room. "Okay, Coach," I say, "what do you suggest we do first?" I place my hands on my waist skeptically, looking at my new fashion guru.

"First thing is that we need to get you some head shots."

"Head shots? What's that? That sounds terrible." I look at her, confused and frightened.

"Kate, don't be silly. Head shots are photographs of you presented in a portfolio."

Thank goodness. I'm relieved; I was starting to think someone was going to be pointing a rifle at my head.

"Where would one get head shots?" I ask. "I'm sure they're expensive."

"Not to worry, my friend. I can get my kids in the art studio to help us out. I have several students in need of some extra credit."

"Great. What should I wear?"

"Hmmm. Well, that may be a problem," Josie says, intently crossing her arms and walking in a circle around me, inquisitively looking me up and down.

"Why?" I try to turn with her as she completes her assessment.

"Well, definitely something other than sweatpants and your Care Bear T-shirt—that's for sure."

I touch my hand to my heart. "What's wrong with Cheer Bear?"

"As pajamas maybe. When we were seven," Josie says teasingly, trying not to laugh.

I stick out my tongue at her. *How rude!* "So, Miss Fashion Queen, what do you suggest?"

"I'm thinking something vintage."

"Vintage?" I look back at her with furrowed brow. "Then why don't I just ask Louise to borrow something from her closet?"

Josie shakes her head. "Not that kind of vintage. Chic vintage. I was thinking we could hit some stores down in SoHo," she says assuredly.

"Okay, but as long as I don't look like Charlie's Angels or something."

"Oh Kate, that's a great idea."

"Josie?" I say with a hint of trepidation.

"Just trust me."

"I'm not so sure, but okay, Coach." I salute her. "Bring on the glam."

I bite my tongue, keeping silent, as Josie begins to talk about my fashion makeover. She pulls out her latest issue of *Vogue* and begins marking various pages for reference. With her natural flair for creativity, Josie's style is more hip and contemporary than mine on any of my best fashion days. I cringe at the idea, however, of relinquishing complete control of my wardrobe. Some might say this need for control is only a reflection of other areas of my life. That could be true, but is it so wrong that I don't want to look like a bad version of a 1970s television star? I can be fashionable and relevant.

"What about this?" Josie points to a picture of a girl in white platform boots. *Wait. On second thought ...*

Chapter 5

It's possible that I have created a tiny fashion conundrum with the idea of half shoes. I mention this as I notice Sara Beth teetering down the hall of *Fancy Feline*. She looks to be wearing a pair of patent-leather Big Bird–yellow high heels. One heel of her shoes is drastically shorter than the other. The closer she gets, judging by the horrendous-looking jagged edges, it appears she sawed down the heel with a kitchen knife. Her powder-pink blouse has a random yellow stain on the upper left corner. I smile to myself and think, *I have to give her credit for color coordinating.*

"Good morning," I say, restraining my laughter as Sara Beth meets me along the narrow corridor. "Nice shoes."

"Morning," Sara Beth says, cheerier than normal. "Thanks so much, Katelyn, for the fashion tip. It's funny, though. I do believe the whole town is sold out of half shoes. I couldn't find them anywhere."

"You don't say." *Oh my, what have I done?*

"I know; I couldn't believe it," she says, surprised, and then she begins to teeter to one side. She catches herself on the ash-gray wall. "So I made my own pair."

"Wow. You made them yourself." I point down toward her mutilated shoes.

"I sure did. And the shirt too," she says, proudly touching her blouse. "Yellow mustard," she whispers.

"Really, that's quite impressive. Very creative and organically minded of you," I offer, trying not to snicker.

I can't believe she believed me. No, what I can't believe is that she ruined a perfectly good pair of shoes.

"Thanks," Sara Beth happily replies in her high-pitched voice. She sputters off down the hall, wobbling all the way.

My goodness, I have to fix this. I have always known Sara Beth is slightly naive, but this is a whole new level of innocence. It's not right to let her walk around wearing hacked-up shoes. *I really should say something.* Quickly, I turn to follow her. I'm not sure how I'm going to reverse the damage, but I hope something clever will come to mind.

"Well, if it ain't Queen Teeter-Totter herself."

How lovely. Clive emerges like a scoundrel from a recessed hallway, his Hawaiian shirt unbuttoned one too many. Gross—I see chest hair.

"And good morning to you too," I say sarcastically. "How was the luau?"

He laughs heartily. "Nice one, Turner. You know, I like your spunk. Sometimes," he says, smirking, and he sashays closer, cornering me next to the office copier. He leans in next to my ear, smelling like my grandpa's musty Stetson aftershave. "I'll let you in on a little secret," he says, his voice low and creepy.

I cough and pull away. "What's that, Clive?"

He leans in again, his dull green eyes wide and fixed on mine. "It would've been a much better luau if you had been there in a grass skirt and a couple of coconuts."

I cough violently as if something's stuck in my throat and begin to ease away around the copier. *How disgusting.* I'm totally mortified, and now I could use a sanitizing shower. Certainly not wanting to continue this conversation, I ignore the comment and decide to return to my desk in search of a cup of water. I can feel Clive's eyes on me as I walk. Yuck—see what I'm talking about? I attract men with issues. A forty-four-year-old man who still lives with his mother definitely has issues.

We're a half hour into our weekly staff meeting, and I can feel the rumblings of stomach pains. Luckily, I have at least half my macchiato left to savor, although a banana-nut muffin sounds scrumptious. Oh, and I made sure I visited the little girls' room before we started, so as to not disturb Louise in all her glory. Louise goes over the budget for another half hour and then asks for updates on our current article statuses. I finished my "How Fat Is Your Cat?" article a week ago.

My ears perk up as Louise begins to discuss an idea about a new section in our magazine. It will be geared toward interviewing famous local celebrity cat lovers within or around the city. I have to admit this is the first interesting idea Louise has had in years. Clive boldly speaks up and says he can snag an interview with former mayor Giuliani. Apparently, they go to the same gym. Even if it's true, I seriously doubt that Giuliani is going to stop and talk to a tall, scary-looking man wearing Globe Trotter shorts, knee-high white socks, and a sweatband. The only reason I know his workout attire is because Clive changes into his gym clothes before he leaves for the day. I usually have to cover my eyes.

I'm still pondering Louise's grand celebrity article idea, when my mouth begins to speak before my brain can stop the words escaping from my mouth.

"I can get an interview with Mya Sasser," I say confidently.

Sara Beth gasps loudly along with a few other hushed shrills scattered around the room.

"Katelyn, did you mean Mya Sasser from the morning talk show?" Louise asks, surprised.

I'm shocked she actually knows whom I'm referring to. I always imagine Louise sitting around with her cats, watching recorded episodes of *Days of Our Lives*.

I hastily look around the room. *Did I just say that out loud? Wait a minute. What am I saying? This is brilliant.*

"Yes, Louise. Mya Sasser from *Wake Up with Rob and Mya*," I say, lightly tapping my pen on my doodling pad.

"I didn't know Mya had any cats," says Susie, our know-it-all girl from HR.

She doesn't, but I didn't exactly say I was going to interview Mya about cats. I ignore the statement.

"Katelyn, I think that sounds like a great idea," Louise optimistically agrees. "When could you have this ready for print?"

Let's see, the modeling contest will be over in three months, so maybe December—that is, if I last that long.

"I think it would be a great way to start off the new year. What do you think?"

Louise stops for a moment. Her expression, as always, is hard to decipher, but I think I see a smile starting to break, the corners of her lips turning slightly upward. She's thinking and nodding her head, and there it is—a full-on smile. It might be one out of a handful all year.

"Yes, I think that sounds like a great idea. We'll make the Mya Sasser interview a prime feature in our January issue."

"Great," I reply cheerily. "I'll get started right away."

The only problem here is that Mya has two dogs, Roscoe and Daisy, and a hamster named Boss Hog (apparently, she loves *Dukes of Hazard*). How do I know this? She's posted this information on her Facebook page. I promise I'm not a celebrity stalker. Okay, so maybe I could buy the dogs a couple of cat costumes. However, there is this little minor detail of a modeling contest, and somehow I've got to tie the two together. An interview with Sasser is a good start.

The entire office is buzzing all day about my article with Mya. All of a sudden, I seem to be the newest *Fancy Feline* rising star. I smile at the irony, when my cell phone rings somewhere in the bottom of my purse. I dig around until I spot its bright purple metal case and stop at the crosswalk as traffic zooms through the intersection of West Fifty-Seventh and Ninth Avenue.

"Hello?" I answer, readjusting my bag onto my shoulder.

"Katelyn," my father says in a tone I immediately recognize as serious and disappointed.

I sigh heavily before I reply. I feel a bad phone connection coming on.

"Hey, Daddy, it's good to hear your voice," I say casually, as if I haven't noticed his unpleasant mood.

"Katelyn, I have something of importance to discuss with you, my dear."

See? I knew it was bad. My father, bless his soul, usually never calls just to chat.

"What's on your mind?"

"Katelyn, are you in financial trouble?"

My father is a man of urgency. Well, I could use a little more incoming cash flow, but I wouldn't characterize it on the scale of the Fannie and Freddie Mac downfall, as his tone infers.

"Not really. I could always use a raise, but I'm doing okay. Why?"

"I received a phone call from a Sylvie from MasterCard yesterday."

"You did? That's odd."

Sylvie's been calling for a few weeks. I've paid that bill, and I wish she would stop hounding me. How did they find my father? That's scary—they'll track you down anywhere, won't they? They certainly don't tell you about that when you innocently sign up for these little pieces of plastic. It must be there in the ultrafine print: "If you fail to make a payment, you'll be tracked down like a common criminal." I never really wanted a credit card. A long while ago, like many college freshman, I was hypnotized by the lure of a free T-shirt with the application. Once you have credit, it's hard not to use it; it would be sort of like someone offering you a hot-and-now Krispy Kreme doughnut and you letting it sit there untouched.

"Oh, that Sylvie. She's a persistent little one, isn't she?" I say jokingly.

"Now, Katelyn, if you're having trouble paying your bills, we can certainly have a look at your budget."

Are you kidding? I really don't need an audit from my father. He's incredibly thorough and worse than Louise. On his budget, there would be no shopping, and I'd be drinking instant coffee for an entire year.

"I had a bit of a problem last month. Somehow I forgot to pay one bill. Oops! I'm sure it happens to everyone." I embarrassingly giggle.

There's only silence from the other end. I'm sure my father doesn't agree. I look up and cross the street with the large group of fellow pedestrians who have been waiting on the street corner.

"Dad, I appreciate your concern. I can assure you that everything is taken care of. I'm up to date on all my bills."

"I'm glad to hear that, sweetheart. Your mother and I worry about you so far away from us."

Dad wasn't happy about my decision to move to New York, and he loves to remind me when he can. My father loves his girls, and I'm lucky for that, so I choose to not pay attention to the gentle reminders.

"No problem, Daddy. Thank you for checking up on me. I love you."

"I love you too, Kate. Take care of yourself, will you? Talk to you soon."

Geez! That was stressful. I hang up the phone and keep walking. I know I need to work on my budgeting skills—I can't deny it. I certainly don't want my father calling about late payments on my credit card—yet another reason it would be nice to win this competition. *Me—a supermodel? I must be delusional.*

❀ ❀ ❀

Today is the first day of the *Runway Star* tryouts. Josie has spent all morning glamming me up for my big modeling debut. I have to give her credit: I don't look half bad. Actually, I look highly fashionable. I'm wearing vintage, of course. Josie has paired a kelly-green, mod '60s cable-knit sweater dress with a large, wide black belt and a pair of black knee-high boots. She has pulled my long, usually shapeless hair up into a sleek ponytail and added a wide black headband. Apparently, the style shows off my high cheekbones. I never knew I had those.

We have worked all week on putting together the portfolio Josie said I would need to make a good impression. I feel sort of narcissistic putting together a scrapbook of pictures of just myself. Josie's art students took the photographs around campus. Surprisingly, they didn't come out half bad either. I've never thought of myself as anything but average, but I could certainly pass for pretty in these pictures. I even question if they were perhaps photoshopped to make me more presentable. When I asked, I received an overwhelming no, but I had to verify any fraudulent activity.

The line for the tryouts is ridiculously long. I have never seen so many girls in one place before. There have to be at least a thousand—girls of all different shapes and sizes, waiting for their own big break at stardom. In a line wrapped around the main auditorium on campus, I stand for what seems like days, waiting to get inside. Glancing around, I can't help but notice the interesting mix of girls who are here to audition. It's amazing what we will do to ourselves to be noticed. One girl about five in front of me is dressed in a black patent-leather catsuit. I'm guessing they're not interested in Halloween costumes for this contest. Then again, they might mistake me for a sixties go-go dancer.

After three hours of waiting outside, I finally get into the main entrance of this old institution of learning. The never-ending line continues into the large brick building. It reminds me of when I was a kid one summer at Disney World. The five of us—Mom, Dad, my two sisters, and I—were waiting to get on the popular It's a Small World ride. My little sister, Kelsey, fainted from the ninety-degree heat, and they allowed us to pass everyone in line. I wonder if that would work here—probably not. It's seventy-one degrees, sunny, and beautiful.

Inside, there's more frenzy as the inner workings of the show are evident throughout the room. Television camera guys are carefully meandering through the crowd of contestants and following them to different predesignated stations. Stagehands are directing others regarding where to go and talking into their headpieces. Huge stage lights are set up at each corner of the foyer, illuminating the unfolding scene. I can feel the excitement oozing all around. I watch the organized chaos and continue to scan the room for a glimpse of Sasser. *Is she here?* I wonder. *What am I going to say this time?* I can't just stare at her again with my deer-in-the-headlight eyes. This might be my only chance for a second Mya encounter. Who knows how long this modeling experience will last? Looking around me, I can see that I have some fierce competition. There are some stunningly beautiful girls scattered about; I already feel like I might be out of my league.

Five exhausting hours pass by, and I've almost read an entire novel by the time I make it to the first station. The pale-looking young man sitting at the registration table looks about as thrilled to be here as my father does when my mother drags him to the shopping mall. The man adjusts his skinny gray tie as if he's choking. I pull out my ID from my wallet, smile, and gingerly hand it to him.

"Please print your name and age here," the young man says unenthusiastically. He points his long, bony finger toward the next empty line on the sign-in sheet and pushes his black metal-framed glasses back on his nose.

"Lots of girls here today," I say merrily, hoping to make him feel better as I take his red plastic pen.

"Yes," he says. He still has no expression on his face other than absolute boredom.

I can't help but feel a bit sorry for him. *Poor guy. He looks like he hasn't eaten in days—sort of like several of my competitors here.*

"Most guys would kill for this opportunity," I continue, probing to get a positive reaction.

"Most guys would, yes," he grimly replies, still with no expression, as he writes my name and contestant number on a name tag.

"Okay. Uh, well, nice chatting with you," I say.

I should introduce him to Shelly at the coffee shop; they'd be a perfect match.

He looks at me bleakly and hands me the name tag. "You too."

I attempt one more forced smile again with no response from the name-tag guy and walk to the next station. Model hopefuls eager to get to their next destination continue to pass me on either side as I pause to pull the paper backing off my name tag. Before I can finish, I spot Sasser about thirty feet away by the main auditorium door. She's chatting with someone from the set crew. I feel giddy inside; here's my second chance. Maybe I should go talk with her. *That's easy, right? No biggie. So what do I say? I could tell her what a huge fan I am and how much I admire her work—but everyone says that, I'm sure. No, I need to be more original.*

I continue to stare at Mya as I'm contemplating something clever to say, when I realize my fingers are stuck to the backing of my name tag. I start to pull off the backing and drop the whole thing on the floor. I roll my eyes and sigh as I reach down for it. *Typical.* Before I can secure it in my hand, it begins to shuffle between the feet of people passing by, almost as if the name tag is willing itself away from me. I want to yell out, "Stop! I need that name tag," as I wait for a stagehand to walk by. I lose sight of the tag for a few seconds, and then my eyes fall on it coming to rest right in the middle of the walkway. I start to walk toward it and then cringe as a girl in four-inch heels steps on it, leaving a nice gash in the left-hand corner of the paper.

Another slew of girls flow on, and I finally see a momentary break in the crowd. I have to retrieve it, or else I'll be nameless and numberless. I start to make my way over, when a man, in phantomlike fashion, swoops down and picks up the now wrinkled and tattered name tag. *Oh, thank goodness.* I smile with delight as he stands up, tag in hand. I'm immediately taken aback by his roguish good looks—he's quite a contrast to the previous guy at the registration table. I feel a little faint as I watch him straighten the bottom of his black corduroy blazer with suede elbow patches. He pushes the strap of a large camera bag back onto his shoulder as he glances around. As his crystal-blue eyes come to rest on mine, I feel for a moment as if he's just rescued me.

"This must be yours," his says, eyebrows arched.

"Ah, there it is," I say playfully, trying to downplay my near panic, twirling the tip of my ponytail. I wonder if he saw the whole fiasco.

He briefly glances down at the tag and then gives an almost impish grin. "Good luck, Katelyn."

I gently take the crinkled tag from his hand. "Thank you," I mutter, my face red with embarrassment.

He casually nods and keeps walking. I turn around in a whirlwind, trying to get another glimpse of him as he confidently swaggers away. Hypnotized, I can't stop watching him walk through the crowd. He disappears out the main doors, and I stand there as if a bolt of lightning has hit me. The phantom guy has certainly made a chivalrous first impression. Staring after him, I feel another girl brush by me, pushing her way through the crowd, and I slightly break from my trance. An announcement is made on the overhead speakers that complimentary lunch will be provided in the school cafeteria for all potential contestants. The thought of nourishment helps me refocus on the task at hand; I attempt to press out the battered name tag and stick it on my shirt. I feel as if I'm forgetting something. Then I see a picture of Mya Sasser underneath a *Runway Star* banner. I twist around; she's gone, of course.

Following the posted signs, I make my way to my next designated area for the tryouts. The gold arrows lead me to a more intimate room where the atmosphere is less chaotic; it is calm and strangely quiet, like a testing center. Inside the room, six round tables are set up. Another student volunteer is standing at the door and hands me what looks like a questionnaire. I scan it briefly as I walk toward an empty table. I hate filling out stuff like this, but I guess this is just part of the process. Sitting down at a table in the back of the room, I begin to read over the four-page packet. The first few questions seem easy enough: name, age, address, etc.—all the essential questions. Flipping to the second page, however, I notice that the questions begin to get a tad more personal. "What is your current height and weight?" *Can they ask that? Okay, well this is a modeling contest. Why would I want to tell a host full of modeling critics my weight? The things we'll do, right? Josie owes me big-time.* I write "five nine and a half" for height, and for the sake of vanity, I decide to round down for my weight. I cringe even as I write the number. Let's just say it's more than it should be.

I hear the sound of a bracelet clinking and look up to see a strikingly beautiful girl sit down beside me, her ebony skin glowing like bronze.

"Hello," she says kindly.

I'm relieved. *Finally, a friendly face around here.*

"Hello," I reply cheerfully.

"This is so exciting, isn't it?" Her expression is one of pure joy and delight as her large gold-hoop earrings lightly jiggle next to her sassy bob haircut.

"Yes, very exciting. I've never seen so many girls in one place before."

"I know. I've been waiting for almost six hours."

"Me too. It's absolutely crazy. Have you read over this questionnaire?"

"No." She looks at me, concerned. "Why?"

"They want to know some personal things," I whisper.

"Really?" She looks scared. "Like what?"

"Like how much you weigh."

"Oh, my boyfriend doesn't even know how much I weigh."

"Well, he will now."

She frowns. I feel guilty for making her feel self-conscious.

"Hey, you have nothing to worry about," I say encouragingly, hoping to make up for my negativity. "You have an incredible figure."

She smiles. "Thank you."

"You're welcome. It's true, though. You're gorgeous. You'll have no problem making it on the show." I reach out to shake her hand. "My name's Katelyn."

"Deidra."

"It's nice to meet you."

"It's nice to meet you, Katelyn."

"Good luck today. I hope we'll be seeing more of each other."

"Thanks, me too. And good luck to you."

"Thanks, I need all the luck I can get." I grin and look down to finish filling out the monster questionnaire.

"Can you two take your chatting somewhere else? Some of us are trying to think here." A sharp female voice projects from the other side of the room.

Deidra and I both turn to meet a pair of stone-cold emerald eyes. It's another haunting beauty—this one has silky fiery-red hair flowing over her tall, extralean frame and translucently fair shoulders. *Where do they breed these girls? I really don't belong here.* I feel like hiding under the table.

Neither Deidra nor I respond to the red-haired beauty. Obviously, some of our competitors do not welcome friendly banter. Deidra sits down at my table, and we both return to diligently filling out our questionnaires. I slowly make my way through all the questions, which include "What is your current occupation?" and "Are you in school?" They want to know where we're from and about our family lives. Thank goodness my family is normal for the most part— my immediate family anyway. I have a few cousins with criminal records, something to do with defacing property—specifically, graffiti, I believe—but I'll not mention those. So I answer simply, "I'm the middle of three sisters. My mother and father have been married for thirty years. I left the South in search of the Big Apple to start my writing career."

After what seems like an endless array of questions, I get to the final one, which is in large, bold print. I assume this must be important—more important than my body-fat percentage, I hope.

"Why do you want to be the next Runway Star?" That's a valid question. *Let's think about this for a minute. Should I be honest? Okay, yes, I have to be honest. I'm not here to be world famous or make oodles of money, although that would be nice. I just want to meet Mya Sasser. Oh, and I'm here for a good story. Um, probably shouldn't mention that just yet. I could say that my roommate made me do it.* I contemplate for a moment and start to tap my pen anxiously on the table. The red-haired beauty and a few other girls in the room look over at me, obviously annoyed.

"Sorry," I whisper softly. *Geez, this isn't the SAT, people.*

Focusing on the last question, I'm at a loss and grasping for an intelligent answer, when the lightbulb in my brain begins to flash. I think of sad and intense Shelly from the coffee shop. Her passionate words resonate in my mind. Quickly, I begin to write: "I want to be the next Runway Star to show the world that women are not just meant to be admired for their beauty. We should also be appreciated for our minds. I want to give young women a voice in an industry that says that beauty is only skin-deep. It's time for change."

I sound like a mantra from a presidential election. Also, I write at the bottom, "Mya Sasser is my hero." I scan over my response for a minute. Shelly would be proud.

Chapter 6

F eeling confident in my politically embellished answer, I gather up my questionnaire and once more follow the signs that lead to the final stop of the day, the auditorium. This is where I last spotted Mya. Maybe she's there inside. Anxiously, I walk in, slowly taking in the grand location. There are rows and rows of plush burgundy-colored chairs and a full balcony that encircles the upper perimeter of the room. Model hopefuls fill the large auditorium from front to back. I can feel the thick tension in the air as I look down at the throng of girls waiting their turn to go before the judges.

I notice that some dreams have already been smashed to pieces, as I pass three girls walking out with tears rolling down their cheeks. *My goodness, so the crying is real. It's like on that singing competition—I always thought it was just staged.* It's definitely not staged.

The shattering of dreams continues, as the judges have just told the next girl standing onstage that she is not what they're looking for in this competition. She looks back, pleading with the judges. "Please, you don't understand—this is my dream."

I start to feel a lump rolling up into my throat, and my stomach is beginning to turn. *How horrible!*

I try to shake my building uneasiness and take a seat beside a girl in a brown cowboy hat. Her long blonde hair is pulled over into a side ponytail, spilling like waves from under her hat.

"Hey there," she says with a noticeable Texan accent. Aside from the accent, the hat and the Texas flag on her ultrafitted T-shirt are dead giveaways as to where she's from. The Lone Star is stretched wide across her rather well-endowed chest.

"I'm Isabel. I flew all the way from San Antonio to be here," she says exuberantly while chomping on her gum. "My granny says I have great legs."

I smile glibly and take a quick glance at her sun-kissed, never-ending legs, one crossed over the other under her denim miniskirt. Her granny's right. And that's not her only good feature. My legs are long, but they look more like shapeless, pasty white blobs, and well, my chest is basically nonexistent.

"Wow, really? That's great. I'm Katelyn," I reply with moderate enthusiasm.

"Nice to meet ya. I just love modeling, don't you?"

I nod. "Yep, sure do."

A wide grin stretches across Isabel's pretty face; her eyes are wide with excitement. She's obviously happy to be here. I'm assuming, based on my initial assessment, Isabel will do well. I'm just hoping to survive the first round.

The announcers ask the next contestant to take the stage: "Vivian Hawthorne, please begin."

I look up toward the deep burgundy velvet curtain draping the background of the stage and notice that the next contestant is the red-haired beauty from earlier in the day. Isabel leans over quietly, and I can smell her cinnamon gum. "I've heard this girl has already been in three magazines. She's real good."

Of course she is. I mean, look at her—she's perfectly poised and ready to take her walk on the catwalk. She also seems to have perfected that model scowl. I don't know why models shouldn't smile; they always look mad. I read somewhere that they are trained to remain calm and show no emotion. Josie advised that I do the same and not smile. Josie's the closest thing I have to a coach, so I guess I'll take her advice. I mean, it seems to be working for ole Viv here.

Vivian continues her walk down the mock runway they've positioned on the center platform. There's no doubt the fiery redhead owns the stage. It's like watching a seasoned professional. She perfectly hits every mark, her long, lean body practically floating on air. We all watch in awe, and we know we're in the presence of greatness.

Josie and I practiced walks yesterday down the hall outside our apartment. I did pretty well, except for the turning-around part. Walking in high heels was the true test. I'm afraid I was a bit wobbly, almost twisting my ankle. In our apartment, there also wasn't a two-foot drop off on either side, as there is today, which makes me anxious. Strategically, however, the boots I'm wearing have wedge heels—more stability, less wobble. Josie says the tactic is about projecting an illusion that I know what I'm doing. At this point, that sort of feels more like a metaphor for my life than what I need to do for this contest.

After another forty-five minutes of waiting, I've heard about every beauty pageant that Isabel has ever been in since she was two years old. It's good to know I'm sitting next to the reigning Armadillo Queen—apparently, it's quite a coveted title. My ears are starting to long for some silence, and the once-filled auditorium is dwindling down to the final group of the day. I'm seriously thinking about backing out, when I hear over the loudspeaker, "Katelyn Turner." *Oh my goodness, it's my turn.* The lump in my throat now feels the size of a golf ball. I have a hard time swallowing. Why am I nervous? I love being in front of the camera. It's never bothered me before. I hosted our high school news channel and interviewed students and faculty all the time. This should be a piece of cake. Then again, people have never been solely focused on me, studying the shape of my body, how I walk, and the expression on my face. I'm much better at just talking.

I take a big breath and walk over to the judges; there are three of them. They seemed so much smaller from down in the audience. The first judge is Camilla Sparks, the modeling agent who was talking to the reporter lady the other day. She owns Sparks International Modeling Agency. From my limited research, I know that Camilla was once a model herself. She definitely knows the ins and outs of the business. I can imagine there will be no getting anything past her, and the white power suit she's wearing today seems to agree. The next judge is the gorgeous Adrianna Watts. She's currently the most photographed and celebrated model in the world, a photographer's dream, the return of the true supermodel. You hear of models and a lot of celebrities who look better on camera or in pictures than in real life. This is not the case with Adrianna. She's even more beautiful in person, with her honey-brown hair swept back behind an aqua silk scarf. So far, she's been the most merciful of the three judges, often giving encouraging advice even when she's turning someone away.

The third and final judge is beloved Italian fashion designer Gianni Botello. A quick Google search informed me that he's popular among the Hollywood A-list. He's famous for his feminine and elegant gowns; actresses flock to him for any red-carpet event. He appears exotic in his navy-blue pinstripe suit and purple button-down dress shirt, with a touch of gray sprinkled about his temples and goatee. His judging of the model hopefuls seems to have been more or less neutral, possibly because his English is limited and hard to understand.

Here goes nothing, I suppose. I take a deep breath and hand my questionnaire and portfolio to a stagehand. I've been told to go to the beginning of the catwalk behind the curtain and wait to begin my walk. I stroll past all three of them, smile, and casually wave. *Kate, really, did you have to wave? That was so silly.*

I wait patiently as the judges read through my answers and peruse my personal portfolio. I take a peek as the three of them are reading through my application of sorts. My stomach turns again as I notice Camilla scrunch up her nose at something on page two. I guess it's probably my body size she's not happy with. I cringe at the thought of them knowing my actual weight. I know it could be better. I really don't have the best of eating habits, not to mention the daily macchiatos, which I'm sure are not helping to prevent the expanding size of my hips. I look down at the floor and close my eyes to gather the last of my remaining confidence, when I hear a faint clank on the hardwood beneath me. I open my eyes and notice that one of my silver hoop earrings has fallen onto the ground. I quickly bend over to pick it up. Before I can stand back up, a stage guy breezes by me, talking into his earpiece, and he bumps me forward. It's like déjà vu from my morning name-tag chaos and the sidewalk crack the other day. Why do people knock me over all the time? Do I look invisible? I'm five nine, for goodness sakes—it should be pretty avoidable. Or maybe my size is the problem.

I lose my balance and sort of tumble down onto my knees, picking a large hole in my panty hose. I knew I shouldn't have worn panty hose. I hate panty hose. I hate them because they induce a claustrophobic-type reaction in me every time I wear them. It's awful. Josie made me wear them today because my legs are so pale. Great, this is perfect timing for a hole in the panty hose. It's the first thing they'll see. They'll think, *Poor girl. Looks like she has a run in her hose. Fingernail polish, anyone?*

"Katelyn, you're up," the stagehand announces.

I quickly put in my earring, swallow hard, and walk to the beginning of the runway. The lights are glaring brightly into my eyes. I blink, trying to focus. At this moment, all I care about is not falling. I look out and faintly make out the outline of the three judges in the distance behind the bright lights. I begin to freak out a bit, and then I hear Josie's calm voice in the back of my mind: "You can do this, Katelyn—even Cindy Crawford had to start somewhere." *Okay, I can do this! Yes, that's it. I'll pretend I'm the beautiful and classic Cindy Crawford.* I only wish I really did look like Cindy Crawford.

I stare out into the dazzling light and try to zone in on Cindy circa 1990. Hesitantly, I step out onto the catwalk. It's slightly unnerving that I can't see to the end of the platform or how much space I have on either side. Silently, I pray that I don't fall off, and I start to walk. The lights become more brilliant with each step, and I try to picture Louise tapping on her watch as if she's caught me late for work. This helps me keep from smiling, although it is hard not to smile when you're purposely trying not to smile. With a straight face, I keep walking forward. I focus my sights down the runway, blankly staring ahead, my sight fixated on Adrianna's aqua headscarf, which is now in clear view. Surprisingly, she smiles at me. It takes everything I've got not to smile back at her. I finally come to the end of the runway and abruptly have to remind myself to stop and turn. I twist my hips and pause, as Josie has shown me. Casually, I glance back over my shoulder and slightly pout my lips, still trying not to smile. Twisting back around, as I turn to leave, I look directly at Gianni and unconsciously give him a wink. *Did I just do what I think I did? I can't believe I just winked at a judge. What has gotten into me?* Suddenly, I feel a rush of adrenaline and exhilaration. I keep trying not to smile as I finish my catwalk. I hear faint applause offstage as I make my way behind the curtain. Deidra's waiting her turn. She's smiling and clapping.

"You were so great," Deidra says, still happily applauding. "Good job, Katelyn."

"Thanks." I blink hard, still a bit dazed from the contrasting lights. "It was fun."

I don't know what came over me. It really was fun. The ironic thing is that I want to go back out there and do it again. The anticipation, the walk, and then the applause—you sort of lose yourself in the moment. I feel empowered. Shelly doesn't know what's she talking about—she would love this. Okay, maybe that's pushing it, but she should try it at least once.

My momentary catwalk high is fleeting, as the stagehand points me toward the judges for my final verdict. No matter what they say, I've had a great time. I neatly fold my hands behind my back as I approach the great and mighty *Runway Star* judges.

Gianni begins with his thick Italian accent. "Nice-a job. I like-a ze way you connect with us, ze audience."

"Thank you."

I think he said he liked the way I connected with the audience. It sounded positive. I'm pleasantly surprised. It also could've been the wink.

Adrianna's critique is coming next. I brace myself again for negative comments. Adrianna pleasantly grins and playfully touches her blue head scarf while twisting in her seat.

"Katelyn, I definitely agree with Gianni—you made a real connection with us and the audience," she says in her soft-spoken British accent. "You seemed very comfortable walking down the runway. That's important in this competition."

"Thank you," I reply graciously.

Adrianna pats the red faux-leather-bound scrapbook in front of her. "Looking through your portfolio, it's obvious that the camera loves you."

"Really?"

"Oh yes, have you had much modeling experience?"

I look out into the roomful of girls now listening to my every word. "No, this is my first time."

"Impressive." Adrianna raises her perfectly arched eyebrows. "I also love the fact that you want to help create a new image for the modeling industry. I think America will love you. I hope to see more of you in this competition."

Wow, my answer worked. That's so great. Thanks, Shelly. I love Adrianna's accent. When she speaks, I imagine the two of us are sitting with the queen, having tea and scones.

"Thanks so much."

Adrianna smiles, sits back in her swivel chair, and takes a sip of her designer bottled water. *Gosh, even her water is chic.* I can see a glimmer of hope for me after all. *Not so fast, Kate—Camilla hasn't spoken yet.* Judging by her expression, I'm not sure she's going to be as kind. Two out of three isn't bad. Unfortunately, for this part of the competition, all three judges must agree for the contestant to go to the next round, so although two out of three isn't bad, it's possibly not good enough for me.

"Katelyn, dear, I will agree that you do have some basic skills necessary in modeling. You have great potential on film, and you certainly have the height needed in this industry. You also can handle the runway very well." She pauses, clears her throat, puts down her glossy red reading glasses, and looks up at me with an austere expression. "But ..."

See? Here comes the but. *That's usually not good.*

"But I have to be honest, my dear. You're simply too hefty to model couture."

Hefty—like a trash bag. I mean, let's just be real here: if you think I'm fat, just say I'm fat.

Adrianna shakes her head in apparent disagreement with Camilla's critique, and Gianni says nothing. I knew my weight would be an issue, but I didn't think I would be humiliated in front of a roomful of people—and soon to be on national television. I fear I might be getting myself into more than I've bargained for here.

Camilla looks quizzically down again at my questionnaire and sighs. "Adrianna does have one thing right, however. America will love you. You have that girl-next-door quality about you that I think is needed in this competition. We will put you through to the next round."

A giddy smile emerges on my lips, and I can hear Deidra cheer from backstage.

"But ..." Camilla begins again.

Here we go again—another but.

I brace myself for the ending, my shoulders slumped forward.

"I need to see a minimum of ten pounds gone before we start airing in three weeks. If it were up to me, I feel you need to drop twenty-five to even think about being in the finals."

I stand there speechless. I don't know if I should be excited that I'm going through or mortified that she called me fat. What show am I on—*The Biggest Loser*?

"I'll do my best. Thank you for the opportunity."

A part of me wants to defend myself, but I should be happy that they're letting me come back, so I'll leave it at that response.

"Good luck to you; we'll see you next month. Now off you go," Camilla says in haste, swooshing her hand my way to let me know she's ready to move on.

I start to walk away, when Camilla begins to speak again. "Oh, and, Katelyn, please remember to make sure there are no holes in your panty hose next time, my dear." She looks at me with a blank stare, eyebrows raised.

I guess she noticed.

I nod. "Oh, absolutely, no holes in the panty hose. You got it."

I happily smile again and then proceed to curtsy, of all things. I walk silently down the steps to the main auditorium floor. I can hear Deidra clapping again from behind the stage, and I feel as if I'm on a sugar rush. America will love me, they say. Then the word *hefty* starts to resonate in my mind—ten pounds in three weeks? I guess from now on, I'll be ordering a grande nonfat macchiato with no whipped cream. *No whipped cream? You've got to be kidding.*

Chapter 7

This can't be happening. Did I really make it onto a reality television show? I must've entered a parallel universe or something—these things never happen to me. To my recollection, I don't think I've ever won anything before. Well, let me stop myself—I haven't won anything just yet. What I don't love about all this is the idea that I somehow have to remove twenty-plus pounds of unwanted fat from my body. The ugly truth is that I guess I was becoming comfortable with my size—and let's not forget about the unhealthy eating habits. I do want to be healthy, and there's no greater motivator than a modeling contest to jump-start the process. *So let me think about this for a minute; I'll step up my cardio a bit, maybe skip dinner a few nights a week, and eat fat-free cheese. Gross. Oh well, I'll try that and see what happens.* Then again, something about my diet plan doesn't seem so nutritious. It's a starting point anyway. Besides, this is all for my chance at meeting Mya and my future career. A girl needs to learn the art of sacrifice sometimes.

I'm on my way to meet Josie and some of her colleagues and students for dinner. Several of them helped put my portfolio together, which was a great success. I'm not sure how to break the news. Josie can be a bit competitive when it comes to supporting Team Josie, no matter what cause she's supporting. She's notorious for camping out on the couch for an entire day to watch the Oscars and will stay on the phone for hours to vote for her favorite celebrity on that dancing show. I have a scary feeling she'll turn our whole apartment into a *Runway Star* call center.

We're meeting up at one of Columbia's premier college hangout spots, the Red Tavern. *Tavern* sounds a little rowdy, doesn't it? Not to worry—I'm not much of a drinker, although I'm of the opinion that never drinking alcohol doesn't make you holy or spotless. I've always thought that it's more about the condition of your heart. I think being mean and nasty is just as bad as waking up over your toilet seat and not remembering how you got there from the night before.

The Red Tavern is hopping tonight with a crowd of college students spilling outside onto the sidewalk as reggae music plays in the background. I spot Josie's red hair, like a beacon. She's standing in the corner on the tavern's connecting patio. Since there's a hint of coolness in the air, I pull on my charcoal-gray cardigan sweater and walk through the crowd. Josie sees me coming and rushes over to greet me, practically knocking down a few innocent bystanders on the way.

"Katelyn, how did it go? How'd we do?" Josie asks, slightly out of breath, as she grabs on to my shoulders. She's so excited that it seems as if she's going to pop out of her own skin.

I hang my head and then look up at her with the saddest eyes I can muster. I want to play with her head for a moment. *This should be fun—she'll forgive me later. I hope.*

"Josie, I'm sorry to have to tell you—"

"What?" Josie asks dismally, her hopes deflated. "Tell me what? Katelyn, no, don't say it." She purses her lips, takes a step back from me, and shakes her head. "Oh, you didn't make it, did you?"

I don't respond and keep looking at her with my sad eyes.

"Did you fall? I thought those heels might be a bit high for you." Josie closes her eyes and drops her head as if she's about to say a prayer.

"No, I didn't fall. It's just, well," I say, trying to sound disappointed while holding back a smile.

"I'm sorry, Kate." Josie shakes her head once more and pushes her lips out into a pout.

I pull from around my back a bright pink piece of paper. It simply reads, "*Runway Star*, Round-Two Pass." Slowly, almost reservedly, I hand it to her.

"What's this?" She looks down at it, puzzled.

A huge grin starts to emerge across my face. "Just kidding."

"What?" Her eyes grow in size.

"Josie, I made it. I made it on the show," I say, grinning.

"You made it?" She looks at me, surprised, and the color begins to return to her face.

"I made it." I keep grinning.

"I knew you could do it!" Josie says, utterly delighted, and she grabs my hands. She starts bouncing up and down, her curly red hair bouncing along with her. "*Runway Star! Runway Star!* We're going to be on *Runway Star!*" she sings.

I look around, hoping that not many restaurant patrons are paying attention to this display of excitement. Josie grabs tightly to my hand, and we quickly walk over to her art colleagues. The whole group is sitting at two black metal tables that they have pushed together. A decorative potted tree is nestled next to the tables in the corner of the patio and twinkles with white lights. All ten of Josie's art buddies are immersed in jovial conversation. One guy, with short dark hair and retro-style Buddy Holly glasses, spots us walking closer and signals our arrival to the others. As we approach, they all suddenly stop talking and turn to await the pending news. Josie smiles and dramatically whirls me around in front of her. She stands by my side and announces, as if she's doing Shakespeare in the round, "My friends, a star is born."

They all raise their glasses together and cheer for me. I decide to play along and bow modestly and blow them all kisses. "Thanks, guys, I couldn't have done it without you."

Glad that's over.

"Great. Let's eat," I say eagerly, and I turn to walk toward the patio restaurant doors.

"Not yet," she says. "We have something else to take care of first." I look at her, confused.

Josie commandingly grabs my hand again in hers and tells me, "Kate, you really had me going there for a minute." She leads me away from the shelter of our semiprivate table in the corner.

I shrug. "I couldn't help it. I wanted you to be really surprised. I figured you'd forgive me."

"Maybe." She raises her eyebrows, and a devilish grin starts to emerge at the corners of her lips. "Now that you're going to be in this contest, I think a bit of promotional celebration is in order."

"Promotion?" I ask, confused. "Josie, I think that's a bit unnecessary. Uh, I'm sure the show will do a great job with advertising."

She ignores me. "Trust me. You'll thank me later."

I think my little trick on Josie is backfiring on me. Josie proceeds to step up onto an empty chair so that she can speak to the crowd below. I start to feel as if I've lost all control of the situation.

"Hey, everybody, can I have your attention, please?" she says in grandiose fashion, tapping a fork to the side of her water glass.

I want to run away, but I seem to be immobile, although this time, my shoe isn't stuck in a crack. Conversations quickly come to a halt. I can hear people placing their drinks back on the tables and shuffling as they turn in their seats. The background music sounds louder than before, like the beat of steel drums in my chest. Slowly, I start to scoot sideways, trying to make my getaway. I turn to my left and see that I have a clear shot of the door to the restaurant. Too late—all eyes are focused on Josie.

"Now that I have everyone's attention, I would like to make a brief announcement." Josie turns toward me. I try not to give her an angry look and grit my teeth into a smile. "My friend Katelyn here is going to be on a new reality TV show. You all are in the presence of the world's next supermodel. Tune in and watch her strut down the catwalk."

No! She didn't just say that.

"Katelyn, don't be shy—turn around and face your fans," Josie boldly continues, and I can feel my face turning as red as a strawberry.

I take a deep breath and timidly twist to face the crowd.

"Folks, would you please give a round of applause for the next *Runway Star*, Miss Katelyn Turner?"

I shyly smile and say thank you, and then I wave them off as if they're making a big fuss of nothing. Geez, this is embarrassing.

Josie jumps down from her temporary platform and happily skips over to me.

"Josie, what are you doing?" I ask firmly, trying to maintain a soft voice to hide my annoyance.

"I'm getting you votes is what I'm doing," she replies confidently, her eyes gleaming.

"Thank you, but don't you think that was a little over the top?"

Josie shrugs. "Maybe, but people remember over the top. They'll vote for you."

"You think?" I roll my eyes.

Josie's right in her own eccentric sort of way, but I'm still not sure if I'm ready for her to introduce me to people as the world's next supermodel. I notice some people laughing at me and not cheering. They probably think it is all some big joke.

"Well, she certainly has my vote," I hear a familiarly smooth voice say from behind.

I turn around to a tall and handsome young man with a head of neatly trimmed, wavy dark hair. I start to gasp but quietly restrain myself when I realize it's the new guy from the Corner Street Coffee Shop, smiling down at me. Now I'm really embarrassed. Of all the places to run into him.

"Hi," I say, startled by his presence.

"Ben, so glad you could make it," Josie says welcomingly, and she leans in to hug the new guy, who now has a name.

Wait a minute. What's he doing here, and how does he know Josie? I feel as if two worlds are colliding, and my head is spinning.

"Do you two know each other?" Josie asks.

Ben glances my way and grins. "Katelyn here is my best customer down at the coffee shop."

I lightly nod in agreement. I feel woozy.

"Oh yes. The coffee shop—I should've known. Katelyn can't go a morning without it. I'm trying to convert her to green tea, but she'll not have any of it."

Coming back down to earth, I smile bashfully. "Ben makes a pretty mean macchiato."

Josie playfully punches Ben in the bicep. "I bet he does. Ben, I thought you were only working at the coffee shop temporarily. Kate, don't let Ben here fool you, whipping up those coffee drinks; this guy is ridiculously smart. Ben's working on his PhD at Columbia."

"Really?" I look at him, surprised.

Ben shrugs. "Yeah, I'm an art buff—what can I say?"

"That's amazing."

I knew this guy had to have more ambition than making cappuccinos all day. He's ditched the usual baseball work cap, which is likely why I didn't immediately recognize him. The low evening sun illuminates the natural amber highlights dispersed throughout his dark locks. I feel butterflies in my stomach.

"It looks like congratulations are in order," he says thoughtfully, and he tenderly touches my back as the butterflies swoosh around.

Man, this guy can really play havoc on my intrinsic nervous system.

"Oh, that. It's nothing, really," I say in a modest tone, waving him off with my hand.

"You should be proud of yourself. I can say one day I served coffee to a famous supermodel," he says, grinning, and he puts his hands in the pockets of his jeans. His fitted navy-blue T-shirt with a gray eagle across the shoulder coordinates nicely with his faded indigo denim.

I laugh at the idea that I'll actually become famous because of this television show. It's all too surreal at the moment. Besides, I have other intentions. I don't want to be a model. I'm a journalist—well, sort of.

Josie pulls out two chairs at a nearby empty table. "Ben, come sit down and keep Kate company." She yawns and rubs her stomach. "All this excitement has made me tired and hungry. I think I'll go inside and grab some food. Can I get you guys anything? My treat? Katelyn, how about some of your favorite chili cheese fries?"

"Sounds perfect."

My mouth almost starts to water just thinking of them. *Chili cheese fries. Wait a minute,* I think. *I can't have those. What am I saying? Who cares? Tonight I'm celebrating. Tomorrow, I diet.*

Ben takes the empty seat beside me that Josie has graciously pulled out for him. I casually glance over as he sits down and pull my sweater in tighter to my body. The night air is starting to become a bit chilly, and I feel shaky—or it could be that I'm extremely nervous with Ben this close in proximity.

"She's pretty excited," I say.

"I can see that," he says with a slight chuckle.

"You know, Josie talked me into this whole thing. We are big fans of Mya Sasser from *Wake Up with Rob and Mya.*"

"Oh yeah, she's hosting the model competition. She was in the coffee shop the other day. Nice lady."

"I nearly knocked her down as I was leaving that day. I was so starstruck I couldn't speak. Totally not like me."

"I hadn't noticed," he says with a playfully sarcastic tone.

"What? I can't help it. My mouth keeps talking before my brain can tell it to stop speaking. It's been a problem since childhood—middle-child syndrome."

"You're in luck. Only-child disorder," Ben says, pointing to himself. "So I'm a great listener."

I smile at his playful banter. His deep brown eyes are fixed on mine. Casually, he slinks back into the metal chair and inquisitively crosses his arms. "So, Katelyn, aspiring model in your spare time, where do you go running off to every day from the coffee shop?"

He's not kidding—I'm usually running or close to it.

I lightly giggle and shake my head. "I'm not sure if you call what I'm doing modeling. It's more like I'm trying to stay upright while I walk on a narrow platform."

Ben laughs heartily.

I straighten my previously slouched posture. "If you must know, I'm actually an aspiring journalist."

"Ah, now, that's more like it. Not that modeling doesn't suit you, but I had you pegged for more challenging work. So tell me—what's the aspiring journalist writing about these days?"

Internally, I cringe at even revealing my pitiful excuse for journalism. Honestly, this modeling gig is far more challenging.

"Cat food," I say with forced confidence.

"Sounds intriguing." Ben smiles covertly.

"Very. You have no idea how complicated cat food can be. It's a vital part of our economy. The ratio of protein to fat—highly important." I try to hold back the laughter as I finish my thought.

It's too late—Ben and I both start to laugh. I can't help but notice the way his eyes sparkle and a faint dimple emerges on one side of his cheek. Did I mention he has the most fabulous lips?

Ben clears his throat and composes himself. "It sounds like you have very complicated work there, Miss Turner. What are you researching at the moment?"

I clear my throat to gather my composure. "I actually volunteered myself to interview Mya Sasser."

"That's great. Is she a cat lover?"

"That's where I have a bit of a problem. I have no idea if she has any kind of affinity for cats."

"I can see where that might be an issue," Ben says, looking at me curiously.

"Yes, it could be, but I'm working out the details. All jokes aside, the interview is my cover."

"Your cover? I'm confused."

"Most of the production is shot during the day, so I needed a reason to be doing the modeling contest. I sort of volunteered myself to get an exclusive interview with Mya Sasser."

"I like it," he says, nodding. "I'm curious, though, how you're going to work with the fact that she doesn't have any furry little felines scurrying around." Ben seems genuinely interested; he leans forward against the table, resting his strong chin on his hand. I feel goose bumps rise up on my arms at the shortened distance between us.

"Like I said, I'm working on it." I giggle and begin to nervously stroke the tip of my ponytail. "The truth is that I'm using this experience to write an inside story on modeling."

"Sort of like a double agent?"

I lightly slap my hand on the table. "Yes, that's it. I'm a double-agent journalist, posing as a model to write a career-boosting article. I like the way you think, Ben."

"Glad I could help," he says as the edges of his lips begin to turn up into a sly smile.

The reggae music begins to increase in cadence in the background while Ben and I continue to chat. Immersed in conversation, I'm oblivious to almost everything going on around me. We laugh about my new venture into modeling and my double-agent journalist life. I learn that Ben is graduating from Columbia in December. He loves painting, mostly a mixture of acrylic, oil, and wax on canvas. I joke and tell him it sounds like a trip to the day spa to me. He assures me it isn't and says he would love to show me some of his work sometime. I start to ask if he's asking me out, but I don't want to seem too pretentious. After graduation, he's planning on doing some traveling in Europe. Eventually, he wants to continue to teach and own his own art gallery one day. I find this out all in the span of twenty minutes or so—not too shabby. I knew my journalism skills would come in handy one day. One thing is for sure: Ben is pretty amazing.

"Here are your chili cheese fries and a large Coke," Josie says happily, returning with a basket of food in hand.

"Yummy, thanks."

"Did I interrupt something?" Josie looks at me peculiarly and then sets down the basket of fries oozing with cheddar cheese and some sort of barbecue-sauce concoction.

"No, no. We were just chatting," Ben says in a relaxed manner, and then he glances down at his watch. He seems startled by the time and starts to rise as if he's leaving. "Listen, ladies, I'm going to let you enjoy your delicious feast. I need to get going."

I reach out my hand to stop him. "No, that's okay. Please stay— have some fries, please," I say insistently.

"Really, I'd love to, but I can't. I've got a prior commitment, but I'll see you on Monday," he replies softly, and he touches my shoulder, the warm sensation again jolting through my body.

"Monday?" I say. *Did we make plans and I totally missed him asking me out?*

"A star needs her macchiato."

Wishful thinking—I had almost forgotten about the coffee shop. I smile in agreement. "Yes, she does."

Ben gives me a wink like the one I gave the Italian guy today and begins to display his nice pearly whites. I feel my face getting hot and flushed. He turns casually and walks away. I watch him as he pushes his way through the crowd, and he disappears around the corner.

"Oh la la. What's going on with you and Benny boy there?" Josie smiles shrewdly.

"Nothing," I say, as if she doesn't know what she's talking about. "He's just a new friend."

"I'll say." Josie lightly giggles. "I could feel the sparks bouncing off you two from inside."

"What?" I shake my head. "It's not like that."

"Well, he's a real sweetheart. He's got a lot of potential, that Ben Roberts." Josie raises her eyebrows as she flattens out the white paper napkin across her lap.

"Why don't you date him then?" I ask, slightly frustrated by her probing comments, and I bite down on a cheese-covered french fry.

"Oh no—me and Ben? No, no, no." Josie waves her hands as she talks. "Ben is super cute but totally not my type, more like a brother. You know how I like my lone musicians."

I roll my eyes. "Yes, I remember."

Josie's last boyfriend was a guy who referred to himself as only the Lone Horse. He had one purple shirt with a black horse on it that he wore all the time. He rarely spoke, and when he did, it was like a soft, gurgling mumble. I could never understand what he said. It was strange. I never heard him sing, but I hope his singing was better than his mumbling. Sometimes I worry about Josie.

"I heard Ben sing once, and I'm sorry to say I think he's completely tone deaf. Not pretty," Josie says as she pulls a stringy piece of cheese off a fry.

I stare off into the crowd, recalling my recent conversation with Ben, and quietly say, "Oh, he could sing to me in any tone he wants."

"What?" Josie looks at me with expanding eyes and mouth gaping.

"Did I just say that out loud?" I lightly gasp and cover my mouth with my hand.

"Aha. I knew you had a thing for Ben."

"No. I don't. I mean, I don't even know him."

"That's the point. You need to get to know him."

"Josie, I can't get involved in a relationship right now."

"What do you mean you can't get involved?" Josie asks, shocked, and she looks at me as if I've lost my mind. "He's a great catch, Katelyn, and he's a Christian."

It's ironic how Josie dangles the word *Christian* in front of me as if it's a great pair of shoes on sale. My roommate is still exploring her "religious options," as she likes to tell me. I try not to push my beliefs on her, but I never hide what I believe.

"I'm glad to hear it, but that doesn't mean he's available or interested. He told me himself that he's going to go backpacking around Europe in a few months. Besides, I can't get distracted with romance. I know you want me to stay focused on the modeling competition, don't you?"

A pensive look drapes her face. "Okay, I see your point."

I knew that would shut her up.

"Well, it doesn't mean you can't flirt with the idea, right?" Josie gives me a roguish smile. "Right?"

I sigh and lightly flip my ponytail. "A girl can dream, can't she?"

"Absolutely! Okay, Miss *Runway Star*, let's forget about romance for the moment. We have to start planning our strategy."

"Our strategy?" I ask, confused. I didn't know we needed one.

"Yes, our strategy. We're in this thing to win it," Josie says with pure conviction. Judging by the fierce look in her eyes, she means business.

"We are?" I ask, baffled again.

"Oh yes, honey, to *win* it! This is our chance to get on the inside with Mya Sasser, and let's not forget about the quarter of a million dollars." She waves a french fry in the air.

I frown. "Who said I was going to share?"

"You have to share. I'm your fashion coach, and it's in the contract."

"What contract?" I ask, puzzled. I think Josie might've lost her mind.

"Well, we'll discuss that later," Josie says as she refolds her napkin. "It's crucial that we have a strategy."

I fear she has lost her mind. But if I won, I would treat her well. I don't think she would turn down a trip to Italy, and we would definitely be moving across town to a new apartment.

"Do you honestly think I have a shot at winning? Last week, you said I was a fashion disaster." I frown again and take a sip of Coke.

"True, but anything's possible. I believe in you. Goodness, look at you—you're gorgeous. It's amazing what a great outfit and some makeup can do."

I smile modestly. "Uh, thanks, I think."

"You're welcome, sweetie."

"Oh, by the way, they said I need to lose twenty-five pounds," I say nonchalantly as I start to eat a few more chili cheese fries.

"They did?" Josie pulls the rest of my fries out of my hands.

I scowl. "Hey, wait a minute—I was eating those."

"Not now you're not," Josie says like an army lieutenant.

"Josie?"

"You're a Runway Star, Katelyn. Runway Stars don't eat chili cheese fries."

"More like *Runway Starved*," I say in disgust, and I take a sip of my Coke.

"No more soda either," Josie says, and she attempts to pull the red plastic cup from my hands. I resist, holding on to the straw with my teeth.

"Katelyn, release the Coke."

I shake my head in defiance.

"Kate, give me the Coke," she says again with determination.

Our eyes fiercely lock on each other. I bite down even harder on the straw and hold on with both hands as she continues to try to pull it away.

"Oh, look," Josie says suddenly, peering over my shoulder. "Ben's walking this way."

Unconsciously, I drop the straw and let go of my cup.

"Where?" I sharply turn around to scan the crowd for Ben.

Josie quickly grabs my soda. "Just kidding," she says, laughing.

I twist back around and give her the death stare. "I don't like you." I cross my arms, pout, and slump back in my chair.

She smiles victoriously and tells the waiter, "She'll have water, please."

Chapter 8

"**K**atelyn, honey, is this the only set of towels you have?" my mom calls from my bathroom, her southern drawl softened by the sound of running water.

My mother and little sister, Kelsey, are visiting for the weekend. This is Kelsey's first time in New York, and she's like I was the first time I came here—eyes glazed over and excited about everything. My mother is only concerned with my less-than-satisfactory housekeeping. I'm seconds away from paying for a hotel room, and they haven't even been here for two hours.

I clear my throat and attempt to choke down the growing agitation. "I'm sorry—I meant to pick up a few more towels before you got here. We can stop by the linen store sometime today if it's a problem. I do have a couple of beach towels you can use in the meantime."

My mother, God love her—and He does immensely—makes Martha Stewart look like an amateur homemaker. I've certainly not followed suit. I decorate based on whatever color makes me feel good at the moment. Mom has a theme for every room in her house with every season or holiday.

"I can't believe you're going to be on a modeling TV show. This is so cool, Kate. You'll make me the most popular girl in senior class—or the whole school, really," Kelsey says excitedly, and she sweeps her long blonde locks up into a loose knot. I try not to roll my eyes.

Kelsey's a senior in high school. She's into her status and popularity. We couldn't be more different. Kelsey will more than likely be homecoming queen. My senior year, I was president of the Future Writers of America club. We had four members.

"Katelyn, I'm not sure this is something your father and I approve of. A modeling contest doesn't sound very Christian," Mom critically comments, now coming to join us in the living room. The scent of coconut hand soap floats through the air after her. She takes a seat on the sofa next to Kelsey and disapprovingly brushes off a piece of lint onto the floor.

"Mom, I'm perfectly capable of handling myself appropriately. What a great way for me to be a good witness of my faith. As I recall, Jesus hung out with the sinners, not the saints."

"All right, I guess you have a point," Mom says begrudgingly. "Please remember, you're representing the Turner family when you're up on that stage. And I don't want to see you in any skimpy bikini." She looks at me sternly, pointing her finger as if accusing me of something I haven't even done yet.

I almost spit coffee out of my nose and sit down my cup on the kitchen counter. "Are you kidding? Absolutely no bikini. They've already told me that I'm fat."

"They didn't!" Kelsey gasps, her eyes wide.

"Camilla Sparks said I was a tad hefty for couture."

"Hefty? What does that mean?" Kelsey makes a perplexed face.

"I know. That's what I said."

"Katelyn, I did notice that you had put on some weight your last visit home," my mother says timidly.

"Mom! I can't help I inherited more of dad's genes than yours," I reply, slightly offended.

"I'm sorry, honey. I didn't mean to hurt your feelings. I just want you to be healthy."

Somehow I don't believe that to be the whole truth. I already know I'm a bit overweight, but I don't need my mother to make me feel worse. It's hard enough when both my sisters inherited the skinny genes and I've always struggled with my weight.

"This is not going to be an easy competition, and Camilla Sparks is one tough cookie. She knows what she likes. And I'm not so sure she likes me. At least I have Adrianna on my side."

"Adrianna? Do you mean *the* Adrianna Watts?" Kelsey asks, her eyes glowing with fascination.

"Yep, the one and only. And, Kelsey, she's even more beautiful in person. Plus, she's incredibly nice too." I ease down onto the blue chair next to my sister, who is notably shocked by my recent minuscule exposure to celebrity life.

"Wow, I'm so jealous," Kelsey says enthusiastically, continuing to look at me as if I'm the coolest thing since Justin Bieber.

It's strange, really. I don't remember a time when Kelsey has ever looked at me as if I'm the cool older sister. I can't help but notice how perfectly proportioned she is. I haven't seen her in a few months, and she's growing up into a pretty young lady. I think about all the weight I have to lose, and I find myself jealous of Kelsey's figure. The wrong sister is certainly in this competition.

"How's Kara doing, by the way? I haven't gotten a chance to talk to her lately," I say politely, trying to change the modeling-show subject.

"She's doing much better now that she's in her second trimester," Mom says, aglow. "Poor thing. She was sick as a dog until a few weeks ago."

Kara is expecting the first grandchild. My parents, especially my mother, couldn't be any more thrilled. Kara is our family's version of the perfect daughter. She never caused any trouble, got straight As all through high school and college, is a respected and wonderful nurse in the community, and married a man of equal reputation. Need I say more?

"I'm glad to hear that she's feeling better," I say sympathetically.

"She and Todd should find out in a few weeks whether we're having a boy or girl." My mother's eyes light up like a Christmas tree.

Here we go again. Mom's already acting as if it's her child and not Kara's baby. Judy Turner has a habit of taking over things that aren't hers to begin with—like the time she decided to plan my high school graduation party and invited twenty of my classmates who weren't even my friends.

"I hope she's having a girl. Girls are so much more fun to shop for," Kelsey replies in the superficial tone of a typical teenager as she gingerly files her fingernails.

"Knowing Kara, she probably doesn't care what it is as long as it's healthy," I sensibly reply.

It's strange to think I'll be an aunt soon. I want my nieces and nephews to remember me as fun Aunt Katelyn, the one who sneaks dessert in before dinner and who doesn't mind when they get their clothes dirty. I'll buy them all kind of fun toys, the ones that make a lot of noise.

By late afternoon, Mom and Kelsey are settled in. Mom finally stops asking for more towels or wondering where my vacuum cleaner might be. I'm assuming my carpet isn't clean enough for her liking, and I find myself already counting the hours until they leave. It's terrible, but I can only handle the two of them in small doses.

On Saturday morning, Mom makes her famous buttermilk pancakes, which are definitely not on my diet. Luckily, Josie left early this morning for an art show, and she'll not know about my overindulgence. For the remainder of the day, I show Mom and Kelsey around the city, visiting all the famous sites: the Statue of Liberty, the Empire State Building, and Central Park. To satisfy Kelsey's shopping needs, I make sure we hit Saks and Macy's to finish out our day. I pick up a new outfit for my next *Runway Star* appearance. Camilla would send me home for sure if I showed up in my faded cartoon T-shirts. I'm learning quickly that I must not only present myself well on the runway but also project the same image every day. That's what Josie says anyway.

Mostly biting my lip and keeping us all busy, I survive the weekend visit. Before their late-afternoon flight, Mom and Kelsey attend church with me on Sunday morning. I want to show my mother that she doesn't have to worry whether I'm still grounded in my faith. Mom was afraid that when I moved to New York, I would want to sow my wild oats or something. I can assure her that the only thing I've sown is five years of my life in a mind-numbing job.

I grab my mom's hand as the worship team begins to play and I smile. The contemporary style is a little different from what my mom is used to, which is the generally more traditional worship music in the church I grew up in. I look over a few times and see her singing the words that are on the big screen. Kelsey is singing in spurts, as she seems to be distracted with some boy she keeps making eye contact with in the row across from us.

As worship concludes with a modern version of "Amazing Grace," even with the strain on my nerves, I think about how good it feels to be here with family. Pastor Jacobs gives an eloquent sermon, taken from Romans 8:28, on how God works all things together for our good. I start to think about the last four years and how I got here. Despite my unhappiness with my job and my unluckiness in love, I know that even though I can't see it at this moment, God does have my best interests at heart. He's working on my behalf to bring about something positive in my life, although sometimes I wish He'd give me a little clue as to what that might be. Then again, it's highly likely I'm missing the signs along the way.

❀   ❀   ❀

"Your water is ready," Josie calls to me from the living room.

I can hear the faint whistling of the teakettle making its announcement as I turn off the water in the bathroom sink. Grabbing a towel to dry my face, now pale without my makeup, I look at my reflection in the mirror. I notice a few more freckles across my cheeks and a faint line across my forehead that doesn't seem to be going away. I have a few more years before I'm thirty. I shouldn't be getting wrinkles yet, should I? I pull my hair up like Kelsey's, swept up in a high ponytail. I wonder why I am the way I am and why my sisters turned out so effortlessly pretty. Why do I have to work so hard at everything I do? It's the constant enigma of my life.

It has been great seeing Mom and Kelsey, but I do enjoy having my bedroom to myself again. Kelsey packed enough clothes for two weeks, and her suitcases practically covered the entire floor of my compact bedroom. Now I can actually see where I'm stepping.

I sip my chamomile tea as I get online to see what's new on my Facebook page. I try not to obsess over Facebook. It's hard not to want to check it two or three times a day. I fill in my "Katelyn is doing what right now?" on my wall with "Sipping on tea and getting ready for bed." I'm not one to update my status every time I get online, and I've never quite understood the need to know what someone is doing at all times of the day, unless you're the Secret Service monitoring the president. There are some people who like to share everything—for instance, my sweet older sister, who feels she needs to give hour-by-hour updates of her pregnancy. I mean, don't get me wrong—we're all very happy for her—but do I really need to know that she was nauseated and didn't keep her lunch down today? Some things are better left unsaid.

Before signing out, I see that I have one new friend request. It can likely wait until tomorrow, but curiosity moves me to take a peek. I'm pleasantly surprised to see the request is from Ben. His thumbnail picture is smiling at me as he's standing on some grand mountain, looking as if he's just hiked Mount Everest. Seriously, what does this guy not do? I feel my heart do that skipping-a-beat thing again. Why haven't I thought of looking for him before? I should've known he'd be on Facebook. Isn't everybody? Well, except Louise, and I keep ignoring a friend request from Clive.

Without a second thought, I decide to click "confirm." My profile updates that I am now friends with Ben Roberts. I feel a bit giddy inside. It's official. It says it right here: I'm friends with Ben. I should call it a night and get off the computer, but I want to see Ben's page. Taking another sip of tea with one hand, I click on his picture with the other. Immediately, Ben's profile comes into view before my eager eyes. I scan his page; it looks as if Ben is quite the popular guy, with more than three hundred friends. Sometimes I wonder if people acquire friends just to look popular, sort of like when I would have any random person sign my yearbook in high school. Well, I must look like a total loser with my fifty-eight Facebook friends. I'm picky, you know. It's a safety precaution. I don't want any old weirdo knowing everything about me.

I type into Ben's comment box, "Ben makes the best macchiato," and post it to his wall. It feels strangely exciting to be communicating with him without a coffee counter between us. I take another sip of my tea just before signing out, when up pops my IM: "Missed you at the shop this weekend."

Oh my goodness—Ben's online. My heart starts to flutter. Should I write back? He knows I'm here. The blank line on the IM is staring at me. What if I say something stupid? And why am I panicking? I can do this. It's just a computer.

My nervous fingers begin to type.

"Mom and Sis in from NC to visit—busy playing hostess and tour guide."

Ben responds before I blink my eyes.

"I bet you make an excellent tour guide."

I laugh and quickly type back. "We didn't get lost, so I think I did pretty well for my first tour. How was your weekend? Did you paint any masterpieces?"

There's a short pause, and I take another sip of tea as I watch for a response.

"No masterpieces this weekend. A little guitar strumming maybe."

I like him better all the time.

"The guitar? No kidding. Aren't you just the modern-day Renaissance man?"

"LOL. Michelangelo—not even close. What's the saying about someone knowing a little about a lot of things but being an expert at none? That's me."

"I doubt that."

"Truth is, I play in the worship band at my church."

So Ben does go to church. This could be promising.

"What church?"

"Abundant Life Fellowship."

"Yeah. Pastor Mike Smith, right? He's spoken at my church before."

"Do you go to New Garden?"

"Yep. We have a happening young-adult group—you should come check us out sometime."

Was that too forward? I'm only suggesting.

"I should do that. So what was the sermon on today?"

I close my eyes and think about today's message.

"God working all things (even my messes) into something for my good."

"Ah, yes, Romans 8:28."

Man, this guy is good. He knows his Bible—definitely a bonus.

"Correct. God has cleaned up my messes a time or two."

"Not you, Katelyn—you seem pretty spotless. I, on the other hand, have been the prodigal son."

I can't imagine the Ben I know being anything less than perfect.

"You, a prodigal?"

"Try me. I've got some stories."

"Do you mind sharing one?"

I hope I haven't overstepped my boundaries there. I don't want to pry.

"Sure. I'm an open book."

"I must hear more then."

I'm intrigued, but this can't be much of a juicy story. There's a long pause as I wait a minute while the IM posts Ben's status as "typing."

"My dad passed away of cancer when I was seventeen. I was angry and bitter. I rebelled against God through most of college, got in lots of trouble, and broke my mother's already-broken heart. It wasn't until my mother bailed me out of jail for a DUI that I realized what a mess I was."

DUI? Not Ben! Shocked, I almost fall off my bed. Okay, so I was wrong. This is juicy—juicy and terrible all at the same time. I can't imagine what it must be like to lose your father. I start to type back but don't know what to say. Sometimes when you've known God since you were a little girl, you forget the depths of His grace.

"Katelyn, are you still there? Did I say something wrong?"

"Oh no, you didn't say anything wrong. I was trying to imagine what it must've been like for you to lose your dad. I'm so sorry, Ben."

I wipe a tear at the edge of my eye.

"It was tough, and I still miss him terribly. The good thing is that my father knew Christ, and I know I'll see him again. That gives me peace in his absence."

I don't know if I could respond with such maturity. My parents drive me crazy sometimes, but to think of life without one of them creates an empty place in my heart. I think for another moment and then type back.

"That's beautiful. There's nothing like the peace of the heavenly Father. Thank you for sharing your story with me."

"Sure. I like to talk about what God's done in my life. So enough about me. How's the world's next supermodel?"

Thank goodness. I thought I was going to have to break out some Kleenex with all that intensity.

"LOL. Praying she has a chance into the next round."

"I'm sure she does. Who could resist that pretty face of yours, Katelyn?"

I'm glad he can't see me blushing right now.

"Apparently, I have that girl-next-door quality."

"I agree. You know you have my vote."

"Thanks."

I pause, take in a big yawn, and stretch out my arms. I can barely hold my eyes open. If my mind and body would let me, I would talk to Ben all night, but I need to quit before I can no longer write coherent sentences.

"I think the pillow is calling my name. So I'm going to have to call it a night."

I wait for Ben's reply and finish off my bedtime tea.

"I understand. A girl needs her beauty rest. See you tomorrow?"

"Of course, what would I do without my coffee fix? Good night, Ben."

"Sweet dreams, Kate."

Chapter 9

"Katelyn."

"What?" I say groggily as I faintly hear someone calling my name.

Am I dreaming? I think I'm still asleep, but it's so real, as if I can feel the warmth of sunlight on my face.

"Katelyn!" The voice is now getting louder and more forceful.

I roll over, put my pillow over my head, and moan. Maybe it will go away.

"Katelyn, get up," the loud voice I now recognize as Josie's says firmly to me once more with increasing agitation.

Get up? Why? What time is it? I sit straight up in the bed and look over at my clock. It's seven thirty in the morning. *Oh no, is it Monday already?* I thought it was Saturday again. I hate it when I do that—such a letdown.

"I slept late today," I say, yawning as I rub my sleepy eyes.

"Yes, and you're going to be late for your feline friends if you don't get up," Josie says in an irritated tone.

"Yes, Mom," I reply sarcastically, teasing her.

"Kate, I'm not your mother. I'm just trying to help you get to work on time."

We've already established that I'm chronically late, but she's right. This could be pushing it.

She looks down at her watch. "Speaking of jobs, I've gotta go or I'm going to be late for mine. Now get up."

Josie hastily grabs her shiny purple tote bag, which she's placed on the floor next to my dresser.

"Yes, Mom," I teasingly say again, and I throw my pillow at her as she quickly slams my bedroom door.

Tossing the covers a side, I scramble to get out of bed and rush over to my closet to quickly find some clothes. I know I was up late chatting with Ben on Facebook. I don't even remember what time I went to bed. Oh, how I could use some grande goodness right now. My head is throbbing as I look in the mirror; my eyes are bloodshot from lack of sleep, and my hair is a tangled mess. I reach over to my dresser, grab my trusty plastic hair clip, twist up my hair disaster, and secure it all onto the back of my head. Unfortunately, there is no time to shower. Oh well, sometimes you've just got to do what you can. I grab my deodorant, rub the baby-powder-scented clear gel under both my arms, and also spray some coconut-scented body spray all over to cover the not-so-fresh odor. To finish my get-ready-in-a-hurry exercise, I gargle some minty mouthwash. Okay, not the cleanest I've ever been, but this should do for now. I grab my green purse, and like a flash, I'm out the door.

Amazingly, twenty minutes later, I arrive at work right on time. Maybe I should sleep in more often. I slip into my cubicle unnoticed by Louise on her time-clock patrol. Sitting down, I'm so out of breath that I feel as if I've just competed in a track-and-field event getting here this morning. Well, it was more like stampede. I almost took out a few innocent bystanders on my mad dash down the streets of New York. I sit calmly and take in three deep breaths to normalize my rapid heart rate and slow my breathing. I can hear Sara Beth playing the *Angry Birds* game on her cell phone.

I finally feel normal again and start my day. I smile sheepishly when Louise walks by with a pile of *Fancy Feline* magazines in hand as I spray my keyboard with the torch-like air cleaner. I love that little gadget. I use it almost every day just because it makes me feel as if I'm using a mini power tool. With keyboard all clean, I pull out my article file and then reach down to grab my coffee cup. My hand slices through the empty air and hits the desk below. *Ouch. Okay, who took my coffee?* I stand up and peek around the other cubes. *Oh, wait a minute—there is no coffee, because I didn't have time to visit the coffee shop today.* I sigh extra heavily and plop loudly down into my seat. No grande goodness—I'm depressed already.

I spend most of my morning researching information on my upcoming Mya Sasser cat story. Mostly, I'm just Googling information on Mya's new fall wardrobe tips. Apparently, metallics are going to be big this year, and I can argue this would likely apply to cat apparel as well.

As I work, I keep reaching down for my phantom coffee cup, and I begin to think of Ben. I wonder if he missed me again this morning. I finally meet a smart, great-looking, sweet guy who believes the same way I do, and I'm forced to keep him at arm's length because of a modeling contest. I must be in a parallel universe or something. Unbelievable, the luck I have sometimes. Then again, the guy is leaving for a foreign country in a few months. Who knows when or if he'll ever come back? Besides, who says he's interested in me anyway? I have a tendency to let my imagination run away with me sometimes. I might be mistaking flirting with Ben simply being a nice guy.

My stomach starts growling around eleven o'clock. Not only did I forget coffee this morning, but I also forgot to eat—definitely not a good combination. I can feel my internal engine starting to sputter, so I decide to go for an early lunch. I clock out around eleven thirty and make my way down Fifty-Seventh Street. I'm craving something grilled and light, so I opt for a yummy grilled chicken gyro and a Greek salad at Sal's Bistro. I eat there a lot because they're always nice. It's one of those places where the entire staff says hello to you as soon as you come in the door. "Welcome to Sal's," they say in unison. It's as if I'm part of the family, and it doesn't hurt that they also have the best baklava around.

I take my time eating lunch and flip through a copy of *You've Got Style* magazine. Adrianna is in countless ads scattered throughout the pages. It's hard to believe she's a real person when I see her in these photos—it's almost like a painting come to life. The idea that this kind of beauty is attainable is truly unimaginable; I don't feel that I could ever achieve it. She looks like a sculpture in one picture as she stands in an open, grass-covered field. A flowing, almost-sheer white dress loosely drapes her long, thin body, and her arms are extended toward the brilliantly blue sky like an angel. I study her serene facial expression and unconsciously try to imitate her, lifting my neck and head like a crane. It's going pretty well until I realize I'm in a restaurant and the other patrons are watching me. One elderly lady with purplish hair is definitely giving me the "you are a weirdo" eyes as she eats her Greek salad. This is likely not the best place to practice, and I must look rather silly. I decide to close my magazine, gather the rest of my things, and head back to *Fancy Feline*.

My early lunch exit from Sal's has given me just enough time for that cup of coffee I missed this morning. I turn the corner and head toward the coffee shop. I wonder if Ben is still there. Likely not, as he normally works the morning shift. Actually, it's not just coffee I need—I think I might be having Ben withdrawals as well. Breathing in the fresh fall air, I'm nearing my destination, when I happen to look over and notice my reflection in the coffee-shop window. The person staring back at me is shockingly ghastly. I look like a vagabond. I have on no makeup, and my eyes are swollen considerably from my lack of sleep. To top it all off, I'm dressed in my comfy, long patchwork skirt. This skirt looks like my grandmother sewed it together, and I paired it with a long-sleeved brown T-shirt with a large sunflower in the center. To look more professional, I threw on a taupe corduroy blazer. The result is that I look as if I just left a Woodstock reunion festival. On second thought, maybe coffee can wait.

I look up from my reflection and see Ben waving to me from behind the counter inside. *Doggone it.* He's spotted me, and it's too late to retreat. I politely wave back. I pop another piece of gum in my mouth to cover up any leftover bad breath and open the door. He winks at me when I walk in and continues helping the current customer at the counter.

Casually, I walk around and look at all the store paraphernalia while I wait for Ben to finish. Maybe I should pick up one of the store's stainless-steel coffee cups while I'm here. I love this light blue mug. A brown tree is painted on the side, with a little bird sitting on one of the branches. This wouldn't be a frivolous purchase. It's my duty to support the local economy, right? I would be saving a few trees with all the paper cups I buy. Why haven't I invested in this before? Josie's always telling me I need to be greener. I decide to grab one before I change my mind.

Walking around the product display, I look over as Ben glances my way. He gently lifts his brow slightly as if to say hello. His customer is a beautiful woman; I'm guessing she's somewhere around my age, but she's about a million times more put together. Her long auburn hair is pulled back in a sleek ponytail, and she's dressed in a black fitted suit that hugs every curve of her supertrim body. She's carrying a large red-leather Gucci bag, and she's gripping her ultrasleek iPhone in her hand. She and Ben seem comfortable in conversation. Strangely, I start to feel a spot of jealousy squeeze my heart. Why is she so cozy with Ben? I hear her giggle at something he says, and I think I feel phlegm rising in my throat.

"Thanks, Ben—so I'll see you Friday," the pretty girl says with a sultry voice. Ben hands her a coffee cup.

He smiles warmly, and I feel my heart sink. "Sure, Jessica, looking forward to it," he replies.

Who is this Jessica person? And why is he seeing her on Friday? I don't like her already. Turning to leave, Jessica takes a look at me, bleakly smiles, and gives me the once-over, glancing up and down at my tattered outfit. I smirk at her and watch her as she confidently walks toward the door. Her cell phone rings. "Jess here," she says snappishly. Her voice drifts away along with the scent of expensive lavender-and-jasmine perfume as she makes her way out the door.

"I thought you skipped out on coffee this morning," Ben says cheerily from behind the counter, still smiling, wiping down the counter.

"Overslept."

"Ah, it happens to the best of us."

"I look like I just rolled out of bed—literally."

Ben laughs. "No, not at all. I like your skirt of many colors. It's very, uh, biblical."

I lightly laugh at his insightful observation. "Now, that's an interesting way to describe it. This ensemble is left over from college."

"I'm only kidding. Katelyn, only you could make that skirt look pretty," Ben insists.

I blush and bat my eyes at his attempts to flatter me. "Funny. Thanks, I think," I say. "I'm surprised you're still here. I thought you only worked the morning shift."

"I'm working a double shift today. Shelly called in with the flu or something."

"That's too bad. Are you sure she's really sick? It could be that whole I hate-the-world vibe she's putting out."

Ben chuckles. "True. We do need to help her discover her inner peace."

"I think she should keep the blue hair, though. It totally suits her. I'm thinking about trying it myself. It would go great with this skirt." I reach down and lightly swoosh the bottom of it.

He laughs. "Nah, I think you should stick with the brunette look, although I'm sure you'd look great even in a paper sack."

He has to be kidding, right? He's such the charmer; he can't really mean that. I look down at my horrible skirt, which I'm going to give to Goodwill as soon as possible. I start to feel self-conscious.

"Thank you. I mean, that's really sweet of you to say. The truth is that you and I know I'm not exactly dressed for the runway today. I mean, not like your friend, of course."

Ben looks at me, confused. "My friend?"

"Yeah, your friend—Miss Matching Red Gucci Bag and High-Heeled Jimmy Choo Pumps." I glance toward the store window.

He chuckles again. "You mean Jessica. I don't know if you would call her a friend."

"Oh," I say hesitantly. "Well, you seemed very friendly with her—that's all."

Ben stops wiping down the counter and looks at me curiously, raising his dark eyebrows. "Why? Does that bother you?" Ben asks as leans himself over the counter closer to me.

"Bother me? What do you mean?" I look him squarely in his eyes.

"I detect a hint of jealousy, Miss Turner."

"What?" I firmly cross my arms in front of my chest.

"Are you jealous of me talking with another woman?" He proudly pulls back his shoulders, pushing out his chest.

I place my hand over my heart. "Me—jealous? Why would I be jealous?"

"I don't know. Maybe you find me likeable, Miss Turner."

"Likeable" is an understatement; I would like to be the mother of your children is more like it. I'm starting to feel uncomfortable with where this conversation is going. Ben starts to lean in again. He's close to my face, his eyes locked on mine. I want to cover my mouth. With the state of my breath, it's not a good time for this sort of personal-space invasion. I would like to brush my teeth first, and a shower might be good as well. Maybe I need to turn this topic around before my heart starts to feel more things than it already does.

"Why, yes, Mr. Roberts, I like the way you make my macchiato. You're a fantastic coffee barista."

Ben's face goes cold. That was a tad insensitive. Couldn't I have come up with a more clever diversion?

"Right, I'm just the coffee guy."

My chest starts to hurt at Ben's frosty expression. I can't let him know that I find him completely irresistible. If I do, then I'll look like a fool in a fool's skirt. Let's face it: a guy like Ben could only break my heart. It's one thing to dress me up in a fashion show, but I'll never be able to compete with a girl like Jessica. She's a goddess in stilettos.

I start to stumble over my words. "Ben, that's not what I mean. You're not just the coffee guy. I'm sorry. You know I consider you my friend, right?"

He nods calmly, adjusting his apron, which has come undone, retying it behind his back. "No need to explain. I got the point."

"You are my friend, aren't you?" I ask playfully, but I'm feeling desperate inside.

Ben leans in again, getting closer to my pale face, inches away from my nose. "Kate," he says smoothly.

I swallow hard. "Yes, Ben?"

He starts to cheekily smile, and I see a cheerful glint return to his eyes.

"I mean, who doesn't want to be friends with the world's next supermodel?"

"That's right," I say merrily, attempting to lighten the mood.

"Don't forget me when you're famous."

"How could I forget you, Ben?" I wink at him. "Now, where's a star's macchiato when she needs it?" I snap my fingers twice with a zigzag motion.

Ben lightly slaps the countertop. "Coming right up, my lady!"

"Oh, can you make that a nonfat macchiato with no whipped cream?"

Ben looks at me as if I've lost my marbles. I frown. "Okay, maybe just a little whip."

Chapter 10

It's been four weeks now that I've been preparing for my debut on *Runway Star*. A grueling four weeks it's been—well, for me anyway. What I mean is that it's been tough, mostly the workouts and dieting. And I can credit myself with the fact that I've done it all on my own. I've had no workout boot-camp experience or celebrity fitness trainer yelling in my face if I had to take a break on the treadmill while having an emotional therapy session. So far, I've lost the ten pounds recommended, along with an additional two pounds. My diet most days consists of cornflakes cereal twice a day and a turkey sandwich for lunch—sort of my own version of Special K meets the Subway diet. Right now, I'm seeing results, and I like it.

To jump-start my weight loss, I also have started visiting the gym a few extra times a week. I mostly walk on the treadmill for thirty-minute intervals, and I've tried the kickboxing class a few times. The elliptical machine was a complete disaster. I have no coordination with moving my arms and my legs at the same time. It was quite a spectacle, so I opted out on anything other than the treadmill, the StairMaster, or the stationary bike. I do, however, dearly miss my full-fat macchiatos, my favorite chili cheese fries, and chocolate doughnuts, as well as other various sugary and fat-loaded treats. I have to admit, though, I do feel better. I have more energy throughout the day and no longer seem to need that three o'clock candy bar. An apple does just as well. The best part is that my clothes are all too big for me. I think I've dropped at least one dress size. I'm practically drowning myself with the amount of water I'm consuming, which I dare say has tremendously increased my trips to the little girls' room. I'm not complaining except for the fact that I have to walk past Clive's desk more often because of the bathroom visits. Other than that inconvenience, I'm getting used to it, and it's not so bad. I think I can keep it up—for a while, I mean, at least until this competition is over. Who knows? Maybe someday I too can get into a pair of skinny jeans.

Round two begins tomorrow, and I'm pretty nervous about making the judges happy. I've met the requirements Camilla asked of me. The question remains: Is it enough? Compared to some of the other contestants, I still have a long way to go. The home audience votes begin in a few weeks, so I have to make it past the next two rounds of competition. If Adrianna is correct in her predictions and America really likes the girl next door, I think I'll have a better shot at them keeping me around. Then again, who ever really knows with these things? It could go either way. For now, I'm having fun if I don't think about actually being in a competition.

The *Runway Star* stage is located at the SBS Studios in lower Manhattan. I arrive there early for the first day of round-two competitions, wanting to make my best impression. I walk into the large building; blue-tinted glass windows surround most of the interior. The building's sleek, contemporary design is intimidating, and I haven't even made it onto the elevator.

The studio lobby is hustling and bustling with employees and apparent visitors going to their appointed destinations within the building. I decide to casually step in line with a group of four men getting onto the elevator. I walk in first and find my spot on the right side near the back as the doors close shut. Three of the four men are now standing in front of me; they're dressed in black suits and typing away on their myriad of smartphones, while the fourth gentleman is standing opposite me in the other corner of the elevator. The shiny black elevator wall nicely frames his white button-down dress shirt, dark jeans, and what looks like a black camera bag. For some reason, out of the corner of my eye, I have this strange sensation that he's watching me.

The feeling continues as the elevator begins to move. I don't want to look his way, so I keep watching the numbers ascend as we travel upward. I'm sure I'm imagining the whole thing. The elevator reaches floor ten, and the three men in black suits get off together, still texting away on their cell phones. Now it's just me standing alone with the man holding the bag. The door closes, and the elevator continues upward. I feel strangely uncomfortable.

"Excuse me, Katelyn Turner," the man says casually, breaking the silence with a smooth British accent.

Do I know this guy? I'm pretty sure I don't know anyone who's British, except for Adrianna, and we're not exactly BFFs.

Mr. Britain shifts his frame. I feel his eyes on me, and I am nearly shaking. Abruptly, I stop chewing my gum.

"You are Katelyn Turner, aren't you?"

I don't know if I should be flattered or terrified that this guy knows my name. Worst-case scenario, the elevator stalls and I'm stuck with this man, who could be a serial killer for all I know. Serial killers can dress nicely too. Okay, I'm probably completely overreacting. I awkwardly turn to blankly glance at this gentleman who apparently knows my name. I see that he has piercing blue eyes, and fashionably disheveled dirty-blond hair frames his handsome, chiseled face.

"Yes. I'm sorry—do I know you?"

I study his face, intrigued, hoping I might remember him from somewhere. Or just in case I make it out alive, I can describe him to the police. Then the memories and synapses begin to work together in my brain; it's the dreamy guy who picked up my name tag on the first day of *Runway Star*. I must say, he has an extraordinary memory. Thank goodness he doesn't want to kill me. Or wait a minute—maybe he's a handsome model stalker.

"Excuse me—where are my manners? I'm Nathan Steele, photographer for *Runway Star*. Did I startle you? I do apologize for my abrupt introduction."

Not a model stalker and doesn't want to kill me. Perfect.

I smile coyly. "Funny, I did think you were a serial killer for a brief second. And you would've been in luck. I forgot my mace today." I pat my purse.

He chuckles to himself with a deep and husky tone. "Good to know. I wish to cause you no harm, my dear," he says with air of debonair reassurance, and he reaches his hand out to greet me. His accent makes me feel as if I just walked into a scene from *Pride and Prejudice*. He'd make a fine Mr. Darcy.

I reach forward to take his hand as the elevator lightly drops onto the twenty-second floor. The jolt causes me to lose my balance, and I suddenly fall into Mr. Nathan Steele, jarring his camera bag.

"Oops! I'm so sorry," I say, embarrassed, and I look up into his amazing sea-glass-blue eyes as he keeps me from falling over. I catch his bag as it flops off his shoulder.

"That's perfectly all right, dear." He gently helps me stand back up, the elevator door now opening to our floor.

"I guess this is us." I giggle, still embarrassed by my tumble on the elevator.

Nathan readjusts the camera bag on his shoulder. "I've seen your portfolio, Katelyn. I must say that you're magnificent on film."

Magnificent? No one has ever used that adjective to describe anything about me in my entire life. It must be a British thing.

"Really? You think so?"

Like a gentleman, Nathan politely leads me out of the elevator.

"Oh, the camera loves you. I think you have a great shot at this contest."

"You do?"

"Absolutely."

"I don't know what to say—thank you, Nathan," I reply, flattered.

"You're welcome, dear. I know I look forward to getting you in front of my camera."

He smiles mischievously and opens the door for me as we enter into the *Runway Star* studio lobby. *Houston, we may have a problem here.* I'm totally infatuated. Who wouldn't be? He's a hottie British photographer.

"Good luck," he whispers.

Nathan softly grazes my arm with the side of his hand as he walks by. The touch is so subtle that I almost believe I imagined it. He continues to smile slyly and swaggers away down the long hallway. Slightly dazed and confused, I watch him walk away and disappear around the corner, when I hear someone speaking to me from the main entry.

"Miss?"

"Yes?" I answer slowly, my mind in a fog.

"Can I help you, miss?" a pretty blonde girl sitting behind the main entry desk asks.

"Oh yes, sorry—I'm Katelyn Turner. I'm here for *Runway Star.*"

"Yes, Miss Turner." She hands me an official name tag and then motions down the long corridor, like one of the girls on the *The Price Is Right* pointing to a prize door. "Please follow the hallway. They're expecting you in the last room on the right."

"Thank you. I'm sorry—I didn't catch your name."

"It's Kierstin."

Of course it is. Kierstin—such a perky name for such prettiness.

"Thank you, Kierstin."

She smiles pleasantly in response, her beautiful white teeth sparkling back at me. She must have those professionally done. They're almost glowing.

"You're welcome, Miss Turner."

I turn around and look again down the hallway, the same one I just watched Nathan disappear down. The studio is posh and glamorous. It reminds me of an exotic spa for the rich and famous. I'm just waiting for someone to come out and greet me with my own luxurious bathrobe and slippers. Large green indoor palm trees have been strategically placed throughout, giving the decor even more an atmosphere of a tropical getaway. The walls are pale green and divided throughout with frosted-glass partitions. A gray slate water fountain is the focal point on the main lobby wall area. Underneath the large square fountain sit two large white leather chairs. An oversized teak coffee table sits in front of the chairs, along with a variety of the most popular fashion magazines neatly spread across the table. Adrianna Watts is on the cover of at least three of them.

I keep staring down the hall, somewhat afraid to move. I feel like Dorothy from *The Wizard of Oz* going to meet the great and powerful wizard. I could really use a dose of lion courage right about now. I might look magnificent on film, but who knows how I will look in a real fashion show—on live television no doubt? As I stand there frozen in my own space, I hear Kierstin in her bubbly voice greet someone coming in the door.

"Hello, Ms. Sasser."

I turn quickly, and there she is—Mya Sasser. She's casually sophisticated in brown herringbone dress trousers and a matching blazer with a peach-toned blouse peeking out underneath. Her oversized Prada tortoise-shell sunglasses push back her perfectly highlighted and styled blonde hair.

Mya returns the greeting, pleasantly smiles at me, and walks down the hall.

"Is everything okay, Miss Turner?" Kierstin asks sweetly.

"Yes. I was, uh, just taking a moment."

Kierstin nods and softly smiles. The front desk phone rings, and she turns from me to answer. "Sparks International, this is Kierstin."

Breathing in deeply, I proceed down the hallway. Mya has already disappeared. This time, I'll not mention another missed opportunity to Josie. I keep walking and reach the large double doors. The doors to the studio are made of frosted glass like most of the partitions and other doors on the *Runway Star* set. Oversized brushed-nickel half-moon-shaped handles give the large doors an extra pizzazz to the entryway. Upon first observation, the expansive open floor plan resembles tropical spa meets industrial New York City loft. The ceilings are high with exposed piping painted in a brushed nickel that matches the door handles as well as most of the other fixtures throughout the space. It's contemporary style at its finest. I wonder if they have anything like this at Target. My apartment could totally use a makeover.

The walls on the large set are painted pale sea green like those in the front office. White marble tiles cover the floor. Extending out from the far back wall is a real-sized runway platform similar to the one they used onstage in the auditorium. Luckily, this one appears to be closer to the ground, which is a bit comforting. I still fear falling off. To the left of the stage are three stainless-steel stools with white leather seats. My guess is that these must be for the judges. All the chairs are identical. I'm surprised Camilla doesn't have one that is specially her own, one that might resemble a throne.

Nestled in the far left corner of the huge space is a large white drop cloth hanging from the ceiling to the floor. A large camera tripod stands boldly in front as if demanding attention. This must be Nathan's nook for photographing the models. I feel a little nervous jolt inside as I remember his words: "magnificent on film." I have a lot to live up to.

"May I take you to the other contestants, Miss Turner?" I break my gawking stare and turn to see a lady with a clear clipboard kindly smiling at me. *How does everyone know my name around here?* I look down and realize that I'm now wearing the name tag that Kierstin gave me. That answers my question, but otherwise, I feel utterly clueless.

"Yes, please," I kindly agree, and I begin to walk with her.

We make our way to the mysterious place behind the stage wall. The atmosphere quickly changes. Set workers of various kinds, including makeup artists, hairstylists, and stagehands, are scurrying all over the place. All the makeup and hairstyling booths are set up along the far wall. More glass partitions separate the dress-up side from the filming side. People are gathered in small groups and hanging out in seating areas placed neatly beside the booths.

I'm early, but other girls have already arrived. Some contestants I recognize from the first day, and some I do not. Everyone's dressed in normal attire today—no catsuits, thank goodness. I quickly spot my new friend Deidra sitting alone by a hanging rack of clothes.

She waves excitedly as I approach her. There was no question that Deidra would make it through to round two. She's even prettier than I remember her from the first day of tryouts. If anyone here fits the model profile, it's Deidra. Her gazelle-like stature, naturally sleek figure, flawless ebony skin, and exotic features exhibit any fashion designer's dream. She's going to do quite well in this competition.

"Hey, Katelyn," Deidra says, smiling brightly.

"I'm so glad you're here," I reply with relief, and I put down my green purse and my old purple backpack next to the rack of clothes.

I don't know why I brought the ratty old backpack. Josie gave me the thumbs-down. This time, I didn't give in to her objection. I guess I felt I needed a security blanket of sorts. I've carried this bag with me since middle school; it's held many of my dearest treasures over the years. And I also needed a good place to stash my SpongeBob SquarePants chewy fruit snacks. These things are only sixty calories a pack and fat free. You gotta love the fat free. They're not the best for my teeth, but at this point, I feel it's a good compromise for the calorie reduction.

"Can you believe all this? It seems so glamorous, doesn't it?" Deidra says with a look of innocence in her eyes.

"Oh yeah, it's definitely glamorous all right."

A glamorous cattle drive is more what I'm thinking. Looking around at everything, it all seems engineered and fabricated. Then again, I guess that's what TV is about, even so-called reality TV. Nothing is quite as it appears. Let's face it: television is about entertainment. It's an audience's way of escaping from the mundane, everyday monotony of life. I'm totally guilty of countless mind-numbing hours in front of the tube. I'm sure I've lost a lot of brain cells over the years due to television watching, or so my father would probably say. He reads books the way I read magazines. If I weren't a contestant on the show, I certainly would be watching it. I'd vote for Deidra.

"Katelyn, I loved the way you walked the runway the other day. You were a natural," Deidra offers encouragingly. She pushes up the sleeves on her denim jacket.

"Thanks, I was mainly trying not to fall off the platform."

Natural is a huge overstatement. I was naturally unnatural.

Deidra giggles. "Me too. It seemed pretty narrow, especially with those lights glaring in my eyes; I thought I was going to dive right off. And please, my friends call me De-De."

"Okay, De-De. Cute, I like it. And you can call me Kate."

"Thanks. I will. So, Kate, have you ever modeled before?"

I start to laugh but catch myself—if she had only seen me in high school. I wore braces until senior year. "Oh no, this is my first time doing anything like this. How about you?"

"Not really. I mean, nothing on this scale. I've modeled for a few local advertisements. I heard about this opportunity on the radio and thought, *I need to do this.* I have nothing to lose."

"And everything to gain." I grin.

"Exactly. I'm hoping this will at least give me some exposure out in the modeling world, or enough to get me on with a credible agency. Not to mention I could use the money to help pay for college."

"Couldn't we all?" We both giggle. "That's wonderful, De-De— so this is your dream, huh?"

"Yes, I guess you could say that. I also want to travel and maybe go to law school."

She says all this with such sincerity and passion. I feel shallow at my reason for being here. This is her dream. I'm looking for a good story and a chance to meet a TV celebrity.

"Well, like I said before, you're gorgeous. My goodness, you have nothing to worry about in this competition. I don't know why some agency hasn't snatched you up already," I offer encouragingly.

"That's so sweet of you to say. I don't know. I mean, that Camilla lady—she scares me." Deidra scans the room as if she's secretly looking for her.

"I don't think you're the only one, honey. I'd guess that she probably scares herself too," I say jokingly.

De-De laughs. "Yeah, she probably does."

"Don't worry about her. At least there are three judges. Adrianna seems like a nice person, and that Gianni guy—I think he's all right too."

"Yeah, I think you're right."

"So what do you think they're going to do with us today?"

De-De casually shakes her head. "I'm not sure. But I think I did hear something about another cut."

"Really? Already?"

De-De frowns and nods. My stomach turns at the word. *Cut* never sounds pleasant, does it? I'm feeling the little confidence I had built up starting to wane. Nathan seems to like me. I'm hoping that will work in my favor. I guess I'll know by the end of the day. I suppose we'll all know by the end of the day who will go and who will stay. It sounds so final, doesn't it? One day you're there, and the next day you're not—it's totally unpredictable.

De-De and I continue in casual conversation as we wait for things to begin. More girls are coming in and gathering in the large studio room. I spot Texas's long legs; she's talking the ears off one of the stagehands and chomping on her gum. She's wearing another supertight low-cut shirt today. I think she's proud of more than just her legs. But you know what they say: everything's bigger in Texas.

I do a quick head count, and I think from my calculations there are almost fifty girls. I didn't realize there would be that many here today. This means they will have to cut a large portion of us this week. I would like to make it at least one more round. Josie will be so disappointed if I don't. She's worked so hard on me. She dressed me in medium-wash boot-cut jeans and a feminine white tunic with flutter sleeves. The top also has a delicate lace design around the scoop neckline, adding that vintage look I keep going for—or Josie keeps going for, I should say. I also bought new brown-suede wedge ankle boots to match. I swear they make me six feet tall, not that I didn't already look like an Amazon woman. Normally, I like small heels or none at all, but this is ridiculous. Josie said the shoes were absolutely necessary to complete the outfit. I bought them to make her happy.

To kill some time, I start looking through the clothes hanging on the rack beside us. Wow, there are some beautiful little numbers here—Balenciaga, Donna Karen, and Versace. Do I say more? We're not talking Old Navy here, folks; this is top-dollar merchandise. I bet these dresses cost over a grand apiece. My entire wardrobe doesn't even add up to one of these divine designs. This one rack of gowns could pay for all four years of my college education.

As I'm looking through the gorgeous display of extravagant fabric, Vivian sashays by, drinking a bottle of water. It's obvious from what seems like a permanent scowl on her face that she disapproves of my casual browsing.

"This isn't a bargain-basement sale, sweetie," she says in a catty manner, and she glances back as if to make sure I've heard her clearly. We make eye contact as she turns up her nose and keeps walking, taking another slow sip of her water. I hold back the desire to stick out my tongue.

"Did you hear what she said?" I ask De-De, who is still standing beside me, hands now on her hips.

"Sure did. I don't like that girl," De-De says sternly, emphasizing her Brooklyn accent. She places her hand on her hip and stares back at the vixen with a defensive glare.

"Yeah, me neither. I get a bad vibe from her all the way around."

"I don't know who she thinks she is, walking around here like she's already won this competition."

"She's definitely trouble," I say, unconsciously placing my hand on top of the rack.

Then, without warning, something terrible begins to happen. I don't know how, but the entire rack starts to move. De-De and I look at one another in disbelief. *Why is it moving? Does this thing have wheels? If it has wheels, shouldn't it have brakes? And this floor has to be unlevel. I mean, this thing shouldn't be moving this fast. Well, maybe I did push it a bit.*

I take off after the runaway rack, but it's picking up some speed. De-De is chasing with me, but we can't catch it. Then, like a bad dream, Camilla appears from around the corner. Everything begins to go in slow motion. She's walking, holding the same designer bottle of water that Adrianna had the other day in her hand. Camilla starts to tilt the bottle to her mouth just as the rack makes its way right for her.

"Watch out," I say, attempting to warn her.

The words come out, but it feels as if there is no sound, as if I'm speaking underwater. I want to cover my eyes as she jumps back, alarmed. The rack barely misses her and comes to a stop as it hits the adjacent wall. All the designer gowns swing back and forth— luckily, none fall to the floor. I stand there stunned, still holding my breath. The impact has been diverted, but there's still wreckage, as water is now spilling down the front of Camilla's once-exquisite red silk blouse.

I cringe as Camilla looks around for the culprit responsible for her accidental drenching. I remove my hands from my eyes, and they meet Camilla's frigid stare. She looks thoroughly disgusted. I'm terrified as her nostrils flare; she looks as if she's about to breathe fire at me from her mouth.

"Ms. Sparks, I'm so very sorry. Here, let me help you with that," I say as I reach to blot her blouse with my shirt.

Camilla pulls back abruptly. "No, thank you. I think you've done enough damage already," she snarls.

She gives me a look that could kill. I can tell she's internalizing her anger. That can never be good. It's probably why she has so many wrinkles around her mouth, with all the frowning and scowling and all. I'm sure that's even after Botox.

"I'm sorry. It was an accident, Ms. Sparks," I say, trying to be apologetic.

She ignores me, doesn't move, and calls out, "Ariel?"

There is no answer.

"Ariel," she says again in her most annoying, nasally, shrill voice. She sounds as if she has a cold, but that's just her normal tone.

Another young, pretty girl comes practically sprinting around the corner. This one is a petite brunette in a short blue-and-charcoal-gray plaid skirt, matching gray sweater, and chocolate-brown riding boots. I assume this girl must be Ariel. She looks a little frazzled carrying her iPad.

"Yes, Ms. Sparks?" Ariel says somewhat timidly, dropping her pen on the floor.

"Ariel, I need some towels. Please, my dear, could you call George down in wardrobe and ask him to bring me a new blouse, preferably something in red?" Camilla hands Ariel her water bottle as she tries to shake out her wet blouse.

At second look, it's really not that bad; the blouse is only a tad spotted—although I guess spotted silk isn't a good thing and certainly not before filming for a television show. This can't be a positive start for me. *Well,* Runway Star*, it was fun while it lasted.*

I start to repeat my apology. "I'm sorr—"

Camilla gives me the death stare again.

Snappily stopping me midsentence, she raises her hand. "I think you've done quite enough already." Camilla turns up her nose, turns around, and disappears behind the stage with Ariel quickly following her lead.

"She's a piece of work, isn't she?" De-De, my one ally, says, considerately coming to my defense.

"No kidding. It was fun knowing you, De-De."

"Don't say that. Accidents happen, Katelyn. She'll get over it."
De-De gently pats me on the shoulder.

"Yeah, I hope you're right. Thanks for trying to help me catch the runaway clothes rack."

I start to laugh a little at the thought of designer gowns chasing Camilla down.

De-De giggles. "No problem. You have to admit it was pretty funny."

"Yeah, it was funny all right."

"No worries, Katelyn. You know what they say in show business?"

"Don't run over the judge with a rolling rack of clothes?"

De-De laughs. "Cute, but not what I was thinking. No matter what, the show must go on."

I smile. "And it shall." *With or without me.*

"How about we go grab some coffee? They have a kiosk over by the stage." De-De points to the runway platform.

"Did you say coffee?"

"Oh yes, I think it's the good kind, too—gourmet blend."

My eyes light up again. "Sounds perfect; that's just the thing I need."

Relieved, I smile and follow De-De in search of liquid therapy.

Chapter 11

De-De and I return from coffee-bar paradise. It's amazing how a warm cup of coffee can calm my nerves. Camilla has made her way back onto the set. She's gotten rid of the red silk blouse altogether and replaced it with a beautiful magenta silk baby-doll-style dress with matte black tights and black peep-toe heels. *Much better choice,* I think. Now I don't feel so bad for drenching her original top. I actually assisted in improving her appearance.

Adrianna, Gianni, and Mya join Camilla, taking their places beside her at the *Runway Star* catwalk. She makes the announcement for all the girls to gather around the runway. Nathan casually swaggers over to the side of Adrianna. He definitely borders on arrogant but has a hint of little boy lost in him that I find attractive. He catches me staring at him and gives me a wink. I feel a slight swoon inside.

"Welcome back, ladies," Camilla says assertively, beginning her introduction.

A cameraman appears beside the group; he's already started filming. *Okay, this is it, the real deal; I'm actually going to be on TV.*

"This is a privileged group. You all were selected to go on to compete for the title of *Runway Star*. This is not as easy as it appears. You will be judged not only on the way you present yourself down a runway, but we will also be looking at how you are captured on film, as well as for the girl that has that extra something special that makes her unforgettable."

I've certainly never been described as unforgettable—the opposite perhaps.

Camilla goes on with her not-so-warm welcome speech to announce that today we will all be doing another walk down the runway. *Okay, that's not too terrible; I did that fine before.* She tells us that twenty-five of us will be going home today. They will be drastically cutting us in half at the beginning. *This is serious business. Let's hope I don't trip walking down the catwalk, or else I can kiss my interview with Mya good-bye.*

Camilla officially introduces us to Adrianna, Gianni, Mya, and Nathan. She describes to us their roles on the show and their backgrounds. Of course, I know just about everything about Mya. One might find that rather creepy. I promise I'm not a celebrity stalker. I just read her fan-club website a lot and follow her on Facebook. I also found it necessary to do some research on Adrianna. Interestingly enough, Adrianna grew up in a small town right outside of London. A talent agent discovered her at a friend's birthday party when she was only fifteen. She's been in the industry ever since. Amazing—at fifteen, I was still wearing a training bra.

Nathan's story is all too familiar. He apprenticed with another big-time photographer and landed himself in the modeling industry. As Camilla goes on and on about him, Nathan flirtatiously laughs and responds, "What can I say? I love beautiful women, and I love them more in front of my camera." All the girls giggle and bat their eyes at his comment. Looking at the expression on Nathan's face, however, and the wayward look in his eyes, somehow I'll bet there is more to his statement than we know. I hear Adrianna cough rather forcefully and roll her eyes. Again, if I were a betting woman, I would say there's a story behind that cough—and Nathan's right in the middle of it. He smells of trouble.

After the introductions, Mya takes her place center stage, and the real filming begins. She welcomes the audience to the show and explains the course of what is to take place over the next twelve weeks. The first three shows are to be prerecorded, and the final ten episodes will be on live TV, with the at-home audience choosing the models who stay and the models who are eliminated each week.

Tonight each of us will do one walk down the runway. This time, we will be wearing a designer outfit of our choosing. We will be judged on our overall ability to model a designer original. I look over at the racks of clothes and think, *I'm so glad that it was Camilla who got the water drenching and not the designer clothes.* I'm sure if the water had spilled on the clothes, they would've personally escorted me out of the building. Josie would have been horrified.

Mya cheerfully tells us that we have only thirty minutes to select an outfit and have hair and makeup completed before our runway walks begin. At the thirty-minute bell, we have to come as we are, no matter how finished or unfinished we might be. Mya explains that in the real modeling world, there are only minutes between each walk down the catwalk. I'm sure this is a test to see how we handle things under pressure. Luckily, we get assistance with our hair and makeup from the stylists and makeup artists on hand.

Mya gives the signal for us to begin our thirty-minute makeover. In a mad dash, girls race toward the hanging racks of clothes. De-De and I take our time, not wanting the stampede to trample us. The cameramen are staying right with the mob, not wanting to miss any juicy footage. It's an absolute mass frenzy as girls push one another to be the first at the racks. I hear loud oohs and aahs as the girls sort through the garments. I think, *My sentiments exactly,* as I felt the same way when I first looked at some of them earlier. Personally, I would just like to have the money they're worth to pay for my education and credit card bill.

The chaos continues as two girls are almost fighting over what looks like a Vera Wang gown. Ironically, it does remind me of a basement sale for bridal gowns where girls camp out for days, waiting to be the first to pick through the bargain-sale designer dresses. I'm waiting for, any minute now, the hair pulling and punching to begin.

De-De spots a dress on a rack and leaves me to find one on my own. I try to push my way in, but it's nearly impossible as one girl after another passes me, pulling garments off the rack. I finally find a rack that has some free space where I can squeeze in and search for my own outfit. I reach in for a white cotton-and-lace dress by Giorgio Armani that I noticed earlier while browsing, but someone quickly grabs it off the rack before I can secure it.

Vivian looks over at me, smirking, the Armani dress folded over her arm. "I wouldn't even try this one; it's way too small for you. Have you thought about plus-size modeling?"

I try to maintain my composure, but internally, I would like to pull her hair out. Vivian prances off toward hair and makeup. I'm really beginning to dislike that girl.

Mya announces we have fifteen minutes left until walks begin. I feel myself start to panic. There's nothing here for me to wear. Everything's been completely picked over. I'm stuck choosing from what no one else wants. They don't have dresses here in my size. There goes my excitement over my twelve-pound weight loss. I'm not even close to where I need to be for this competition. Maybe Vivian is right after all.

I'm starting to feel discouraged. There are only a few of us left searching for an outfit. Everyone else has made her way to hair and makeup. The cameramen are moving away from us and making their way toward the rest of the flock. Finally, I look up to see one stunning dress on a lone rack in the corner. It's a Carolina Herrera red-and-blue poppy-print silk dress. It has a halter-style neckline, so it shouldn't fall off, which is a plus. I walk over to take a closer look. I hesitate to try it, thinking it will not even come close to fitting me, but I grab it anyway and toss it over my arm. As a last resort, I decide to grab some sort of brown garment hanging at the end of the adjacent rack. Quickly, I take both my dresses and press on.

Moving as quickly as I can, I make my way over to the dressing area to see which designer original will fit this body in transition. There are stagehands all around, assisting us with our outfits. Apparently, this is what a true backstage at a real fashion show is like: controlled chaos. It's no surprise, however; I've seen this on the Style channel many times. I'm not really excited about someone helping me dress myself, but at this point, I guess I'll have to deal with it. Running out of time, I try to slip on the Carolina Herrera and think that it just might work. I'm having a hard time reaching for the zipper. A stagehand notices my struggle and quickly comes to my rescue.

"Can you pull in your stomach a little?" she asks me as she tries to force the zipper upward.

"Sure," I say, and I squeeze as hard as I can, although I feel as if I'm going to pass out.

"Is it going to close?" I ask her, barely able to breathe.

"I don't think so. Do you have something else?" She stops trying to fasten the gown. The last thing I need at this point is to bust a zipper on one of these things.

"Yes. One more." I hurriedly point to the blobby brown garment lying across the chair beside me.

She quickly helps me out of the lovely Carolina Herrera that I'm obviously still too large to fit into and hands me what looks like a burlap sack with armholes.

What's this? I think to myself. This can't be an actual dress. It's the ugliest thing I've ever seen.

Out of options, I slip the dress on, and the young assistant ties the ropelike twine around my waist. I look over at myself in the large mirror on the wall. I look like an oversized sack of potatoes. *French fries, anyone? Gosh, how I would love some french fries at this moment. Yes, drizzled in chili and gooey cheese. Oh, what am I saying? Stop it, Kate. Let's get back to reality, shall we?* Did I mention that I look hideous?

Mya calls out the final five-minute countdown. I start to panic. I'm standing here in a brown paper sack with a belt, no makeup, and hair not done. Great, I'm going to be incomplete—incomplete for my first television runway walk. Could this get any worse? Then I think, *In your case, Kate, probably so.* I close my eyes for a brief second to ask for divine intervention. *God, should I really be here?*

Judging by the course of today's events, I'm resigned to the fact that I will be cut from the show tonight. Maybe it wasn't meant to be. Just like Ben and me—the idea is great in theory, but the timing is terrible. For the first time, I start to feel my heart sink, because I want to do well in this competition. But look at me—I'm a walking disaster. I take a deep breath and examine myself one more time in the mirror. Somewhere in the back of my mind, I hear the famous words of Josie, my fashion coach extraordinaire: *Fake it till you make it.*

Let's think about this in the correct perspective. There are plenty of fashion shows where—no offense to anyone—the designs are ridiculous and outlandish, things no average person would wear in public. So what's a little burlap? No biggie. It's not about the clothes I'm wearing but about how I wear the clothes. If I appear confident even though I'm not and I hate the dress, no one will know. It's not as if I have to wear it home.

I sigh deeply, knowing that no matter how horrific the outfit, the show must go on, and right now, I've got to find some shoes. I run over to the shoe-and-accessory room. Thank goodness there are many choices in my size no doubt. Tall women have large feet, and they've accommodated for that fact with plenty of shoes in my size. This makes me feel much better. I quickly spot a pair of Frye red cowboy boots that are fabulous. I grab a dark brown suede cowboy hat on the way out and head over to hair and makeup with three minutes to spare.

José Lopez is my appointed hairstylist. I can't understand half of what he's saying. His Spanish accent is a little heavy, although his boisterous, funny personality isn't lost behind it.

"Katelyn, I want to make your hair flowing and buu-ti-ful, *sí?*" José says, and he runs his fingers through my hair, fluffing it out as he talks.

I nod. "Sounds perfect, José. Hurry and work your magic." I nervously look over at the large clock on the wall, seconds and minutes ticking away.

He keeps talking quickly as he gathers my hair into loose pigtails. He wants to tousle the ends slightly to create a windblown effect, as if I've been working out on the ranch all day or riding my horse. Well, at least that's what I'm imagining anyway.

Amanda is my makeup girl. She speaks perfect English. Serious in her work, she steps back and studies my face for a brief moment as José combs out a tangle in my hair. I try not to wince. I know there is no time for gentle hands. Amanda quickly blots some powder and decides to dust my eyes with a gold shimmer, along with simple black mascara on my lashes. She says I have the longest lashes she's ever seen, and she wants to make them stand out. To finish off the look, Amanda paints a pale pink gloss on to my lips just as Mya announces that our time is up.

Shoo, that was close. I exhale heavily. José gently places my hat on my head and kisses me on the cheek. "Good luck," he says as best as I can understand him.

"Gracias," I say, and I return the kiss on the cheek.

"I want to see you back next week. Okay?"

"I'll do my best." I smile and proudly walk over to meet the rest of the girls at the runway.

Mya calls each contestant up one by one. As we're waiting, a cameraman and another stage assistant ask us a few questions individually. They ask me about the experience so far. I say that this is much harder than I thought it would be but that I love the challenge. Then they ask the big question again: Why do I want to be the first *Runway Star*? Of course, I pull out the ole Shelly reason: I want to bring a change to the fashion industry and give women a voice in an otherwise stereotypical fashion world, or something like that. The funny thing is that I'm starting to believe it myself.

After the short interview, Mya announces me for the first time onto the show. It's surreal to hear Mya Sasser say my name out loud. I'm completely psyched as I reach up to adjust my hat. *Okay, here goes nothing.* I repeat my inner mantra: *Fake it till you make it, Kate.* I look out at the runway and imagine I'm the best supermodel in the world, again channeling Cindy Crawford. I will myself to think that I'm much thinner than I appear to be, especially in this potato-sack dress. Josie and I have been working on my walk—or "strut," as she calls it—since the original tryouts, and I have to say, it's gotten quite good. I mean, at least I think I can mimic a runway model on TV pretty well. I put on my most serious face and begin to walk.

With each step I take, I can feel the judges' eyes watching every move I make, from the top of my head to the tips of my feet. It's unnerving. I try to ignore them and do my best. I keep imagining I'm in Paris or Milan and that I'm wearing the most exquisite gown. Everyone wants it, but I'm the lucky one to wear it today. I want to laugh inside, because seriously, this dress I'm wearing is anything but beautiful. I look as if I need someone to make a donation in my honor—it's that bad. I guess the boots and hat make it work somehow, and I keep walking. I finally make my way to the end of the runway. Lifting up my chin, I turn out my hips and attempt to keep my body as straight as possible. I slightly pucker my lips as if to say, "I'm beautiful and confident, and you know you want this dress." I have to strain to hold my position and expression, because I feel as if I'm going to burst into boisterous laughter. I manage to keep it together, finish the turn, and purposely keep my gaze over the judges' heads, avoiding any eye contact. I tip the front of my hat just before I walk away, and I sassily kick up one boot in the back as I turn to go. I feel the rush again of being onstage, and I hear De-De cheering for me in the background. Vivian greets me with an annoyed look on her face as I pass by and head backstage. She didn't think I could pull it off either. Well, I showed her, didn't I? Once again, I'm just glad I didn't incur any injuries on my walk down the platform.

After what seems like hours, I'm on my second pack of fruit chews as the last girl does her walk down the *Runway Star* stage. Tension is thick in the air as the judges leave to discuss who will be in the top twenty-five. I think I did well, but you never know with these guys—or what could be going on in Camilla's mind. I hope she's not holding my ruining her blouse against me.

It only takes the judges about an hour to deliberate and make their final decisions of the day. We gather around the catwalk, and Mya begins to call us up in groups of ten. The three judges give each girl criticism and praise. Then, without warning, they ask five girls to step in front and ask the girls in the back to leave. As if a baby has awakened from a deep sleep, the crying and sobbing commence. I've never witnessed anything quite like it. The tightness in the pit of my stomach increases. Most contestants accept the verdict gracefully, but a few girls beg and plead until stagehands escort them off the stage. I can't help but feel bad for them. Wait a minute—oh my goodness, I could be next.

Two groups have been ushered through the cutting process, with ten girls now removed. Group three is De-De's group. I'm nervous for her, but of any of the girls here, I can't imagine she would be eliminated tonight. She looks stunning in the dress she chose. It's a black flapper-style dress with spaghetti straps, adorned in intricate crystal embroidery. She looks as if she stepped right out of the Roaring Twenties. Her walk down the runway was flawless. The judges thought so as well, and they reward her with only high praise. Mya calls her and one other girl to step forward, and seconds later, Deidra Douglas advances to the next round of *Runway Star*. Sheer, jubilant excitement is all over her face as she exits the stage. She runs over and barrels into me with a hug.

"Congratulations," I say as we embrace.

"Thank you. Good luck to you."

"I need it. Honey, look at my outfit."

"It's not about the outfit. You really sold it on the runway."

"You think so?"

"Yes, you did," De-De replies encouragingly.

We stand there together and watch the next group viciously cut in half. Camilla is brutal to some of these girls, telling one girl she looked like a clown and walked like a duck. Camilla tells another girl that she had blubbery legs. I feel for the girl, thinking of how hard I've worked over the past month to lose a few pounds.

After the last verbal slaughter, there are only ten of us left to be called. The suspense is evident on all of our faces. I'm hoping they've saved the best for last. Isabel from Texas is also in the final group, and I think she did pretty well. De-De cheers me on as we're called back onto the runway. Mya calls me first to step out. I feel a small cringe inside.

"Katelyn, I'm pleased to see that you took my advice and have worked on your physique," Camilla says, beginning her critique.

My physique—well, isn't that a colorful way to put it? I try to smile graciously at her comment.

"You've improved, but I would still like to see you more in the caliber with some of the other model hopefuls here. Designers create their gowns for a leaner silhouette."

"Okay." I politely nod in agreement.

I want to shout out that I've lost twelve pounds. That's more than "improved."

"But ..."

There's a long pause. *But what?* I can't breathe.

"I will say this: you made me love a burlap dress, so good job."

Seriously? She liked the dress. And she liked me in the dress. Camilla Sparks thinks I did a good job. She must've forgiven me for the blouse. I hold back the urge to jump around as if I've just scored a three-point shot with only seconds on the clock.

Adrianna puts down the pen she's been taking notes with. "I completely agree," she says. "I felt as if I've been watching you for years on the runway. You did your job, taking a rather obscure design and making it believable. I loved it. I want that dress."

A huge smile spreads across my face. Adrianna wants this dress. I can say I wore it first.

Gianni chimes in as well in his Italian accent. "Beautisimo." He kisses his fingers and opens his hands as he answers. His comments are typically short and sweet due to his ever-obvious limited English.

All Dressed Up

I start to blush. Maybe I have a shot at this competition after all. The critiques and praises go on with each girl in this last group. Even though I received good remarks, it's still questionable if I'm going on. This thing about not being lean enough could be the deciding factor. I know I did my best. If Camilla thinks I'm about to starve, she can forget about it.

It's time for the verdict, and Adrianna takes the lead, separating us into two rows. The pattern of separation tonight has been jagged, so I have no idea how to predict where I stand based on positioning of rows. I am in the back row with Isabel, along with an extremely skinny yet demure girl named Chloe, whose raven-black hair is cut in a pixie style. We all received mixed reviews. The judges feel Isabel might be a pretty face and more of a catalog model than couture. They told Chloe that she has the perfect body for couture but that her walk was crooked and lanky. This could go either way. Nervously, I try to avoid putting my nails in my mouth as we await Mya's announcement.

"Front row," Mya begins. She hesitates, letting the anxiety build for everyone. "I'm sorry, but you all are going home tonight. You are not the next Runway Star."

My eyes expand in size, and I feel myself strongly exhale in relief. Once again, I hear De-De cheering for me. I've made it. I've really made it. Josie is going to have a coronary. I think I might too.

Chapter 12

There's something about Fridays that seems to induce a fresh infusion of enlightenment into my otherwise numb brain. Maybe it's just a rise in my serotonin levels because the weekend is quickly approaching. I have two hours until I can technically leave work for the day, and I'm doing a little online browsing. Today I've learned that I never knew how many different ways there are to wrap a scarf—there are twenty different things one can do with this small piece of fabric. I'm amazed. You can loop it, dangle it, or place it over your shoulder. I usually just do the most common one: twist it around my neck. This can prove hazardous, however, because by the time I put on my coat, I almost have a choking hazard.

I start to zoom in on a beautiful magenta-and-gold Moroccan scarf, when I notice a looming shadow in my computer screen. I turn around in my swivel office chair to see Louise practically hovering on top of me. Her intense stare is frightening. I jump a good inch out of my seat and wave my hand across my desk, knocking over my silver tin of multicolored Sharpie pens.

"Louise," I say, startled, and I quickly minimize my scarf parade. "I didn't hear you walk up."

Louise is famous for sneaking up on people. She doesn't do this intentionally; however, a simple greeting would be appropriate in most cases. Strangely, Louise's behaviors resemble those of a cat. She moves in silently, and you don't even know she's there until she "meows" at you.

"Katelyn, may I see you in my office, please?" she says in her usual subdued manner.

I can never tell if I'm in trouble or not. I have no idea how long she has been standing behind me. I might be getting a talking-to about the unprofessionalism of surfing the web on company time. I might have to come up with a clever way as to how I can relate scarves to cats. Who doesn't need a scarf? Even a cat needs the right accessories. Okay, so I know I should really be working and not shopping online. I say this as I reluctantly click close on the tab with the shimmering pink scarf.

"Sure, Louise, I'll be right in," I say, trying not to act worried.

Louise walks off, and I bend over to pick up the pens now scattered across my desk and on the floor. I start to sit back up, when Sara Beth pokes her bright-eyed self around the cubicle. She smells like cotton candy.

"Katelyn?" she whispers, chomping her large piece of gum.

The sound of her voice and her unannounced presence startle me, and I jump again, hitting my head on the underside of my desk.

"Would everyone stop doing that?" I say, frustrated, rubbing my head.

"Doing what?"

"Sneaking up on me."

"I wasn't sneaking up on you, Katelyn," Sara Beth innocently replies.

"No. I know you weren't. You know how Louise is. She makes me a little jumpy sometimes."

"She does that to everyone, Katelyn. What do you think she wants?" Sara Beth's eyes are wide with interest, and her sparkly pink sequin T-shirt is almost blinding me.

"Who knows? I've been on time every day this week, so she can't get on me about my tardiness," I say proudly.

"I wanted to thank you again for that inside tip on the half shoes," Sara Beth says thankfully, now leaning on the side of my cubicle. She straightens a picture on my cube wall of Kelsey, Kara, and me from last summer's family beach trip.

"No problem. I couldn't have you walking around New York City in a fashion flop, could I?"

I told Sara Beth that the half shoes didn't go over so well during fashion week and that they had already been pulled from most retail stores. She totally bought it and was relieved that she'd made her shoes rather than financially investing in the look. I've really got to quit coming up with these outrageous stories. As innocent as it sounds, technically, I'm lying, and that's not the person I want to be.

I finish gathering my pens and securely place each one back in my tin pen container. Casually, I stand, straighten out my gray skirt and black V-neck sweater, and walk over to Louise's office. Her door is partially open, so I politely knock. I say a quick prayer and ask God to give me favor in my meeting. Louise is harmless, yet she makes me nervous.

"Come in," Louise says with no change in her monotone voice.

I walk in and take a seat in a boring old calico-print wingback chair. I think Louise's entire being must revolve around cats. Then again, at least she knows what she loves. I have yet to find my true passion for anything other than peanut M&Ms or most anything involving food and eating. I sigh for a moment. Wow, I think I'm actually envious of Louise.

"Katelyn, I'd like to know where you are with the Mya Sasser interview," she says, her face serious.

I swallow hard, look out her window, and watch the construction workers filling a pothole.

"Hmmm. Oh yes, the Mya Sasser interview. I've been meaning to discuss that with you, Louise. There seems to be a slight problem with scheduling."

"What do you mean 'scheduling'?" Louise asks, confused.

"She's booked up for months," I say, and I wave my hand as if it's no big deal. I'm sure that's got to be true. A celebrity like Mya has a ton of things to do. Okay, didn't I just say I was going to quit telling things that were not true, half truths included?

"Are you going to complete the interview for the New Year's issue? If not, I think Clive's interview with Giuliani would work just fine."

Clive shimve. He's not taking my spot as the lead article. I think I need to come clean with Louise about the modeling thing. I'll promise to get some sort of interview with Mya. I'm not sure, however, if there will be any cats mentioned in this article. We'll think of this as a suggestion interview. Maybe Mya doesn't know she needs a cat, and I can somehow convince her otherwise—that is, if I can get twenty minutes alone with her. And at this point, I would be perfectly happy with five.

"Louise, I think I've come up with a way to get around the scheduling issue."

"Go ahead—please explain," she says as she sits back, looks at me intently, and crosses her arms.

I clear my throat and say a prayer at the same time.

"Well, you see, my idea involves a minor little modeling contest."

"A modeling contest?" Louise looks at me strangely. "What does that have anything to do with cats? I know you like to help dress our employees, but this magazine is not about fashion, Katelyn."

I guess Louise is more observant than I thought. I wish she would let me help her with her own garment choices. The faded navy-blue polyester pants, green Henley long-sleeved shirt, and bright white tennis shoes she's wearing today are truly not working in her best interest.

"Hold on, Louise. I'm not finished," I say calmly. "I know that Mya's going to host a reality TV show called *Runway Star.*"

"What does that have to do with our magazine or your story?"

"I think it would be a great idea if I go undercover as a contestant."

Louise's eyes look completely blank. "I'm not following."

"Louise, stay with me here for a moment." I stand up and start talking with my hands, gesturing for her to look outside. "Think about it. You said yourself that you wanted to bring on new readers. I'm sure many of the viewers watching this show will be in that youthful demographic that you want to appeal to as subscribers. You also said that we needed to embrace change and mix things up a bit. What a great way to do that very thing."

Louise is still staring at me blankly with an occasional glance outside. I feel as if I'm giving a political speech. The idea of change is always a great way to subliminally bring someone to your side. Whether it's the change you're looking for is the real question.

I attempt to rev up my passionate plea as I continue, pacing the room as I speak.

"Louise, I want to do more than just a causal interview. I believe it's important to get to know Mya as a real person and not just a celebrity who happens to have a cat. Who would expect that from *Fancy Feline*? Mya Sasser is the darling of daytime television. Everyone, cat lover or not, will want to pick up an issue just to read about her."

Louise pauses for what feels like an hour. I peer closer to make sure she's still breathing. This is completely out of the box for her. I could be seriously going down in flames. Go ahead and sign me up for the cat-food convention.

"Katelyn, I don't know why, but I trust you on this," Louise says cautiously.

"You do?" I say, surprised.

"This magazine needs something new and fresh. I think you're just the one who can bring in a new crowd of readers."

"So you're saying that it's okay for me to do this?" I ask hesitantly. "I may be out of the office quite a bit."

"Just bring back the story."

I practically leap out of my seat and rush over to hug her.

"Thank you, Louise. I promise you'll not be sorry."

I realize I'm hugging her tightly, and she looks uncomfortable with my arms around her. I quickly disengage. Suspicion confirmed— Louise is definitely not a hugger.

"I want a weekly progress report and pictures."

"Absolutely. You got it," I say merrily, and I skip out the door.

I can't believe my lucky stars—or, rather, my answered prayer from above. Louise just gave me permission to be on a reality TV show. Looks like I'll have to buy Mya Sasser a cat.

❀   ❀   ❀

"Pick your color," says the petite Asian girl drying off my right foot. The left one is still soaking in the unnaturally cobalt-blue water. I'm leaning my head on the top of the massage chair, feeling the mechanical balls knead out the knots in my back. I look up at the wall of vibrantly colored nail polish and point to a bright purple color at the top.

"Katelyn, you're not picking that color, are you?" Josie asks with consternation.

"Yes, I love purple. Purple makes me happy."

"And I love Mambo Melon, but I'm not in a modeling contest. You need to go with something more neutral. A French pedi is much more appropriate."

"Okay, Coach, whatever you say, but as soon as this is over, I'm going Grapetastic," I say gleefully, and I smile at her like a spiteful teenager.

Josie rolls her eyes. "Now, finish telling me about what happened with Louise."

"So she calls me into her office and wants to know how the article is going."

"Uh-huh. And did you tell her about *Runway Star*? Don't you think she's going to be suspicious when you're gone all the time and then she sees you on TV?"

"Well, yes. So I've come up with a way to do both."

"You have?"

"Yes. I really hate being dishonest. That's not my style."

"True. What's your plan then?" Josie says.

"The truth—I told Louise I needed to go undercover and compete on *Runway Star*."

"Just like that—you told her that you were going to be in a modeling contest?" Josie looks at me skeptically.

"She agreed to let me do the show. Louise said she trusts me to do the job. The timing's perfect. She wants something new for the magazine, so I used that to my advantage. I was so excited that I hugged her."

"You hugged Louise? I bet that she about fell out of her chair."

"Almost. You know Louise; she's not one for physical contact. It's sad, really. I think Louise needs to find love in her life—love from something other than her five cats. I'm thinking about setting her up on one of those matchmaker websites."

"Katelyn, you need to stay focused on you for the moment."

"Maybe, but I'm keeping my eye out for her. There was this set producer at *Runway Star* that might be her type."

"What would Louise's type be?"

"I don't know—one of those introverted types who likes to spend hours alone doing crossword puzzles."

Josie snickers at my description of Louise's perfect mate. The nail girl kindly smiles and politely asks for my other foot. I pull it dripping out of the now-lukewarm water, and she quickly places a towel to pat dry.

"I do, however, have a slight dilemma."

"Really, what's that?"

"Louise wants me to have weekly pictures to go along with this article."

"I don't connect. How's that a problem? You can take pictures, can't you?"

"Josie, come on. You've seen my pictures. They're hit and miss even with a digital camera. Usually, they come out blurred. For something this important, I need a professional. Maybe you could come with me. You're great with a camera, and you have that artistic edge."

Josie frowns. "I would love to help you out. But I'm swamped with work right now. I have midterms to grade and tutoring almost every afternoon. As much as I would love to come and be in the presence of Mya Sasser, the timing couldn't be worse. Don't you have someone on the *Fancy Feline* staff that does photography?"

"Not anyone I trust to bring to a modeling contest. I don't want them to know everything going on. I need someone a bit more discreet. What about one of your students? They did a great job with my portfolio."

"They have class during the show taping. And besides, you're right—I think you need a seasoned professional for this task. This is for your big break, remember? It's not only for *Fancy Feline*."

Josie thinks for a moment; her brow furrows, and she pushes a red ringlet behind her ear. "I've got it. I know the person for you. He's absolutely perfect. And I think he has some extra time in his schedule right now."

"Great. Who is it?"

Josie looks at me warily. "Ben."

"Ben? You mean my coffee-shop Ben?" I shake my head. "I don't think that's such a good idea."

The nail girl looks up at me. "No hot stones."

Oops, I've confused the poor girl. I smile and direct her to keep doing what's she's doing. "The stones are fine." She places the soothing stones on the backs of my calves.

"Come on, Kate—he'd be perfect for the job!"

I'm not sure about this suggestion. I would be spending more time with Ben. As tempting as it sounds, I'm not sure my heart could handle the proximity.

"Yes, I suppose he would be. I don't know, Josie. I can't pay him. Do you think he'd do it for free?" I ask, trying to come up with a logical reason why this idea will not work.

"For you, I think he would do quite a lot."

"What are you talking about?"

"I'm telling you, Kate—there's something there with you and Ben. I've seen the way he looks at you. And the things he posts on your Facebook page seem more than friendly to me."

"Josie, stop it. Don't fill my mind with flighty ideas of love. Ben's my friend. I want to keep it that way. I need his professional skills at the moment."

"So you do need him."

"Yes, I do, professionally speaking."

"Okay. But I'm telling you, Katelyn—sometimes God works in mysterious ways."

I find this reasoning interesting coming from a girl who's currently fascinated with Scientology.

"Let's not forget that sometimes you get burned when you think something is more than it really is," I say cheekily.

"I see what it is; you're scared of getting hurt," Josie says emphatically.

"No. I'm just being realistic."

Okay, yes, I'm scared of getting hurt, which would be inevitable in this case. I'm certainly not going to let Josie know that little detail.

"Who ever said love should be realistic?" Josie flips a page in her magazine. "I mean, look at Romeo and Juliet or Jennifer Lopez and Mark Anthony."

"One dead and the other divorced," I bluntly remind her.

"Good point." Josie frowns. "Okay, not the best examples, but you and Ben could totally work."

"Josie, let me remind you that our friend Ben is going to Europe for who knows how long."

"So?"

"So who's to say that he won't meet a pretty little Parisian girl who speaks sweet nothings in French to him all day?"

"Maybe but doubtful."

"And I think he might have a girlfriend."

"What? Ben doesn't have a girlfriend." Josie pauses and narrows her eyes as if she's remembering something. "I don't think he does.

He never talks about anyone at work, although he has asked about you a few times." Josie smiles playfully.

"He did? What did he say?"

"Now, why should I indulge such information if you think Ben doesn't like you?"

"I didn't say that he didn't like me. I've always made a fabulous friend; however, it never really extends past the friendship stage. Let's face it: I'm sure I'm pretty forgettable." I hunch my shoulders, a little discouraged.

"Don't do that!" she exclaims.

"Do what?"

"You always put yourself down. You can't know what Ben thinks or feels, nor can you predict the future."

"I know that, Josie, but I think I know what's best for me. What I don't need is to get wrapped up in a relationship that could potentially leave me empty-handed."

"All I'm saying is to keep the door open. You might be surprised at what's inside."

Josie might have a point; however, I'm not sure I'm ready to agree with her on the matter.

"I'll consider it, but only after the competition is over, my article is completed"—I pause—"and Ben makes it back to the States without a European girlfriend or dumps the one he currently has."

I give Josie a stern look as she exaggeratedly rolls her eyes. I don't believe, however, that there will be any need for future renegotiation. I'll let Josie dream about my romance with Ben. Right now, I need a photographer.

"Deal." She reaches over and shakes my hand.

The nail technician starts to paint on the purple polish. I politely correct her that I would like the French pedicure. I tell her to paint a white flower and add a purple minirhinestone. Josie objectionably glares at me. I figure this is a perfect compromise. I shrug and smile in delight.

Chapter 13

I know this is probably a bad idea, but I take Josie's advice and decide to ask Ben to help with the article. I really don't have any other choice. I'm desperate—desperate for a photographer, of course. Ben, being the sweetheart that he is, graciously agrees in our instant-messaging conversation on Facebook. I don't go into great detail, so I hope he doesn't change his mind. He doesn't know that I want him to follow me around the model set. What guy wouldn't jump at that opportunity?

Ben has some free time this afternoon, so I'm meeting him at Columbia to discuss the specifics of our photography arrangement. He asked me to meet him after the art-appreciation class he's teaching, located somewhere in the Fine and Applied Arts Building. I've only been here a few times to see Josie, and I'm not that familiar with the building. It's pouring buckets outside today, and my child-size Hello Kitty umbrella is not getting the job done. Did I mention I hate umbrellas? They're cumbersome. Luckily, between the umbrella and my purse, I've managed to shield most of my body from the rain—but my bronze ballet-style shoes, not so much. With every step on the linoleum, my feet make a squishy sound. I'm here early so that I can watch Ben in action; however, it's taking me a long time to find the right classroom in this huge building, so I'm only going to see the last part of Ben's lecture.

After meandering down a long, dark corridor, I finally find Ben's classroom. I peek inside to make certain this is Ben's class, and sure enough, there he is, standing at the front of the room. He's pointing to a slide of a painting projected onto a large screen; he's even wearing a tie. *Can he get any cuter? Stop it, Kate. No thoughts of love and fancy today. This is business only.*

Gathering my composure, I wait until he turns his back to the class and then fully open the door. My shoes start to squish, and I quickly close the door—so much for my silent and inconspicuous room entry. I think for a second and decide to do the only thing I know to do: take off my shoes, sneak quietly into the back of the room, and take a vacant seat at the top, nestled in the right-hand corner. The light is rather dim in the large, spacious auditorium-style classroom, and I think I'm pretty well hidden. Ben turns around to face the class again. He continues explaining about this painting of what looks to me like sad, droopy clocks lying on the beach. This painting is by the renowned artist Salvador Dalí and is titled *The Persistence of Memory.* I've definitely felt like those clocks on occasion, when my mind has run amuck. Ben keeps expounding, and I never knew there could be such a wealth of knowledge about one painting. Most students are intently engaged in the presentation. A few, however, are only there in body, which is evident in their blank gazes. I can hear one guy's faint snores in the corner. The ratta-tap-tapping of keyboards accompanies Ben's lecture as students type away on their laptops and iPads. I wish I had had a fancy gadget like these in college. They are handy for taking notes, not to mention providing an additional diversion for a boring lecture. I would've been privately shopping the Internet just like this girl two rows down. I can't quite make out the screen, but it looks like a fabulous handbag she's scanning.

Ben concludes his lecture on the Dalí masterpiece. I don't quite see all that he does in the painting, but he is the expert, and he can see the true intent of the artist at hand. I continue to listen closely as he speaks with passion and enthusiasm. His presentation moves me yet fills me with a hint of sadness at the same time. It's the same feeling I felt in Louise's office the other day. I wonder what it feels like to love what you do.

I wait in the back as Ben packs up the laptop and projector at the end of class. A small handful of students are waiting to speak with him, posing questions about today's lesson as well as about upcoming assignments. I continue to watch and wait behind the procession. One eager young girl, dressed in what look like purple Victoria Secret sweats, stops to ask him a question. She looks to be crushing on him a bit. She can't hide that pure look of infatuation on her face. Who can blame her, really? If I had had a hot guy like Ben as my college professor, I would've secretly adored him too and probably would've majored in art, all for the sake of love. Ben still hasn't noticed me standing here. I don't know how. I'm a head taller than all the other students, it seems. He appears to be interested in each question that he answers. I think that level of interest and attention makes a good professor. I watch and wait as he patiently speaks to each student. The questions end, and the last student leaves. Ben starts to gather up his notebooks and bends down to unplug the projector cord.

"Mr. Roberts, I was wondering if you could please explain to me the color and patterns used in Van Gogh's *Starry Night*," I say in my serious, studious tone. I know nothing about this particular painting, just that Josie has a poster of it hanging above her bed.

He stands up, a bit taken aback by my presence, but he quickly composes himself. He coughs and clears his throat.

"Well, you see, Miss Turner, the colors represent a greater presence than the objects themselves," he replies in a reflective, studious manner.

"How so?" I cross my arms and look at him keenly.

"You see, the colors are an outward projection of an inward desire."

Why does he always make me feel as if I need one of those little personal fans? *Note to self—never ask Ben to describe a painting unless I want to look like a gooey schoolgirl in love.*

I have to break away from this intensity. "Impressive. You really love art, don't you?"

"I do. There's something so raw about taking paint and creating a picture of life on canvas," Ben enthusiastically replies.

"I watched you teaching this afternoon, and it made me envious," I say, slightly discouraged.

"You? Envious of me teaching a roomful of college kids?" Ben says, confused, as he closes his laptop. "I saw two students sleeping."

"It's so apparent that you love what you do. You have a passion that I haven't found in anything. Lately, I feel like life is standing still, and I want to move forward, but I'm not sure where to go. It seems so easy for you."

I don't know why I just divulged such personal information. Ben walks closer to me; I'm standing beside the first row of desks. He perches himself in front of me on the edge of the long countertop-style desk.

"You know why it's easy for me, Katelyn?"

I lightly shake my head. "No, why?"

"Because I finally stopped trying to please the world and decided to do things out of my love for God before anything else. And when you do, God opens up His world to you."

Suddenly, a warm sensation flows over me like a balmy breeze in the summertime. I can almost see a dim light beginning to unfold its radiance inside of me. I have to turn away briefly to catch the tear at the corner of my eye.

"Katelyn, did I say something wrong?" Bens looks at me with sincerity.

"No. Not at all, Ben. You couldn't have said anything more right." I lightly laugh. "Maybe you should add counselor to that list of numerous talents you have."

He blushes and puts his arm around my shoulder. "Katelyn, we, as believers, are all called to encourage one another in Christ."

"I never thought of it that way before."

"Hey, we're all in this together, you know. This world and life are crazy enough to try to make it through the ups and downs on our own. We're meant to lean on one another."

"Thank you. I don't know where all that came from." I turn away, embarrassed. "Must be the rainy-day blues or something."

"No problem—that's what friends are for, remember?"

"Thanks, but I'm sure it was more than you wanted to hear."

"Katelyn, you can tell me anything anytime. I mean that." He smiles and looks down toward the ground. "Of course, I'm sort of a sucker for pretty bare feet."

I look at him, confused, and then realize I'm twirling my shoes in my hands. I try not to laugh. Somewhere in all of this, I forgot to put my shoes back on.

"Are you making fun of me?" I say teasingly. "Can't a girl go barefoot sometimes? Maybe I just wanted to be free of my chains."

"I see that." Ben winks at me as he slips down from the desk's edge.

"Truth is, the rain gave me squeaky shoes," I whisper.

"Well, come on, squeaky—can I buy you a hot dog in the park?"

"In the rain?" I say, looking at him, confused.

"Sure. Why not?"

"Okay, I'll let you hold my Hello Kitty umbrella," I tease.

"For you, my lady, I will." He smiles.

I laugh and hand Ben the pink umbrella. He props it on his shoulder, and together we head out the door.

❀   ❀   ❀

To our favor, the rain has cleared up, and the clouds have peeled themselves back to a bright and sunny afternoon as Ben and I walk along in Central Park. We both decide on an ice-cream cone instead of a hot dog. I spoon out a cold bite of double chocolate chip into my mouth and feel guilty as a thin girl runs by changing the volume on her iPod.

We find a nearby bench nestled under some large oak trees and decide to sit down; my chocolate ice cream is now dripping down the side of my chocolate waffle cone. I catch a falling drop of melted chocolate with my finger and place it in my mouth.

"Good catch." Ben offers me a napkin.

"Thanks." I smile and wipe the remaining sticky, gooey ice cream from my finger. "And thanks for helping me out with this project. I really do appreciate it."

"What guy would object to taking pictures of beautiful models?" Ben slyly grins.

"That's exactly what I thought you'd say. Trust me—there is plenty of beauty to behold." I bite into the bottom of what's left of my waffle cone.

"Personally, I think there is only one beauty that outshines them all."

I roll my eyes and laugh at his continued attempts to flatter me. "Ben, you know, you really don't have to keep doing that all the time."

"Doing what?" he asks sincerely.

I start to explain what I mean but then figure I don't want to make things awkward. I need to keep this relationship as strictly business as possible. It's important that Ben be working at his best for these shots.

"Nothing—I'm sorry." I try to change the subject. "Ben, we have to be discreet with why you're hanging out with me on the set."

"I understand. Secret double-agent journalist—I remember."

"Exactly." I grin. "The show allows for one guest pass each week to accompany me on the set. There are certain restrictions for pictures. One, you can't be in the dressing area, of course."

"Bummer. I think I may have to back out then."

"What! You can't back out!" I say with alarm.

"Kate, I'm only kidding." He laughs, reassuring me, and gently touches my knee.

I lightly jab him in the side of the arm. "You really like to get me going, don't you?"

"I can't resist. You're cute when you're flustered." He grins again.

I scrunch up my nose. "Funny," I say, and I quickly move on. "No pictures are to be shot while the set photographer is shooting, and absolutely no videoing."

"I think I can abide by those rules."

"Great. The next round starts this next week. Do you think you can make it?"

"I'm at your disposal, Miss Turner."

"Well, I don't know about all that, although my apartment could use a good cleaning."

Ben chuckles. "I'm pretty good with a vacuum."

"I'm sure you are." I smile and shake my head at this tomfoolery.

"Seriously, Ben, are you sure this will not interfere with anything else you've got going on—the coffee shop or classes?"

Girlfriends?

"Not that I can think of at the moment. If so, I can work around it. I promise I'll give you only star-quality work."

"I do appreciate this; however, I don't know how long this will last. I could be kicked off any week."

"No worries. I think we'll have time to get the shots you like. I have a feeling you're going to be on the show for quite a while."

"You're too kind, sir," I say, flattered again.

Ben's cell phone rings, sounding like a shrill old-school telephone. *He really should think about changing that ring tone. It might wake the dead.* Ben reaches down to view the incoming call, and a serious expression stretches across his face.

"I'm sorry—will you excuse me a minute?"

I nod. "Sure, go ahead."

Ben gets up and walks to just within earshot. "This is Ben," he says in a muffled tone. While I'm waiting, I watch a young man throwing a Frisbee to his golden retriever. The dog runs freely through the open field; the Frisbee is only a few feet ahead. The retriever runs ahead of the flying disc, leaps into the air, and completes the catch. I clap to myself at the dog's successful trick.

I glance over at Ben, and he looks engrossed in conversation. He briefly looks my way. "I'm sorry," he mouths.

I wave my hand and smile. "It's okay," I mouth back. He smiles kindly and turns his back to me, continuing to talk into the phone. I don't know whom he's speaking with, but it seems important.

A few minutes pass, and I'm engrossed in watching the dog perform his tricks. I feel a hand on my shoulder, and I jump.

"I'm sorry, Katelyn; I didn't mean to startle you."

I look up, and Ben is still gently touching my shoulder.

"That's okay. I was enjoying watching the retriever over there chase that Frisbee. He's really good. I didn't hear you walk up. Is everything all right?" I ask, concerned at the serious expression still plastered upon his face. Without thinking, I reach over and reassuringly touch his hand.

"Everything's fine. Unfortunately, I'm going to have to cut our afternoon short. I have an unexpected meeting," he says, noticeably disappointed.

"No problem."

I try to react nonchalantly. I don't want to pry into his secret comings and goings. *Where is he always running off to?* I wonder.

"I'm very sorry. I hope we can do this again another day," he says warmly, tenderly looking down at me with those deep brown eyes.

"I'm counting on it. You still owe me a hot dog," I say teasingly.

"That's right—I do." He grins and looks down at his watch as if he's in a hurry. "Can I walk you home?"

"No, I'll be fine. Thanks. I think I'm going to stay a few minutes and watch the dog."

"I'll see you for coffee then?" he asks eagerly as he's walking away.

"Coffee," I confirm, nodding.

He pleasantly smiles, turns, and starts to jog hurriedly back down the sidewalk.

Interesting. Where does he go all the time? I remember the night at the tavern, when he had another important engagement. He left in a hurry. And I think about his supposed appointment with the girl in the coffee shop. I'm starting to think Ben might have the Jason Bourne syndrome. *That's it! Ben's really a secret agent working for the CIA or NSA or someone like that. Maybe he's not even American.* I always thought that with his wavy dark brown hair and matching eyes, he has a rather exotic look about him, and he does seem to know a lot about a lot of things. I bet he's not really an art teacher and his stakeout is the coffee shop. I would guess the pretty girl from the coffee shop, Jessica, is his partner. That would also explain the sudden need to go to Europe in a few months. He's not really traveling; he's doing spy work. *Yes, I've got it. Ben's a spy.*

Chapter 14

Josie quickly debunks my suspicions, and I come to the temporary conclusion that Ben is likely not a spy. I emphasize *likely*, because how can I really be sure? It's not as if a spy is going to tell you that he's a spy. He's like Clark Kent—off to save the world, I suppose, or maybe I just like to think he is.

Today is the next round of *Runway Star*. I'm more nervous than usual with Ben here watching me when I have no clue what I'm doing. I hope I don't slip and fall on the runway. I've told him to focus more on Mya than me and to use his artistic eye in capturing the right moments. Ben's already waiting in the lobby when I arrive at the Manhattan studio. He's smiling that adorable smile of his, holding a black Nikon camera bag, and wearing jeans and a brown David Crowder Band T-shirt.

"Are you ready for all the fun?" I ask sarcastically.

"Absolutely!" he says enthusiastically, raising his eyebrows.

"Ben, if I haven't said it before, I really appreciate your helping me out with this," I say, twiddling the worn leather fringe on the zipper of my backpack.

"Yes, you've said it before, and really, it's not a problem at all," he offers considerately while lightly touching my arm.

"I know we haven't discussed fees. I feel horrible that I can't pay you at the moment, but I plan to when I can. You can send me a bill. Maybe we can set up a payment plan."

"Kate, I'm not sending you a bill, because you're not paying me."

"Yes, I am," I insist. "You're not doing this for free."

"Think of this as a gift."

"Ben, I can't."

He puts two fingers gently to my lips before I can finish speaking and looks me directly in the eyes. I feel the electricity jolt through my body.

"Yes, you can," he sweetly but firmly replies.

I roll my eyes and smile. Okay, so I'm going to let him win this round, although I'll have to come up with some clever way to pay him back, such as making sure he has extra tips in his tip jar at the coffee shop.

"You're hard to resist sometimes, you know, but I'm warning you—I'm pretty stubborn when I want to be."

"I've noticed." He widely grins. "Shall we?" He points toward the elevator. "Lead the way."

I motion him toward the elevators facing the opposite direction, and we turn together.

"Ben, so what happened with your phone call the other day in the park? It seemed important." I know that's stretching things, but I have to ask.

Ben looks caught off guard. "Nothing really," he says. "Work stuff."

Work stuff? He offers no details. *I knew it. Josie's got it all wrong. He's a spy.*

Ben and I take the elevator to the twenty-second floor. Minutes later, we enter the *Runway Star* studios with Ben's guest badge hanging around his neck. He has full access inside the studio all day. The atmosphere is the same as before: organized chaos in a tranquil space.

"This is where all the magic happens. Do you remember the rules?" I ask anxiously.

"Sure do, boss," he casually replies, and he gives me an army salute. "Trust me, Kate. I've got it all under control. You don't have to worry about me."

"I know. I'm sorry. This place makes me a little jumpy."

It could be that Ben makes me jumpy.

"Relax—you're a star already. You'll do fine; just be yourself. You've made it this far, haven't you?"

"I'll try my best."

I leave Ben to himself as I go to meet the other contestants. He sits down in the designated visitor section and starts to fiddle with his camera. Deidra's waiting for me at the stage.

"Katelyn, you brought your boyfriend with you. He's so cute," De-De says cheerily.

This is totally her assumption. I've never told De-De I have a boyfriend. I don't want to lie and say that he's my boyfriend, but the whole idea would go well with my cover. A little voice inside says to stick to the truth. I look over at Ben, who is twisting a larger lens onto his camera, and I feel weak inside. I ignore the small voice and decide not to clarify my relationship with Ben. Ben is a boy, and he's my friend, so "boyfriend" is technically an appropriate definition.

"That's Ben. He really wanted to come and support me. He's taking a few pictures for me. A memento, you could say."

"That's great. I would love to meet him later," De-De says sweetly, glancing his way. Ben sees us watching, gives us a smile, and waves. We wave back and giggle like schoolgirls.

"Sure," I say, hoping I can avoid the actual introduction. I knew I should've stuck with the plan.

"Come on, De-De—let's go see what José has planned for my hair today," I say exuberantly, flinging my hair behind my shoulders. She giggles, and we skip arm in arm like little girls playing dress-up.

For the remainder of the day, the overall production goes as smoothly as possible. I'm sure Ben has been bored out of his mind. It would be like me watching ESPN all day. Lucky for me, there are no walks down the catwalk today, so there's less of an opportunity for me to fall and make a fool of myself. I overhear from one of the set producers that Mya has been offset filming her own separate monologues. I feel like it's been a complete waste having Ben here today—other than for my support, I suppose.

Today the plan is that we all will meet individually with one of the set producers for an interview and inside photo shoot. I'm waiting my turn and watching De-De from the side of the set. They've dressed us all in the same outfit today: a Carolina Herrera floor-length pink taffeta ball skirt with a white cotton dress shirt. It's a simple, elegant choice with the magenta pink leaning on the side of edgy. We all look exactly alike, with the exception of our varied mix of hairstyles. José has styled my hair straight and ultrasleek for this ensemble, with Amanda adding rosy pink lipstick and exaggerated smoky eyes.

De-De's perched upon a large Queen Anne–style sofa covered in black velvet with a rich, vibrant pink damask print framed in gilded wood on the wall behind her. In another setting, this might appear a bit tacky, but somehow it looks perfect and cozy beneath the long white drapery—an eclectic mix of new and old with a modern twist.

My interview goes well with no major catastrophes to report; of course, it only involves talking, which is more my specialty. Okay, not always, but today I do quite well. I grin and chuckle when asked about the burlap-bag dress from last week. I give credit to José and Amanda for putting on the finishing touches, a true team effort. I go on to say that it isn't so much about the dress or the outfit but about how you present yourself in the dress that matters. The role of the model is to sell the dress even if she thinks it's the most hideous thing she's ever seen. It's true. I mean, really, have you ever seen the average woman walking down the street in some of these wild creations that come off the runway? Surely not. I'm learning that it's all about an idea, sometimes larger than life, and that idea, however outlandish it might be, gets translated to the seasonal clothing line for the everyday woman. Fashion isn't all about skinny models and crazy creations. There's a science behind it. And of course, at the end of day, it's also about money and what sells. My job is to sell whatever I'm wearing the moment I walk down the runway.

At the completion of the contestant interviews, all the model hopefuls gather around the Queen Anne sofa for a group picture.

Nathan has us pose however we choose. I stand beside De-De. We playfully hug each other like old friends. Vivian stands beside us, her arms folded, giving her best scowl.

Ben cuts out before the end of the shoot. He texts me to say that he has another unexpected meeting. An unexpected meeting is suspicious. Why doesn't he just tell me where he's going? I'm left to my own imagination, which is not necessarily the best for me. Ben also asks me to meet him at his apartment later for dinner. He says he feels bad for leaving me stranded in the park the other day and wants to make it up to me. I'm trying to look at this dinner as a business meeting, because we also will be looking over the shots he took today. The at-home voting for *Runway Star* begins next week, and I need Ben's help with this article. It's vital that I stay focused as much as possible—that is, focused on business, not Ben or me and Ben or whatever might be going on with Ben and me. I'm totally clueless.

❀ ❀ ❀

On my way to Tribeca to meet Ben at his apartment, I don't know why I'm so nervous. I'm not used to meeting men for dinner in their apartments. In fact, I'm not used to meeting a man for dinner anywhere, much less his place of residence. So this is a vast improvement. I am bummed that I had to change back into my regular clothes. Can you believe they wouldn't let me keep or even borrow the ball skirt? I guess my jeans and purple plaid flannel shirt will have to do for now.

I love this area of town. I'm not sure how he's swinging this desirable neighborhood. He said he shares this apartment with three other guys to keep expenses down, which makes complete sense; living in New York City can put you in a serious financial situation if you're not careful. The price of a small apartment here could buy you a three-thousand-square-foot house on several acres of land in the South. Many people rent, and having a roommate is typically a necessity. Because he's an assistant professor with no tenure, I assume

Ben is on a limited income, which is likely why he's working three jobs. However, I'm still toying with the spy theory.

Ben's neighborhood is a safe part of town, but I'm still cautious as I arrive at his apartment. For someone who grew up in small-town USA all her life, big-city life can be uncertain. I tend to be overly paranoid at times. Timidly, I go up the stairs to apartment 2F. I hear the sound of a baby crying in an apartment nearby as I reach the top of the stairs. Two normal-looking young men pass by me as I'm walking down the hall. Kindly, they smile, almost as if they know me. I smile in return. Still, I'm skeptical, and I watch them over my shoulder as I knock on Ben's door.

"Come in—it's open," I hear Ben say pleasantly.

I slowly open the door, walk into the loft space, and shut the door behind me. It smells divinely of garlic and oregano.

"I hope you don't leave that open all the time. I could've been any weirdo off the street, you know."

Ben stands behind a large kitchen island with an extensive stainless-steel countertop.

"Oh, but you'd be my favorite weirdo," he says teasingly as he walks over to greet me.

"Funny. Ha-ha. I'm serious, Ben. Do you just leave the door open all the time like that? This is New York City, not rural North Carolina."

He takes my purple backpack from me and places it on one of two oversized brown leather recliners. I quietly laugh to myself and think, *Men and their cozy chairs.*

"Chris and Sean just left, and I knew you would be coming any minute, so I didn't bother with locking it again. Why? Are you worried?"

Sean and Chris must be the normal-looking guys I passed in the hall. His roommates appeared clean, neat, and friendly. *Maybe they're all spies.*

"Worried? About you? No, Ben, you're a big boy. I'm sure you can take care of yourself."

"Thank you. I'm glad you think so." He chuckles and retreats back into the kitchen area.

I smirk at his comment and plop myself onto one of the leather recliners.

"What smells so wonderful?" I ask, referring to the aroma that's now causing me to come close to salivating.

"Just a little Italian cuisine. It's my specialty."

"I'm impressed—about the food, I mean."

"Why, Kate, my dear, I can make more than a macchiato," he says teasingly as he drains the pasta from the stainless-steel pot, steam rising and almost covering his face.

"Touché."

"So what do you say to a little food before work?"

"If you put it that way, I guess I can't resist. Not to mention the smell is intoxicating."

He smiles at me from the kitchen with a lingering look in his eyes.

"I've been known to make women feel that way," he says, grinning.

"Ben Roberts, you sure are full of yourself tonight, aren't you? I think you did too much schmoozing with all those pretty models today."

Even though we're just friends, I still can't help but engage in some mild flirting.

"I think it's because you bring out the best in me, Kate."

"I can see that—or at least the chef in you, I should say."

"Yes, you could say." Ben pulls what looks like meatballs out of the oven. "It's almost ready. Please go ahead and make yourself at home. We keep it clean here." His smile boasts a hint of teasing.

I walk around, inspecting the huge, open loft area. Ben's right. All joking aside, it's incredibly clean for a bachelor pad. Like the modeling studio, it has an industrial feel about it, but it's not so spa-like. Rich gray tones cover the walls, with black-painted exposed piping above. The kitchen, however, looks like the set of the Food

Channel, with sleek mahogany wood cabinets and stainless-steel countertops.

"Nice place you have here. This kitchen is amazing."

"It's pretty sweet, eh? But I can't take any credit for the design; it's actually Sean's place. Sean and Chris are both sous chefs at a couple of up-and-coming restaurants in town. Sean renovated the kitchen last year."

"That certainly worked well in your favor. So how do you know Sean and Chris?"

"We play in the church band together—Sean on bass guitar and Chris on keyboard."

"Well, it's quite lovely." I do another sweep of the room as I'm walking about and focus in on a large painting of a black lab resting on what looks like the same wood floor. The painting's blue, gray, and black hues look extra vibrant against the darker gray walls and balance perfectly above a rustic wood dining table. The dog is looking up with sweet, sad eyes. He looks strangely real, as if I can almost reach out and pet him.

"I love the dog painting. Did you paint this?"

"Yep."

"It's incredible. Is this your dog?"

"Sure is."

I look around. "Where is he?"

"Oh, he's not here. I keep Tango at my mom's house. She lives in upstate New York, where I grew up. There's much more room for him to run free than here in the city."

"I can understand that, but don't you miss him?" I continue to concentrate on the painting.

"Sure I do. One day, when I have a place of my own, I may bring him to live with me. I'm so busy right now; he would be a latchkey dog."

"I would love to meet him one day."

"I think we can arrange that."

I continue my tour and notice several blank white canvases in the corner of the dining area. The canvases vary in size, and one particular canvas sits on an easel, turned in the opposite direction.

"Are you working on something?" I start to walk around to take a peek at the large canvas.

"Yes, but don't look at it yet. It's not ready," Ben says suddenly, and he quickly comes over to block my view of the canvas.

"Okay, but what is it?" I eagerly ask. My curiosity is definitely piqued.

"Um, just something I'm working on."

"What is it exactly? Why so secretive?" I tease.

"It's rough still, and I don't like to show my work until it's finished. I'm funny that way, I suppose," Ben says with more repose, and he picks up a black sheet lying on the table and covers the canvas.

"That's cool. I get it." I stop standing in front of Ben, who is now guarding the picture. I'm dying to see this painting. It could be nothing but a blob of color for all I'm concerned. I smile coyly. Ben starts to move aside.

"Come on—just one peek?" I playfully scoot past him.

He stops and gently holds me in place before I can reach the painting. "No, Katelyn. You'll just have to wait."

I sigh heavily. "Okay," I say, pouting a bit. "I'll wait. Ben, I never pegged you for such a perfectionist. If I didn't know you any better, I would think you were hiding a portrait of a nude woman back there."

Ben clears his throat, making a choking sound, and then continues with a seemingly forced laugh. He turns me around and casually walks me over to the couch.

"Kate, you're so funny. You have such an imagination."

I sit down and lightly rub my hand over the olive-colored microsuede couch. I'm still dying to get a look at that picture. I knew it—Ben is a spy. The painting might not even be a painting at all. It could be a map of some sort, plotting out his next top-secret mission.

"How did it go after I left today?" Ben asks, quickly changing the subject. He walks back into the kitchen, as the sauce is starting to boil on the stove.

"Nothing too exciting—they interviewed all day and took a few shots after you left. I'm sorry if you were bored. I feel like I wasted your time. Mya wasn't even there today."

"I don't see that as a problem. It looks like I have an excuse to spend another day with you," he says reassuringly.

I smile pleasantly in response. "Well, don't get too cozy. I'm not sure how long this modeling gig will last."

He stops what he's doing in the kitchen and looks up at me. "As long as you're having fun, I would enjoy it. Are you?"

"What?" I look back at him blankly.

"Having fun?"

"Yeah, I think so, but it's just strange. It was all sort of a joke at first. I honestly never thought I would make it past the first round."

"Why?"

"Come on, Ben. We both know I'm not the model type."

Ben wipes his hands on a kitchen towel, walks over, and sits down beside me on the couch. He looks at me with genuine warmth in his eyes. "I think you underestimate yourself. You're a beautiful girl, Kate."

Now I know I'm blushing. He said I was beautiful. I want to rebut, but I know I need to simply accept the compliment.

"Thank you."

Sensing my hesitation, he gingerly touches my hand. "Well, the judges obviously think so too, or they wouldn't move you forward."

"I guess you do have a point there," I say, trying to sound agreeable. "It's just strange—now that I've made it this far, I have this weird desire to go further. I've started to brace each week for disappointment. Does that sound crazy?"

"No, it would be crazy if you said you wanted to fail and not finish something you started. I don't think you're someone who gives up so easily."

"True. My father says it's the Turner stubbornness, but I like to think of it more as perseverance," I say assertively, turning to face Ben on the couch and pulling my legs underneath me. "Like I'm still dying to have a peek at that picture you've got over there." I nod toward the mysterious painting.

Ben shakes his head. "Kate, I'm keeping my eye on you."

"You really should, you know."

He lightly laughs. "You know what I think, Miss Turner?"

"No, tell me."

"I think you actually like modeling."

I open my mouth to respond, but Ben quickly continues. "I think it's something you never thought you'd like to do, but surprisingly, you do. Now you're struggling with losing something you enjoy."

My eyes open wide with surprise; it's as if he can read my mind. He has just pinpointed exactly what I've been feeling but didn't know how to define. *He must be using his spy interrogation methods on me.* "You're right. I do. I like being onstage, and I get this rush of sorts when I walk down the runway. I mean, not as big a rush as I get from writing a good story, but it's still a rush. It's just different. I can't explain it, really."

"I know that kind of rush," Ben says, and he softly looks into my eyes and places his strong, warm hand over mine.

"You do?" I feel my heart moving up to my throat. Ben gives me a rush like falling over a giant, roaring waterfall.

"Sometimes we find a rush in unexpected places."

I look back at him as if I could melt like ice cream on a summer day. *Oh my goodness, is Ben going to kiss me? He can't kiss me; that would mess up everything. On second thought, he's already kissed me a thousand times in my mind, so we might as well make it official. No, he can't kiss me. What am I saying?* He's still looking at me with "I'm going to kiss you" eyes when the smoke alarms starts to beep incessantly. The fresh smell of burned carbohydrates takes over the previous pleasant scent in the air.

"The bread!" Ben quickly jumps up, removes his hand from mine, and runs toward the oven.

Saved by the bell—the moment is lost to burning bread. I sigh in relief and disappointment all rolled into one. Ben scrambles to retrieve the black, crispy garlic toast from the oven. I walk over to help him in the kitchen, the smoke alarm still wailing overhead. He jumps up onto the counter, reaches up to turn off the blaring signal, and knocks the pan of bread onto the floor. Not thinking, I reach down and pick up the still-hot pan. I let out a loud "Ow!" and drop the pan back onto the floor.

"Ow, ow," I say, holding my hand. I'm jumping around in circles, wanting the throbbing to stop. "Hot pan! Hot pan!"

Ben quickly comes back down off the counter. "Katelyn, I'm so sorry. Are you okay? Here, let me see your hand." He reaches for my injured palm.

I quickly jerk it back, afraid, not wanting him to touch it.

"I won't hurt you—I promise. Now, let me see your hand," he says gently but with a firmness that reminds me of my father. I offer my hand to him reluctantly, like a scared little girl.

Ben takes my hand softly and places it under the cold water now flowing from the faucet. I start to pull back at first, but he holds my hand tightly and doesn't let me move. I submit, attempting to trust him by allowing him to hold my hand under the cool water. He's right, of course—the water feels soothing and helps to ease the pain pulsing throughout my tender palm. I look up at him adoringly as he sweetly holds my hand under the water, the throbbing in my heart now overshadowing the pain in my hand. I know I'm falling deeply for this man, who seems to be everything I've been waiting for my whole life. Closing my eyes as the water continues to ease the pain of my hand, I try to forget the bittersweet ache in my heart.

"Does that feel better?" Ben asks, and I open my eyes.

"Yes, thank you. I wasn't thinking when I picked up the pan."

"No kidding. Next time, you might want to grab a pot holder," he says jokingly.

"Gosh, I'll have to remember that."

We laugh, and I slowly pull my hand from beneath the water as he turns off the faucet. Ben lightly pats my hand dry with a clean kitchen towel. I softly smile and keep my hand wrapped while he cleans up the burned toast off the floor.

"Sorry about the bread," Ben says disappointedly, and he throws the last piece into the trash.

"No problem—I'm watching my carbs anyway."

"Well, don't watch them too much or you'll float away."

I smile, take a sip of water, and take a seat on one of the barstools next to the kitchen island. I watch Ben, content, as he finishes preparing dinner. We eat at the kitchen island and enjoy the feast in casual comfort. As I suspected, the food is absolutely delicious. Of course, knowing Ben, I wouldn't expect anything other than fabulous. Is there anything this guy doesn't do well? I'm starting to wonder. I think he's pretty wonderful.

Over dinner, we talk about many things. Ben tells me a lot about his father and what it was like after he died. He and his mother struggled to make ends meet, and the pain of the loss sent Ben into a dark place. He shares that he experimented with alcohol and tried a few drugs. After the DUI, he lost his driver's license for a year and spent lots of time on the bus as he did odd jobs in the city. When he wasn't working, Ben found solace in painting and spent a lot of time listening for God's voice in the pain. I listen, mesmerized, as he talks about how he would paint for hours and God would speak to him through the colors, the lines, and the images he would see in his mind. Somehow, there in the still silence, he found healing and peace.

Ben's story moves my heart with compassion as well as embarrassment. I take a quick inventory of myself as he's talking, and I'm ashamed of my frivolous attitude about life in general. I complain about not being like my sisters or not having the best job or whatever shallow thing I can think of to complain about. Truly, I have never been in need of anything before. Somehow, today I find myself in need of simple gratitude to God for all the good things I have.

Ben and I continue our conversation long after dinner. We joke about the burning hand. I share with him how I ruined Camilla's blouse and about my burlap-dress experience. We laugh until my stomach hurts. We never even get to the topic of the article. Tonight I don't seem to care. I glance over at the clock lighting up on the microwave in the kitchen. It's getting pretty late, and I should probably head home for the night.

I push my hair behind my shoulders and raise my arms, arching my back into a yawn. "Ben, I really should get going now. I didn't realize it was so late."

He glances at his watch. "Yeah, you're right; I didn't realize what time it was. Do you need me to walk with you?"

"No, but thank you; I'll be fine. I'll just catch a cab."

"Let me at least pay for it."

Before I can say no, Ben's already rushing toward what must be his bedroom, and he comes back with cash in hand.

"You really don't have to do that. You made dinner for me. I think I can pay for my own way home."

"Absolutely not. I insist," Ben says kindly. "My mother taught me better."

"Please tell your mother that her son has grown to be quite the gentleman." I smile as he places the money in my hand. "Thanks for a wonderful evening. The food was fabulous."

"It would've been just food without you here," he says, opening the door for me, and I feel myself blushing again as I turn around to say good-bye.

"Thank you."

I smile, and without thinking, I reach up and lightly kiss him on the cheek. Ben looks at me warmly. I quickly divert my eyes. *Why did I just do that?* It was totally an impulse. It's true. Loneliness leads to stupidity sometimes. I look up, and Ben is sweetly grinning. He looks deep into my eyes and starts to move in to return the kiss. I've lost the willpower to resist. I close my eyes and wait for his lips to meet mine, when a familiar smell of jasmine and vanilla begins to tingle beneath my nose. My senses are suddenly on full alert as I hear the sound of stilettos making their way down the hall. I turn from Ben to see the ever-beautiful Jessica walking toward apartment 2F. She's dressed in tight dark-washed skinny jeans and an off-the-shoulder spandex white top, with a black leather jacket tossed casually over her tanned shoulder. She's wearing the same red high heels from the other day and carrying what looks like a white overnight Prada bag. Her auburn hair, instead of being pulled back, is hanging down this evening, perfectly styled and flowing around her shoulders.

What's going on here? Confused, I look over at Ben. A perplexed look seems to drape his face. Who is this girl, and why is she visiting Ben at this hour? He never mentions Jessica. He never talks about her. I wonder if when he has an "unexpected meeting," he is running off to see Jessica. Obviously, something more is going on here than a casual friendship. He even said himself that he wouldn't call her a friend. She's definitely not one of his students. Maybe I've been wrong about Ben. Maybe I've missed the mark on this imposter of a gentleman. He's good at a lot of things; obviously, he's good at juggling multiple women, too. I feel myself getting angry and jealous. The moment I start to let my guard down, in swoops trouble. My hopeful heart now starting to break, I can't think about anything else but getting away from this place.

"Ben, did you get my text?" Jessica says with an aggravated tone, sashaying around me as if I'm not even there. She kisses him on the same cheek I just kissed and disappears like a ghost behind the door, her red high heels tapping on the hardwood floor. Our beautiful evening starts to dissipate like the jasmine-and-vanilla perfume.

"I guess your next appointment is here," I say rather coldly. "I know you wouldn't want to keep her waiting."

Ben turns to glance at Jessica and then rapidly back at me. He looks deep into my eyes as if he can see the hurt and confusion I'm trying to mask behind my charade of a smile.

"I'll see you later. I have a lot of sleep to catch up on. Thanks again for dinner," I say, trying to get the words out before my eyes become clouded with tears. I take off quickly down the stairs.

"Kate, wait."

I choose to ignore him, not wanting to hear his explanation of why there's another woman meeting him at his apartment. Right now, I'm not sure if I would believe him. I especially don't want him to see me cry. I keep walking and don't turn around to look back. Half an hour later, after a blurry cab ride, I arrive back to the safety and sanctuary of my apartment. Josie's sitting up, watching Jimmy Fallon make jokes about the latest celebrity beauty who's going to jail. She's eating ice cream out of the carton. I don't say a word as I grab my own pint of double chocolate-chip mocha out of the fridge.

"Hey, what about your diet?" She starts to interrogate me.

I look at her as if to say, *Back off, sister.* "What diet?"

She quickly picks up that I don't want to be bothered this evening and doesn't say another word. We sit in silence, and I eat away my sorrows.

Chapter 15

"**M**aybe she's just a friend," Josie says calmly.

"A friend with benefits," I snidely respond as I shuffle through my closet, looking for something to wear to tryouts tonight. I throw out a few items I know are not *Runway Star* worthy. "I mean, her bag was large enough to carry a small child."

"Katelyn! You're totally jumping to conclusions without any facts. Ben is about as pure as you'll ever find a man these days. That is saying a whole heck of a lot in this sex-hungry society."

"How do you know that?" I ask, surprised.

"Ben's always been pretty open about his faith. I know he dated a staff member from the English department a year ago. Word got around that she actually dumped him because he wouldn't sleep with her. He's saving himself for his wife, he told her."

"Seriously?"

That makes me feel even worse. He is the perfect man. Then what's he doing with Jessica? I'm confused.

"Just because he's a virgin doesn't mean he knows how to treat women," I snidely retort, and I blow a lock of hair out of my eyes. "He's very good at juggling us about."

"Katelyn, have you ever told him that you had feelings for him?"

I huff about, still looking through my clothes. "Well, no! Why would I tell him that, when he's leaving in a few months? Forgive me, but what ever happened to the guy pursuing the girl? I'm a bit old-fashioned."

"He's not going to Mars or the other side of the universe, Kate. Long-distance relationships have been known to work, you know. I think it's very obvious he likes you. You might be giving him mixed signals. If you haven't told him how you feel, then he's fair game. He can't read your mind. If he doesn't know you like him, then he's free to get to know more than one girl."

Josie makes a valid point. I hate it when she's right, although she makes dating sound like trying on dresses.

"If it's any consolation, I don't know who this Jessica girl may be. I'll bet from the way you're describing her that she's much more interested in Ben than he is in her. She doesn't sound at all like his type."

"Maybe this is one of those cases where opposites attract. All I know is that this girl is all the things I'm not. Why would she be visiting Ben that late at night?" I sigh. "She just walked in like she owned the place."

I continue shuffling through my limited wardrobe, throwing out things at will. Josie ducks as I toss, and she keeps talking.

"That's good, Kate. You should want to be all the things this Jessica isn't."

"Why? She's gorgeous and glamorous, has a body to die for, and looks successful and confident in her own skin. Why would Ben settle for me?"

"Because if Ben wants the real thing—and knowing Ben, he does—you're the real deal. If you ask me, he's not the one settling here. You are."

Okay, that hurt. I feel as if the oxygen just got sucked out the room.

"What's that supposed to mean?" I say defensively.

"It means that you're settling to believe that you're not the best choice."

I'm not settling. What's she talking about? I'm being practical here. Why is she taking Ben's side? I'm so mad at her right now. I feel my face getting red and hot.

"Fine! If that's what you think about me."

"The truth hurts sometimes," Josie says sternly. "I'm just telling you what I see."

"Well, you see wrong! You don't understand."

I huff and puff and make my way to the bathroom. I slam the door and then turn the shower up hot so that the steam can fill the room and help calm my frustration. I sort of see what Josie's getting at, but I keep picturing myself next to Jessica; the matchup is not as equal as Josie makes it out to be. I'm not out to compete with this girl, whoever she is. Even if I were, I don't think I could win. It's true that Ben doesn't know how I feel. I've never said it out loud, because I don't want to make a fool of myself. It seems Jessica has been around since long before I came into the picture. It's none of my business anyway. As much as it makes my heart ache, I'm putting away my feelings for Ben Roberts. There are more fish in the sea. *Right, Lord? Or am I throwing back the best catch ever? Why is love so complicated?*

❀   ❀   ❀

It's a sunny New York City day as I make my way back to the *Runway Star* studio. My heart, however, is not feeling so sunny. The conversation with Josie is still fresh on my mind. I know she meant well, but her words sting. As my friend, she was being my advocate, and I was wrong to get angry. I truly don't believe she understands my situation. I know if she actually physically saw Jessica, she might see what I'm up against and feel differently. Or maybe she's right. Maybe I'm settling, as she says—settling to be second best. Then again, when I think about it, I've been doing that all my life— accepting the things I felt were impossible to change.

Ben texted me early this morning. He said that he would like to meet me at the studio, and he wants to talk to me about last night. I'm not sure if I want to talk to him. Somehow I have to clear all of this from my mind if I want to be successful in this competition.

I need to focus. That's it—more focus. The studio is bustling as usual, with model hopefuls dashing around the set and stagehands preparing for tonight's show; enthusiasm fills the air. Nathan is prepping his area with cameras and other various equipment. The man is actually working today—what a concept. I haven't seen him snapping many pictures. I was starting to think he was just here to look pretty—not that we need any more pretty people here. Everyone is so pretty that it's ridiculous.

I gather that today is a full day of being in front of the camera. This is a modeling contest, so it makes sense that cameras would come with the territory. The last shoot we did was basically a group picture. Today it looks as if it's me against the camera. I know taking photographs isn't a battle, but growing up, it sure felt that way. I always dreaded picture day at school. It seems something always went wrong, usually involving wardrobe or hair or a combination of both. In first grade, I spilled chocolate milk down the front of my favorite pink dress at lunch. I'm crying in the picture. It was horrible. My sisters still tease me. Unfortunately, not much has changed in the spilling department. I hope that today I can avoid dropping anything on my outfit—or anyone else's, for that matter.

Speaking of my spilling victims, Camilla Sparks is making her way on set. She looks almost angelic tonight in her flowing pale blue blouse paired with a pair of white pants and strappy silver high heels. An angel in disguise is more like it. Judging by her constant disdainful attitude, it seems she would be a difficult person to live with. She has a hard-edged and, I've heard, relentless personality. One thing is true, though: Camilla knows her stuff, or else she wouldn't have her own modeling agency or this show. So I have to give her kudos on her overwhelming accomplishments. She's practically bathing in money. Honestly, money is nice, but I would rather find happiness in love over wealth any day. One without the other is empty, it seems. I mean, look at Camilla. She probably has more money than she knows what to do with, but she seems to be terribly unhappy. Lord knows I wouldn't want to end up like her.

I'm not perfect, and I'm probably being judgmental toward someone I don't know well—just as Josie feels I'm being judgmental toward Ben. Is it possible that I've missed the mark? Maybe God has another Prince Charming for me after all. *If you do, Lord, this time, maybe I could get the white horse and everything. Oh, and the sword too.* I always liked fairy tales. I realize that God isn't a magic genie in a bottle. Life doesn't always work that way. He gave us the power of choice. I obviously keep making the wrong ones.

The tension heightens as Adrianna and Gianni arrive on set to complete the trio of judges. Mya appears and asks all the contestants to meet around the catwalk. I'm eager to see what the challenge of the day will be. Soon the camera begins to roll, and Mya comfortably takes what has become her usual spot onstage, front and center.

"Welcome back, *Runway Star* contestants, and welcome back, America. Tonight we're down to the top twenty-five model hopefuls and one more step closer to naming your next Runway Star," Mya says in her vivacious introduction.

The camera pulls away from Mya and pans over to all of us girls as the director cues us to express our excitement. I smile and politely wave as the camera goes by, while some other girls jump, clap their hands, and wave exuberantly at what will soon be an at-home audience. Isabel, standing out front, does a Texas-like holler as if she's at a rodeo. Vivian just stares haughtily at the camera with no smile as usual, and De-De gives a comfortable, easy smile with a simple wave—no need for all that craziness. The cameraman thinks so too. He shakes his head at all the commotion and moves the camera back to Mya.

"Tonight, ladies, we've got the cream of the crop. Now it's really going to be your chance to shine. Your challenge this week is to wow the judges with your ability to work not only a runway but also the camera. Our handsome photographer, Nathan Steele, will be your personal photographer on this challenge."

The camera quickly pans over to Nathan, who looks debonair standing in his makeshift studio. He's wearing a charcoal-gray

Armani suit and bears a striking resemblance to Jude Law with his blond, perfectly messy hair. Nathan smiles, winks, and then also coolly waves toward the camera. I start to feel slightly queasy. This should be interesting. My last mock photo shoot was with some art student hippie wannabes. I wasn't nervous at all. And today I feel like a nervous wreck, as if I'm going in for a final callback interview or something. This is going to take more mental effort, I'm afraid, with the human version of a Ken doll taking my pictures. De-De is all smiles, of course. Why shouldn't she be? She's a modern-day Cleopatra. She could wrap herself in toilet paper and look glamorous in front of a camera. I keep my fingers crossed that I get a better outfit today than burlap and twine.

Mya cues us that the tape is rolling, and she asks the judges their advice for the contestants as well as thoughts on this week's challenge.

Camilla brazenly begins, "You know, it's one thing, Mya, to be able to walk down a runway, but this is our chance to see who truly has that extra something special."

Camilla looks over at us as if we're her naughty children.

"Ladies, the camera will never tell a lie. Your face could be seen in thousands of magazines, on billboards, and could even be plastered right in the middle of Times Square. You have to be fabulous."

Mya lifts her eyebrows and then glances over at us with a sympathetic expression. She quickly turns back to the judge panel.

"Thank you, Camilla. Adrianna, what are your tips for our *Runway Stars* this week?"

"Just be you and have fun out there," Adrianna answers kindly.

"Good advice. Thanks, Adrianna. Gianni?"

"Most bea-u-tiful lade-z, enjoy and make love to ze cam-rah," he answers in his broken English, and he blows kisses our way.

Make love to the camera. Is that what I think he said? Gross. Someone really needs to help this man with his English. My parents are going to be hanging their heads in shame when this segment airs on national television next week. They'll put me on the church prayer list for sure.

"Well, everyone, you've heard the judges' advice. However, let's keep the lovemaking to a minimum, shall we?" Mya winks at Gianni and then turns to us and smiles optimistically.

"Girls, in this challenge, you'll be matched back up with the hair and makeup team you've worked with the last few weeks. This week, you'll also be paired with a stylist who has already chosen a wardrobe for you. So no crazy mayhem at the clothes rack this time, okay, ladies?"

Thank God. I could do without another man-versus-the-trampling-herd survival experiment. How would Bear Grylls handle that? I'd like to see. Grylls might be able to survive for days in the wilderness, but women fighting over designer clothes—now, that's another test altogether.

Mya pivots around and looks directly back into the main center camera. She looks elegant tonight in a little red strapless minidress. Her hair is simple with soft waves.

"After tonight, we will have our final twelve contestants. It's then up to the at-home audience to pick their favorite. One of you will go home each week until we reach our final contestant, who will be crowned the winner of *Runway Star*."

A stagehand cues us again to clap and act happy, so we do as the camera sweeps over us.

"Good luck, ladies. Stay tuned out there. You'll not want to miss what's coming up next. We'll be right back after this." Mya points her finger toward the camera.

"And cut," the show director announces, and everyone seems to breathe a sigh of relief. Like mice when the lights come on, we all scatter to our designated places.

"My Katelyn, so glad to see you, senorita." José greets me with a peck on the cheek.

"I'm glad to see you, José. Thank you for making me beautiful. I wouldn't be here without you," I say, and I return the kiss on his cheek. I mean that sincerely.

"Oh, stop—you are fab-ulouz. You give me chills when you walk down the catwalk."

"*Gracias*, José. That's so sweet of you to say."

"*De nada*, my dear."

I believe that's "you're welcome" in Spanish. I'm getting better at translating or trying to understand his English, but between the two of us, we're still speaking Spanglish. It works for now, and as a last resort, there is always finger-pointing or charades.

I sit down at José's station, and he swivels me around to face the mirror. He takes down my hair out of its messy ponytail. It's still wet underneath. I decided to shower and go this morning. I figured the stylists would do all the work. At least I was hoping for that anyway. I didn't want to spend any more time in the apartment with Josie than I had to after our little spat.

As José is combing out my tangled locks, Amanda, the makeup girl, appears along with another fresh-faced girl. This must be the stylist that Mya spoke of in her intro. I'm pleased to see that there aren't any rawhide or burlap gowns in her arms. Call me crazy, but is an elegant outfit too much to ask for around here? I guess, for me, the question is this: What can I fit into these days? I think I've lost a few more pounds. I haven't checked recently. After last night's stab to the heart, I haven't been able to stomach much of anything today. Then again, my lack of appetite could also be because I indulged in some emotional eating with that pint of ice cream I put away last night. I can't say I've been totally starving.

Amanda introduces me to Ashlyn. She's going to be my personal stylist for the show. Right from the get-go, I like her. Ashlyn graduated from Columbia a few years ago. She is completely sympathetic for me over the potato-sack dress, and she says she will try her best to make sure I never have to wear anything like that again as long as I am on this show. Ashlyn says I truly pulled off the look and modeled it perfectly. I guess I'm better at this whole thing than I thought.

José styles my hair in long, loose, wavy curls. The things he can do with a curling iron amaze me. I usually just end up burning my head, my neck, or the tips of my fingers. I try to stay away from hot hair appliances. After last night's hand scorching, I should really try to stay away from anything hot, for that matter. Amanda keeps my makeup soft and adds a light pink gloss to my lips. From the head up, I think I look pretty good. Man, these people are miracle workers. Seriously, it's incredible what a little makeup and a great hairstyle can do for you. Maybe I should think about incorporating some of these things in my daily routine. I can do light pink lip gloss. Who knows? I might even give that Jessica character a run for her money with Ben. *There I go again. My goodness, I've got to stop thinking about that boy. I need to put him out of sight and out of my mind.* I've still yet to see him on set today. Maybe he's not coming.

Ashlyn holds up the dress I'm going to be wearing. I gasp. It's exquisitely elegant—a Marchesa full-length red silk evening gown. The top is fitted and is an asymmetrical one-shoulder design—that's how Ashlyn describes it. The bottom flares slightly at the knee and flows smoothly to the floor. My favorite part is the pretty little red rosette neatly attached at the top of the shoulder.

"I can't believe it fits," I say, shocked, as Ashlyn zips up the back with no problem.

"It sure does. It looks perfect." Ashlyn steps back, admiring the dress.

Wow, see what a little extra hard work at the gym and some lovesick loss of appetite can do for your figure? Did I just say lovesick? Let me rephrase. I mean disappointed—that's all. I'm just disappointed.

With dress, hair, and makeup complete, I move from the dressing area to take a look at myself in the full-length mirror resting against the adjacent wall. I'm taken aback at this strange person coming into clearer view as I approach the mirror. I barely recognize her. As I inspect this image in more detail, for a moment, I feel like I used to feel when I was a little girl playing dress-up with my mother's clothes. In those days, anything seemed possible. I'm engrossed in an outward beauty that I've never been aware of before. As I gaze intently at this reflection, I hear an affirming whisper in my spirit, and I know it can be only be God speaking to my heart: *This is what I see when I look at you.* I'm awestruck by the gravity of the moment. It's not an audible voice but, rather, a still, small, piercing thought that I know couldn't have been my own. I would never think this is what God sees when He looks at me. I think He sees a big ole mess, because that's what I normally see. On the contrary, God sees me as His beautiful creation. I feel all dressed up in His perfect love for me. Why do we choose to believe the lies of the world—the world without God that says you must look a certain way to be beautiful? No matter what I see on the outside, God sees me as beautiful. I look again and start to wipe away the tear that is making its way out of the corner of my eye.

"You look like an angel."

Nathan appears, and his reflection joins mine as he softly speaks over my shoulder. His breath is warm on my neck. I continue to peer at him in the mirror. He places his hand on the small of my back, and it shoots a tingling sensation throughout my body.

"Interesting. I always imagined angels in white, not red."

He smirks at my sarcasm and then purses his lips and looks at me with a glint in his eyes. "White is so drab. I like my angels in a bold color."

"Somehow I'm not surprised." I smirk in return.

He lightly laughs. "I like your spunk, my dear. I think you've just given me an idea."

"What do you mean?"

"I have a new inspiration for your photo shoot today."

I look at him, confused and slightly concerned.

"You'll see."

At that, he raises his eyebrows, slowly removes his hand from my back, and swaggers away. I watch him walk across the studio, his blond highlights shimmering in the light shining through the frosted windows. I keep watching in a clouded daze. Then he casually looks back as if to see if I'm still looking. *Doggone it. Why am I still looking?* He smiles almost victoriously and keeps walking.

I hear a faint cough to the left, and I snap out of the daze.

"You look incredible." Ben suddenly appears beside me.

So he has made it after all. I was starting to think he was a no-show. His smile is strained, and I can feel the tension between us. I hate conflict. I have to quickly squelch this awkwardness. I need him for this project.

"Thank you. I'm glad you could make it," I say, cool and calm.

"I wouldn't miss it."

"Mya's here today, so I think you should get some great shots."

"Sure. I'll do my best." He lightly pats his camera. "I'll just be over there." He points toward the visitor section.

"Okay. Good luck."

"And, Kate?"

I hesitate to answer. I don't want to talk about last night. What's done is done. Ben doesn't need to explain. I don't want to hear the rejection; the experience was enough for one lifetime.

"About last night—" Ben starts, when Mya makes an announcement for all girls to make their way to the main stage. Thank goodness. I am at a loss for words at the moment.

"Ben, I've got to go. I'll catch you later."

He nods as if he understands the meaning behind my silence and walks toward the designated guest area. I meet De-De by the dressing area.

"Everything okay?" De-De says, concerned, and she looks back toward Ben.

"Sure. Why?" I say. I try to maintain my cool composure, which is growing more stoic by the minute.

"Ben looks like he just lost his best friend or something. You two didn't break up, did you?" De-De asks with alarm.

Break up. Interesting—why does it feel that way, when we were never together?

I start to say no and then remember I've pledged to tell no more half truths, yet all I can say is "Maybe."

Chapter 16

I see now what Nathan's inspiration was all about as I'm standing here in grown-up angel wings. My photo shoot today consists of me in this spectacular designer dress, looking as if I've signed up for a bad Christmas pageant. I don't mean a poorly acted Christmas pageant—no, this is more like an expanded version of *The Best Christmas Pageant Ever*. I am playing the angel gone postal—oversized wings, handgun, and all. Nathan has me prancing all over the set as if I am one of Charlie's Angels on a hot pursuit. Actually, it is a lot of fun. I am getting into character. I seem to have Nathan going anyway. I'm interested to see how the photos turn out—good enough, I hope, to keep me around for one more week. Once again, we wait. They will be having a special taping on Monday night to pick the top twelve. This time, I have an entire weekend to bite my nails instead of one night.

Ben is nowhere to be found after shooting wraps for the day. De-De says she saw him leave shortly after Nathan started snapping pictures of me. I guess he got what he needed. I'll check with him later. I'm pretty tired after a long day of pretending to chase criminals. I need a long, hot bath and a cup of hot chocolate. Anxious to get home and into something comfortable, with backpack slung on my shoulder, I step out onto the busy Manhattan sidewalk. The hustle and bustle of life is all about me. A police siren here, a car horn blaring there, and voices chattering away—I stop to take it all in. At times, I miss the simpler way of life back home, but I've grown to love the sights and sounds of this city.

"There's my naughty angel."

I sharply turn around, and there's Nathan, standing suavely in the doorway. He's changed out of his suit and into a black leather jacket over a fitted charcoal-gray shirt and dark-wash jeans.

"If I were an angel, I'm sure I'd be doing good deeds, thank you very much," I sarcastically retort. I don't mean to be cranky, but that's what you get when you mix tired and hungry.

"I never said you wouldn't be nice. Nice doesn't mean you can't be naughty."

What is this guy's deal? I'm starting to get a little irritated and also starting to blush. Nathan can be intimidating. I'm having a difficult time keeping up with his flirtatious comments.

"Why, Nathan, I'm not sure what you mean."

"I mean that simply, I think you looked absolutely amazing today."

"Thanks. I had fun. You're a great photographer."

"Well, I've had a lot of experience."

I'm sure he has. I'm not just referring to his expertise with a camera. Nathan's got "player" written all over him. I'm sure he has romanced quite a few women in his all of maybe thirty years. I'm not sure if I want to be added to his list.

"It takes talent, too. I think you certainly have an artistic eye," I offer as a friendly gesture.

It's true; he does. I've been looking at some of his spreads in recent fashion magazines. Adrianna Watts tends to be his favorite muse. The backdrops of her photo shoots seem to be on some tropical island, with Adrianna bearing a lot of skin—too much skin for me to even think about showing at this stage in the game. I mean, the weight is coming off, but I would rather model the newest and most fashionable winter wear than minibikinis. Also, my mother would kill me.

"Artistry comes naturally when you have such a beautiful canvas to fill."

Man, oh man, is he full of it or what? Sometimes I don't know how to respond—play along or call his bluff.

"Nathan, do you use that sort of flattery on all the ladies? I hope you know I'm not so easily swayed."

He throws his head back a bit and chuckles as if caught in a lie.

"Why, Katelyn, I'm only stating the obvious. You know, you're allowed to accept a compliment. You're quite stunning, my dear. It makes my job easier when I have great talent to work with."

"Thank you."

"Hey, it's still early—what do you say we go for a drink?"

"Together?" I look around to see if he's talking to someone else.

"Yes, together. I promise I'll be good." He looks at me with eager eyes.

I can't help but smile. The man is simply gorgeous. What can a little drink hurt? And I am hungry. I guess my bubble bath will have to wait.

"Oh, all right then. One drink, and then I have to get going."

"You worked hard today. Let's have a little fun, shall we?"

Nathan smiles and casually puts his arm around me. The leather of his jacket smells new and complements the hint of rustic, woodsy cologne on his neck. This guy has a way of putting a spell on me. I wouldn't say it's a good one. I feel sort of pulled toward the dark side. I have an uneasy feeling in the pit of my stomach every time I'm around Nathan, as if I should know better. Tonight my usually strong will can't seem to completely resist this man's charms. Then again, it could be that Nathan is a fascinating diversion from my recent heartache.

We head around the corner, near Sixth and MacDougal, to an upscale restaurant called Marisol, famously known for their fancy surf-and-turf cuisine. I've never dined here before, only gawked as a passerby at the patrons sitting behind the extensive front windows. Nathan gestures for me to take his arm as the host generously greets us at the front door.

"Mr. Steele, so glad to see you, sir," says the kind gentleman in a crisp white dress shirt and black pants. I should've known Nathan must be a favorite here.

Inside, a rich decor welcomes us. Expansive wood beams adorn the high ceilings, and a mixture of dark-stained wood and white subway tiles fill the walls, complementing the natural exposed brick. Mirrors sit strategically behind chestnut-toned leather-trimmed booths with tables dressed in bright white linens. As we walk toward the back of the restaurant, I peer upward at the amazing hand-blown amber-colored glass globes hanging at different heights like chandeliers.

The host ushers us onto the second floor and promptly seats us in a prime location. It's a cozy table for two in the rear corner that overlooks the main floor. Judging by his comfortable attitude, I guess this must be "Nathan's table." I would venture to say that a number of pretty women have sat in this spot, unknowingly captivated under the dim candlelight. I feel my stomach starting to turn a bit. Maybe this isn't such a good idea. Wait a minute—I shouldn't be so hard on myself. This is not a date; it's totally innocent, and I do need to eat.

The waiter arrives and offers us a menu. Nathan orders the most expensive merlot listed. I know they say red wine is good for your heart, but I just don't like the idea of drinking something that looks like my own blood. It's sort of creepy. I order a Coke, full strength. I vow to get back on my diet tomorrow and wean myself from so much caffeine in one day. Between the three cups of coffee this afternoon and now the Coke, I'll probably be up all night—no beauty sleep here.

"Hungry?" Nathan asks, and he opens up the black leather-bound dinner menu.

"Starving! The carrot and celery sticks they give us at the studio are not quite what I would call filling. I assume it's not proper to offer models real food at work."

He laughs jovially. "You might have a point there. I hope it's okay for me to say, Katelyn, that I've seen quite a transformation in you over the past few weeks. I know the others have noticed too. I think you're a definite contender for the finals."

"You think so?" I take a sip of my Coke.

"Yes, I do. I've worked with quite a few models, and there's something extraspecial about you. It goes deeper than your beauty. An inner light, I would say. It's definitely captured on film."

I'm actually flattered. But does he use the inner-light line on all the girls?

"Thank you, Nathan. I think people need to see beyond the stereotype. Models can be more than beautiful; many of us have brains, too. I mean, look at De-De; she wants to go to law school. I think that's pretty amazing."

"And that's what makes you so different. You're the kind of person that sees the potential in everyone. You don't only focus on yourself."

"Not always. Please don't put me on a pedestal."

"We all deserve a pedestal now and again. Tell me, my dear— I'm curious: What is it that you desire in life?"

Well, that's a loaded question. I desire many things. Right now, I would love to have the juicy steak that a lady at a nearby table is biting into.

"This whole modeling thing was just something I sort of stumbled into. I never thought in a million years that I could be doing something like this—or wanted to, for that matter. I want to be a successful journalist. I work at a lesser-known magazine at the moment."

"Interesting." He takes a slow sip of his merlot. "What do you write about?"

"Cats."

"Really?" He furrows his brow slightly. "Are you joking?"

"I'm sorry to say that I am not joking." I give a faint smile.

"Fascinating." He pauses and peers at me with those icy blue eyes. "Do you like cats, Katelyn?"

"A few, but not usually my pet of choice," I whisper, not wanting to offend any nearby cat lovers.

"Well, that's a problem. I think modeling suits you much better, if I do say so."

"Yes, well, thanks."

I look over and notice that the lady at the next table is now eating a decadent side of mashed potatoes. I never knew potatoes could look so pretty, as if they've been pressed out of a decorating bag.

"I hope you find your passion in life, Miss Turner. I'd love to snap some award-winning shots for you in the future."

Nathan winks at me and raises his glass. I raise my half-full glass of soda, and we clink them together in a toast. For a moment, I think he might be honestly interested in me, not just the person he sees in front of the camera. I feel my guard dropping.

"Well, okay, but on one condition."

"What might that be?" He leans in closer across the table.

"They have to be spectacular."

He lightly laughs. "Why, my lady, for you, I wouldn't have it any other way."

Gosh, there is just something tantalizing about that British accent. It captivates me every time he speaks and is completely romantic.

The nice waiter arrives again. I, of course, order the steak and potatoes. Judging by the lady's plate, they look to die for. Nathan orders some sort of braised lamb with roasted fennel and couscous. I'm sorry—call me unrefined, but the thought of eating an animal I used to sing nursery rhymes about makes me downright sad. *Couscous* sounds like the overthrow of a dictator, not something one eats.

As our waiter turns to go, another waiter, carrying a basket of bread, hurriedly walks by, and the two collide. Fresh-baked bread goes tumbling down to the floor. In the moment of slight chaos, suddenly, images of burned toast and Ben flood my mind. I can almost feel his strong hand holding mine under the cool water.

"Katelyn, are you all right?"

Still gazing at the bread and thinking of Ben, I hear my name in the fog. "What?"

"Are you all right? I seem to have lost you to a daydream."

"Oh, that, yes—I'm fine. Just thinking about the article I'm working on," I say as I fidget with my utensils.

Nathan reaches over to still my hands. "I see. I should hope it might have been me you were dreaming about."

I giggle. "Why do I need to dream about you when I have the real thing right in front of me?"

Did I just say that? I doubt he would appreciate my thoughts on Ben Roberts at the moment, not to mention any chance of Nathan paying for my meal would be lost. I can't let Nathan think he's got me all figured out.

Following the main course, Nathan insists that we share dessert. Who am I to turn down dessert? I figure that by now, I've gained back all the weight I've lost this past week, so why not have dessert? What are a few more hundred calories going to hurt? As I suspected, the dessert is worth the indulgence. We share a decadent crème brûlée, made with Madagascar vanilla beans and topped with fresh berries. I would describe it as nothing less than amazing. Nathan certainly knows how to wine and dine the ladies. Maybe I've been a tad hard on him. I smile tentatively across the table as Nathan takes his last sip of wine.

It's almost ten o'clock when we arrive back at my apartment building. Nathan sweetly offered to walk me home. Thank goodness he did pay for my meal. I was worried I would be eating ramen noodles for the next two weeks. I'm not sure what to make of this evening. It came about rather unexpectedly. Nathan really is a nice guy despite the heart-breaker label I placed on him. He's funny and gorgeous and has an incredibly promising career. He has everything a girl could want—or rather, it seems he does. He's loaded with potential. As I think this, I feel an uneasiness grip my chest. The thought occurs to me that I really should ask him if he's a believer. You know, that whole unequally yoked thing doesn't work too well in the Christian life. God did say that such unions could cause some problems. Lord knows I don't need any more man *problems.* I don't want to potentially spoil the evening, so for now, that question can wait.

"This is me," I say as we stop hand in hand just outside the front of the old brownstone building.

We've been holding hands for a long time—for at least four blocks—and I'm becoming fond of the feeling.

"Can I walk you up?" he offers softly.

The cool night air blows the scent of his cologne in my direction. It makes me gleefully lightheaded.

"Oh no, that's not necessary. I had a fun time tonight, Nathan. Thank you for dinner." I smile lightly and meet his gaze.

"It was my pleasure. I'd like to see you again, if that's all right. It'll be our little secret." He leans in as he whispers these words, and he grazes my hair with his cheek.

Is he serious? He looks at me with the most sincere expression, and those blue-crystal eyes sparkle like diamonds in the moonlight. I swallow hard, thinking, *This is totally not happening to me,* and I'm not sure how to react.

"Um, sure. That's all right, I guess. I would like that too."

That's all right, I guess? That's the best I could come up with? Very smooth, Katelyn. Yeah, that was about as smooth as a broken fingernail without any good nail clippers handy.

Nathan reaches down, pushes a wild strand of hair out of my face, and gently places it behind my ear. Staring into his eyes, I breathe in another whiff of his earthy cologne, and I feel almost hypnotized by the fragrance. He moves in like a cunning lion—sure, steady, his eyes fixed on my vulnerable gaze. I'm not sure if I should feel terrified or exhilarated by the attention. Slowly, he pulls me close, his arms tightly around my waist. Without warning, I feel his lips fully on mine; his kiss is strong and powerful, almost demanding my response. I feel as if I should pull away, but I can't let go. I'm not sure if I want to. I can't think of a time that I've ever been kissed this way—not that I've had that many opportunities. This kiss has left me weak all over.

I feel weak as my mind and body are caught between worlds when the door to the apartment building shuts firmly behind us. It startles me, and I break the embrace. Glancing over my shoulder, I quickly notice a familiar brown baseball cap. It rests on the figure that is standing motionless on the steps leading down from the brownstone. Our eyes lock. It's Ben.

Chapter 17

What's Ben doing here? Did he just see the kiss? I hope he didn't see the kiss. Judging, however, from the way he's stoically standing there, he probably did. I don't know the protocol for damage control in these types of situations. I'm not familiar. What am I saying? I have nothing to be ashamed of here. So why is my heart racing, and why do I feel as if I might be sick?

I continue to lock eyes with Ben, my mind thinking of the other night outside his apartment door, the moment when we almost kissed. What is going on in the universe? This can't be my life.

I turn to Nathan. "Can you excuse me just a moment?" Nathan nods and benignly smiles.

I walk slowly to Ben, my head drooping as I go. It's strange somehow, but I feel guilty.

"Ben," I say timidly, wanting to address the increasingly awkward moment.

"Kate," he solemnly acknowledges.

Why did he have to call me Kate? I love it when he calls me Kate.

"What are you doing here?" I ask quietly.

He looks at me, expressionless—not cold and not sad, but as if I'm not even here, as if he's looking right through me.

"I was returning your article file. You left it at my apartment last night."

"Oh. Well, thank you. I didn't even know it was gone."

"Sure," he says, still solemn.

He peers at me curiously, as if he's as confused as I am. I don't know what to say next. He looks adorable in his rugged navy-blue fleece pullover, jeans, and hiking boots.

"I gave the file to Josie."

I lightly giggle with embarrassment. Ironically, this reminds me of when my father caught me kissing Robbie Fogelman behind the bleachers in high school at a football game—not a good thing, considering Robbie turned out to be our class felon. He stole numerous videos from Blockbuster, copied them, and attempted to sell them as originals. I always wondered how he had so great a selection of movies to watch.

"Oh, okay, of course you did. I really do appreciate it, Ben. I would've been going crazy without it."

"I thought you would need it, so …"

He would know. I'd have been taking pictures with my cell phone if it weren't for Ben.

There's an awkward pause, and then Ben casually tilts his head toward Nathan. "Well, it, um, looks like you're busy. So I, uh, guess I should go."

I turn back to glance at Nathan. He seems to force a smile this time and raises his eyebrows, suggesting a hint of growing impatience. I close my eyes, feeling as if I'm caught again between two worlds.

Swiftly, I turn back to face Ben, my head spinning. "Yes, well, um, thanks for stopping by."

Ben shrugs and clenches his jaw as he peers over at Nathan. "No problem."

He starts to walk away, and unconsciously, I reach out to grab his arm.

"Ben, wait," I say with a hint of desperation, my heart feeling as if it's bouncing all over the place.

"Yes?" This time, he looks at me with a glint of sadness in his eyes. I wonder if anything will go back to the way it was before.

"Thank you again."

I want to say more, but saying anything else wouldn't help the situation. He nods, gently touches my hand still holding his arm, and gives me that familiar wink I've grown to love. My heart aches inside as he leaves me standing there. I'm fixed in place, unable to move, as I watch him walk away.

"Katelyn, is everything all right?"

Nathan? Oh goodness, I almost forgot about Nathan.

"Absolutely, yes, everything's fine," I say emphatically.

That's a total lie; everything is not fine. I might be going crazy.

"Are you sure? You just seemed a bit shaken by that chap there. This guy—he's been on the set with you recently, hasn't he?"

"Yes," I say halfheartedly, not fully answering his question.

"Katelyn, is he your boyfriend?"

"Yes," I reply once more, still thinking about Ben standing there helplessly on the stairs. Nathan looks at me strangely, eyebrows rising again.

"No, no. I mean Ben's my friend, who, yes, happens to be a boy." I lightly laugh to myself and continue to stumble over my words. "He's been helping me with a special article. I'm letting him tag along on set. What guy couldn't resist inside access to a bunch of beautiful models?" I giggle and slide my hands into my jacket pockets.

Nathan exhales, his breath taking shape in the cool air. "Good point. What a lucky chap, having a friend like you."

"Sure. I guess so." I shrug and stare contemplatively in the direction Ben traveled. He's long disappeared around the block.

"Well, it looks like we both have some work to do, my dear. I will have to say good night then. I have lots of photos to go through for next week. You're pictures, especially—I can't wait to see how they turned out. They're going to be spectacular." Nathan endearingly touches the tip of my nose with his finger.

How sweet. Why does he have to be so nice? Nathan seems to be a good guy. I do like him. But I really like Ben, too. *What is wrong with me?* I've never had so many guys to choose from—or even one good choice, for that matter. This is all new to me. Anyway, why do I keep thinking Ben is free? He has Jessica—end of story.

"Thank you. I have to admit, Nathan, that you're quite the distraction—from work, that is." I smile fondly and gaze up at him; his diamond eyes are still twinkling in the light.

"I certainly like the sound of that, and I should like to continue to be your distraction some other night."

He kisses me tenderly on the forehead and walks down the brick sidewalk.

Josie's practically waiting at the door for me when I come dragging into the apartment. She seems highly irritated, with her hands on her hips and her foot tapping—definitely a dead giveaway of a bad mood.

"Glad to see you decided to come home," Josie says in her motherly voice. "I was starting to wonder."

"What are you talking about?" I say in defensive mode.

"I'm talking about *you*, down there with the photographer guy while poor Ben is up here waiting to see *you*."

"You mean Nathan. His name is Nathan."

"I don't really care what his name is."

Geez, what's with the inquisition? I'm not sharing my Marisol leftovers with her.

"How was I supposed to know Ben was coming by? He didn't tell me that he was coming over. A simple text would've been nice."

"He brought your work file and pictures." She points to the prints lying on the kitchen counter. "You and Nathan looked rather intimate. I'm starting to worry about your virtue." Her harsh tone cuts through the tense air.

I shut the door to our apartment so that the whole building doesn't hear about my virginity status.

"Josie, you can't be serious. My virtue is perfectly intact. Trust me. And don't tell me that you're taking Ben's side." I throw my hands up in the air. "There isn't even a reason to have sides. Let's be practical here—Ben is in a relationship, so why shouldn't I be too?"

"I really think you have Ben all wrong, Katelyn. He obviously cares about you. He came all the way over here just to return your file. He was concerned that you would be upset if you didn't have it to write your article. We both saw you down there with pretty boy."

So he did see everything.

"What did Ben say?" I walk toward my room, taking off my boots in the hallway, trying to balance myself on one foot at a time with one hand on the inner wall. Josie follows and stands at the doorway as I toss my boots into the open closet.

"Nothing—he didn't need to. There was something in his eyes; you could tell he was hurt."

"Hurt? I don't know what on earth for. He's never said he was interested in me. He's my friend and business associate. After seeing his trashy girlfriend last night, I'm sure that's all I'll ever be."

Okay, that was mean; I don't know anything about Jessica. She might not be trashy at all. She just dresses the part well.

"I know what it is." Josie leans gingerly against the doorframe. "It's your pattern."

"My pattern?"

"Yes," she says eagerly, as if she's about to reveal to me the secrets of the universe.

"I'm glad you've got it all figured out. Please, do tell." *Great, here it comes—an analysis of my emotional threshold.*

"It seems, my dear friend, that you continue to be afraid of getting hurt, so you push guys away, like you're pushing Ben away." Josie points an accusing finger at me.

She really knows how to knock a girl when she's down. I'll agree that sometimes it's better to keep someone at arm's reach instead of letting him get too close. It's easier to do the rejecting than to be rejected. I know—I've been on the losing end more times than I want to remember. I'm even more terrified of getting hurt with Ben. The more I get to know him, the more I want to know and the more I find myself falling deeply for him. I've had crushes before, but the way I feel about Ben is radically different. It's as if God took my what-I-want-in-a-man list and designed him perfectly for me. If Ben doesn't truly feel the same way about me, I'm better off not knowing.

I moan and then sigh deeply. "I'm just so confused." I place my hands on my chest and fall backward onto my bed. "Ben's seeing a mystery girl, and I still have no earthly idea why Nathan Steele seems interested in me."

"Ha!" Josie laughs. "That's easy. He just wants to get into your pants. That's all."

"What!" I say, shocked, and I sit straight up. "Well, thanks a lot, Josie."

"Be careful with him, Kate. Nathan could do more than break your heart."

"Ugh, I'm such a mess." I sigh and flop back down on the bed again. "What am I supposed to do?"

Josie's expression quickly shifts from frustration to compassion. "It sounds so cliché, but it always points in the right direction when followed correctly."

"What's that?" I look at her, puzzled.

"Your heart."

"My heart?"

"Yes, you need to follow your heart."

I grab my pillow and hold on to it as I roll back over to face the ceiling. I notice a couple of my glow-in-the-dark star stickers have fallen off the wall, sort of like my sanity.

"Follow my heart. Josie, it sounds so easy, but my heart feels like it's spinning out of control."

Josie sits down next to me on the bed. "Have you really searched your heart and prayed about it?"

"No, not really, I guess." I frown.

This is weird—Josie telling me to pray.

"Well, I suggest you start there."

Josie gently pats me on the head and silently leaves the room. I can't believe how blind I've been. It takes my religion-of-the-month-practicing roommate to tell me what I knew to do all along. Why is it that we often search in all the wrong places before we decide to seek the One who has all the answers? I should have done that first, and maybe I wouldn't be in such an emotional mess.

I toss and turn during the night, but sleep won't come. I can't stop thinking about Ben and Nathan. I'm in quite the predicament. Then again, Nathan doesn't know how I feel about Ben. Ben doesn't know how I feel about him or Nathan. I'm not even sure what I feel about either one of them at the moment. At three o'clock in the morning, after hours of insomnia, I decide to get up and find a change of scenery. I need to clear my mind if I'm going to make any progress on this article. I haven't started writing it, and Louise wants the intro completed by Monday. My last meeting with Louise did not go as easily as the previous one. There were no hugs or pleasant exchanges. Louise was stern in her demeanor and not as forgiving. She was as shocked as I am that I still do not have an introduction. She even has Clive on standby in case I'm not finished in time. There was a tone in her voice that hinted at a threat of demotion if I do not follow through with what I said I could deliver—although I'm not sure how anything other than being fired could be less than my current assignment as cat-food staff writer. Whatever she means, Louise means business, and right now, I still need my job.

I walk quietly past Josie's room into our living room, heading straight for the kitchen. I feel another emotional-eating binge coming on and open the door to the fridge. Luckily, we're out of ice cream, and all I can find are milk and cereal—not too calorie laden, I suppose. I grab a bowl and a spoon and opt for the Fruity Pebbles, the rainbow of colors slightly lifting my dreary mood. I sit down on the couch with my cereal and the article file Ben brought back, along with the pictures he's printed for me. The sweet, crunchy rice flakes combined with the cold milk taste yummy. I enjoy a few bites and then set down the cereal bowl on the coffee table. I pick up the article file and begin to flip through Ben's photographs. They're really good—and not like your average run-of-the-mill photos. Ben has an artistic eye for lighting and the positioning of people in tune with the setting around them. There are candid shots of the models, a few pictures of the judges, and some really great ones of Mya. I smile as I make my way through the pictures. An oversized yellow Post-It covers the last photo in the stack. I trace my fingers over the words as I read.

Katelyn,
No star shines brighter than the Star that's within you.
Good luck. I'm thinking of you.
—Ben

I gently pull off the Post-It, and underneath is a black-and-white photo of me intently gazing at myself in the mirror. It's an amazing picture—a rare moment of self-discovery captured through a camera lens. Ben watched it all unfold and thought enough to capture it here for me to remember forever. I feel the tears break through the surface, and that same still-small voice I heard earlier returns softly to my ear. The tears keep flowing as I realize that I don't have to figure this out alone. Thank goodness—I was starting to think I had fallen into the love abyss. I realize that as with most things, I'm probably making this thing more complicated than it needs to be. Oddly enough, I've decided to take Josie's advice to pray and let God lead my heart to the right place. Yes, God does work in mysterious ways and sometimes through the unlikeliest people.

A few hours later, I find myself caught between sleep and the distant voices I hear on the television set. The shrill beep of a telephone abruptly awakens me. Its whistle-like noise accelerates the arrival of a pending headache. In the early morning light, I reach over for my phone, which is lying on the coffee table beside my unfinished bowl of Fruity Pebbles. I rub my swollen eyes and look at the caller ID on my cell phone. It's my mother. I notice that the time on my phone is five thirty. That's early, even for Judy.

"Hello?" I drowsily answer.

"Katelyn," my mother says, her voice sounding slightly frantic.

"Mom, is everything okay?" My heart starts racing.

"No, everything is not all right. Kara's in the hospital."

"What's wrong? Is the baby ..." I hesitate, afraid to ask.

"Kara was in a car accident on the way home from work last night. It was raining, and she hydroplaned. She and the baby are fine. She gave us all a scare. We thought she might go into early labor."

I breathe a sigh of relief. "Thank goodness. I'm glad she and the baby are okay."

"They're keeping her for a few days for observation."

"Good. I appreciate you calling to tell me. Please tell her I am praying for them both." I begin to pick up my used Kleenex strewn about on the coffee table. I think I cried myself to sleep last night.

"Sure, sweetheart. I thought you would want to know."

"Please keep me posted on any changes. I'll come home if she needs me."

"Honey, we always need you."

I smile inside. I know my mother can be a bit high maintenance at times, but she does love me.

"Oh, Katelyn?"

"Yes?"

"Did you ever find out what those black spots were on your wall and carpet?"

I drop my handful of Kleenex onto the floor. I spoke too soon. On my mother's last visit with Kelsey, she was convinced that we had black mold. She complained that her lungs were constricted all weekend. The black spots were speckles of black finger polish that splattered after I dropped the bottle on the floor. I just never corrected her. I didn't want the lecture on appropriate cleaning methods.

"Possibly," I quickly answer, and I move on. "Mom, I've gotta run. Tell Kara I said to get better soon and that I love her."

"Okay, dear. Have a lovely day."

"You too. I love you."

"I love you too. Bye."

I plop back down on the couch, leaving the Kleenex on the floor, and curl into my favorite position. The sun hasn't risen yet. I can hear Josie snoring like a freight train from her bedroom, and I turn up the TV to drown out the sound. I thank God for protecting my family and drift off to sleep.

❀   ❀   ❀

The smell of fall is in the air as I enter Corner Street Coffee Shop. A few brightly colored leaves blow in after me. I reach up to take off my red toboggan as the heat of the warm shop immediately welcomes me. Despite recent events, on Monday morning, I decide to stick to my usual routine. I know Ben and I left things a bit awkwardly the other night, but it's official—I'm done crying a river over Ben. I realize that avoiding him will only make matters worse, and after all the work I did on this article over the weekend, I could really use a macchiato. Fortunately, there's a short line this morning, and Shelly is working the counter. At first glance, I don't see Ben, and I assume he must be in the back, grabbing more coffee or something to restock out front.

"Can I help you?" Shelly says to me as I walk up to place my unoriginal daily order. Then she does something unexpected: she smiles.

"Katelyn, I didn't recognize you."

I've been trying to look more presentable lately, ditching the normal sweatpants and cartoon-figure screen-print T-shirts as well as the haggard hippie work wear. Today I've opted for a light gray wrap dress, black tights, and a pair of black Mary Jane–style low-heel pumps.

"That's okay. How are things with you, Shelly?" I ask, trying to be polite.

"Not so bad, I guess." She leans in across the counter and whispers as if she's about to give me secret information. "I've been watching *Runway Star*."

I follow her lead and whisper back, sounding surprised by this revelation. "You have?"

"Yes. I highly support your platform," she says, still whispering.

My platform? This isn't the Miss America Pageant, and I'm not running for office, although one must remember whom I'm talking to here. *Okay, whatever. I'll just go with it.*

"Good luck. You have my vote," Shelly continues, still whispering. She looks around to make sure no one has overheard our conversation.

I'm flattered. This revelation from Shelly is a compliment. I still can't tell her that I used her women's-lib speech as inspiration and that it probably helped me get on the show.

"Thanks, Shelly." I smile softly. "Is Ben here today?"

Immediately, she grunts and answers in her more familiar, unhappy tone, "No, he's out of town. Gone home, I believe."

That's odd. Why would he just up and go home? That's not like Ben.

"Gone home? Do you happen to know why?"

"I think it was something about his mom—an emergency," she replies with a bit of concern in her voice.

"What's wrong with his mom?" I ask, now worried.

"I don't know the details; I just know he got a call yesterday. He left and said he's not sure when he'll be back."

I stand there sort of stunned, not knowing what to do next. *Should I call? Is someone sick? What if there was a death? I certainly hope not. When will he be back? What am I going to do about the article?* I start to feel panic inside my mind racing at all the questions.

I hear a loud grunt and cough behind me and notice the increasing sound of more footsteps as people enter the shop, forming a line behind me.

"Katelyn, can I get you something? We're really busy and, because of your Benny boy, short staffed as well."

Shaken from my anxious thoughts, I softly reply, "Oh yes, I'll have my usual."

Shelly looks at me blankly.

Seriously? I come in here practically every day and order the same thing.

"A caramel macchiato with whipped cream."

She starts to repeat the order, when I remember my diet, and I interrupt. "Oh, sorry. Could you make that a nonfat macchiato with no whipped cream?"

Shelly rolls her big eyes and proceeds to yell out the order as someone I don't recognize walks out from the back. I sigh heavily. I miss Ben already.

Chapter 18

A metamorphosis of sorts has taken place within me over the last few months since this *Runway Star* competition has begun. I've transformed in ways I never thought possible—body, mind, and soul. New York City has even transformed in the process, with Christmas lights and its magical storefront-window creations. Macy's department store looks like a winter wonderland, and the massive Rockefeller Christmas tree lights up the night sky for blocks.

It's hard to imagine that we've reached the final stretch in the competition, with only a few weeks left until the show's finale. Every week, I think I will go home, and every week, I'm surprised to still be here. America has been kind and still likes the girl next door. Luckily, I've never even been in the bottom two. I thought for sure I would go home after the underwater-photo challenge—it was a total disaster. I'm what you would call hydrophobic. I like to walk along the beach and take a light dip in the pool. Anything past waist-deep water sends me into a panic. This particular challenge required us to hold our breath and pose underwater—in a dress, no less. The dress was a relief in that I avoided a bathing suit, but the shoot did not go well, with the water pushing the weight of the organza fabric up toward my face. The pictures made me look as if I had just seen the devil himself—sheer terror, with arms flaring as tried to push the skirt of the dress away from my head. It was hilarious—I received the pity vote on that one.

Last week, the elimination show was a real nail bitter, leaving the top three contestants. Vivian, De-De, and I now remain to battle it out for the first *Runway Star* crown. Texas Long Legs happened to be the unlucky one voted off last week. Camilla constantly ridiculed her, telling her she was static, boring, and only able to do one pose, which consisted of pushing her chest out, exposing her voluptuous bosom. America finally agreed. Isabel shouldn't worry, though—I'm sure Victoria's Secret is just waiting to give her a call.

Vivian is definitely the favorite of the judges. She gets rave reviews each week. One can't deny that her photos are spectacular. Her personality, however, is not. I'm still trying to find a redeeming quality within her. She hasn't made the quest easy for me—or anyone else, for that matter. Viv has made it apparent that she's only out for herself, and if you get in her way, you'd better watch out. She bullies the stagehands and ridicules all the other contestants. I've gotten the hint personally on several occasions, and I try to stay clear of her as much as possible. In addition, there have been some odd happenings on set that I wouldn't doubt Miss Vivian had a hand in—for instance, a peculiar situation in which Isabel's toothpaste was tinted with blue food dye. Isabel looked as if she had eaten blue cake icing. Her teeth were stained for two days. No one, of course, would admit to the wrongdoing, with hints of sabotage being whispered around the set. I have my own suspicions. Camilla has already been on several of the top news stations doing damage control and has released a statement: "We are investigating any attempts at inappropriate behavior from any of our contestants or staff. Any attempts at hindering a contestant's participation will be viewed as an immediate reason for disqualification."

Despite the disruptions on set, I'm bracing myself for what I feel will be my final walk tonight, because I simply can't imagine that I'd be chosen over Vivian or De-De. The idea that I might go on to win this competition seems impossible, yet I suppose stranger things have happened. If I were to win, I have to admit, it would be fantastic. Think of all the places I would get to see—Paris and

Milan, to name a couple. And think of all the things I could write about. The list is endless.

Who knows? Doing all that traveling, maybe I would run into Ben somewhere along the way, too. I've tried not to think about Ben. I've done a pretty good job, too, and that "out of sight, out of mind" thing certainly helps. I found out from further investigation from Josie that Ben's mother had a small stroke, and that is why he had to leave unexpectedly. As a fellow professor, Josie's in the know and keeps up with him through e-mail and coworkers. He had to hand over all his classes at Columbia to other professors, and his shifts to another barista at the coffee shop. Josie says he'll still graduate; he'll just miss all the pomp and circumstance of walking across the stage and receiving his doctoral degree. I have yet to e-mail, text, or Facebook Ben, as I don't want to be a distraction to him or myself. He has bigger issues to deal with than me and my petty problems. I pray for his mom every day.

As if things couldn't get more down to the wire, I've still yet to have my big moment with Mya Sasser, and I'm running out of time. Louise has already extended my deadline well past the original due date. Tonight might be my last shot. I need to come up with a solid plan, but getting to talk to her is like trying to break into Fort Knox. Crowds of people constantly surround her, usually including her own personal aides or the producers discussing the script. I can only continue to admire her from afar. She really is as sweet and bubbly as she appears on *Wake Up with Rob and Mya*—a genuine sweetheart. I think we have a lot in common. I can definitely see us as girlfriends. We could go shopping together, share hair and makeup tips, or hang out at the park with the kids. Okay, maybe that's pushing it a bit. I really am a good babysitter.

Josie's here tonight for the semifinals to help me obtain a few more shots of Mya for my article. Ben captured some great pictures that I can use from the one time he was on set with her. I'm not worried about that portion of the article; I am growing more concerned that the article has yet to mention anything to do with cats, although Mya did wear a leopard-print skirt during our jungle-style photo session. Did I mention that I had to wrap an enormous snake around my shoulders during that shoot? My whole body was numb with fear, but the result was a serious expression across my face that Nathan and the judges said came off as sultry.

Josie and I enter the set, her mouth gaping. A look of complete elation drapes her starstruck eyes as she scans the *Runway Star* studio. Camilla's chatting with a set producer standing on the catwalk as we walk by, and Josie looks at me, eyes opening wider. I can almost see her pupils dilating.

"Is that …?" She starts to point.

I quickly but gently grab her hand and shake my head. "Yes, but let's not point at her, okay? I'll introduce you later."

Josie smiles giddily like a kid in a candy store. It feels sort of like role reversal. Usually, Josie is the calm one, and I'm easily excitable. I suppose after being a part of things here for the past several months, the newness has worn off.

"*Hola*, senorita. *Como estas?*" José says in his exuberant style as he greets me with a kiss on the cheek. I enter the dressing room with Josie by my side.

"*Bien, gracias.*" I kiss him back on both cheeks.

"Tell me, Kate—who's your lovely friend *aquí?*"

He walks over and immediately touches her red hair. Those curly locks are definitely any stylist's greatest hair challenge. I can see his mind working already, new hairstyles probably flashing all over his imagination.

"José, this is my roommate, Josie."

"Jo-ce. You have the most exzi-ting hair, *sí?*"

Josie reaches up and touches her springy red corkscrew locks, a look of shock on her face. "I do?"

"Oh yes, I can do lots of things." He smiles and lifts his eyebrows.

"Really? I've never known what to do with it."

"Oh honey, let José fix it for you. It will be aaamazing."

I'm pretty sure he meant *amazing*.

"José, you're so sweet." I pat him on the shoulder. "I'll have to bring Josie by your salon one day soon."

"Please. I will do it. And for Katelyn, José will do it no charge."

Josie's eyes grow wider once more. "Really, you would?"

"*Sí*, no problem."

"Oh, thank you, Mr. Lopez."

"No, please call me José."

"Thank you, José."

"You're welcome. Have fun visiting da show."

Josie smiles and turns to look at herself in the mirror on the wall. "Katelyn, I can't believe it. José is going to style my hair. Maybe I can finally look like Nicole Kidman instead of Ronald McDonald."

"Josie, you have never looked like anyone from the Golden Arches," I say. "Umm, but what I wouldn't give for some french fries right about now." I lick my lips at the thought.

"When you win this whole shebang, I promise to let you have a few fries."

"Just a few?" I say, frowning.

She grunts. "Okay, well, maybe a whole Happy Meal then."

I do love Happy Meals—something about getting the toy inside still makes me feel as if I'm seven years old. I smile in victory. "That's more like it."

I walk Josie over to my wardrobe rack. I pull out a champagne silk organza dress from the Chloé spring collection. Josie gazes in awe.

"It's okay. You can touch it," I say teasingly.

"It looks so delicate. It's probably worth the cost of a new Prius."

I laugh. "Probably. I don't want to know how much it costs. Then I'd be afraid to put it on."

"Well, I hope you're not getting too used to this special treatment and fancy clothes. I want to still be able to shop with you when this is all over," Josie says, pulling out a Jean Paul Gaultier peasant-style blouse from the rack. She gingerly touches the ruffles along the front.

"Not to worry, my friend. I'm still a bargain-shopping girl at heart."

I continue to pull a few more pieces to show Josie, when Mya casually strolls by and peeps into our dressing area. "Good luck tonight, ladies," she says in her sweet-as-apple-pie tone.

Josie stands there aghast, like the first time I met Mickey Mouse at Disney World. She's giddy with happiness.

"Kate, was that—"

"Yes, but don't point."

"She's so pretty. Prettier in person, isn't she?"

"I told you, and she's super nice."

"So have you finished your article?" Josie whispers, and she leans in as I place a dress back on the rack.

"Not exactly."

"I thought you told me you were almost finished."

I did tell her that I was almost finished. And I am—well, sort of, except for the Mya portion.

"Did you get the Mya interview?" Josie whispers again, using quotation-mark gestures with her fingers.

"No."

"Don't you think you're running out of time?"

"No kidding. I'm working on it. She's never alone to talk to, and we're always so busy on set—any last-minute suggestions?"

Josie ponders for a second. "No, but I'll think about it." Josie moves to the side as José motions for me to sit down so that he can begin his magic on my hair.

"I guess I need to go find my seat. I don't want to be in the way of making you even more beautiful." Josie smiles sweetly, reaching in to give me a hug. "You do look beautiful, by the way."

"Thank you. Now go have fun."

"I will."

Josie starts to walk off, when a little bell starts ringing on her phone, indicating an incoming text. She quickly pulls out her cell, looks down, reads the message, and looks up with a pleasant look on her face. "FYI, Ben's mother is doing better. He thinks he might be coming back to town in a few weeks."

"Oh, really?" I say, trying to sound casual. José takes my hair out of the hair clip. "Did he ask about me?" I can't believe I just asked that, as if my mouth were disengaged, absent from my brain.

"Not today," Josie replies.

I look at her with surprise. "What does that mean? Does he sometimes ask about me?" My heart starts to flutter.

She looks at me, not wanting to respond, as if she's sworn to secrecy. "Maybe."

"What does he ask?"

"Oh Katelyn, I said I wasn't going to get involved."

I realize I shouldn't be probing her for information, but it's not my fault she put me in this position. I look at her with pleading eyes. "Please?"

"Kate, you know you basically broke the man's heart."

"I did not," I say, protesting.

As she says this, Ashlyn and Amanda walk in with all the essentials to make me catwalk ready.

"I'm not so sure. I've never seen him light up the way he does around you."

"Are you talking about Mr. Steele? We see you two talking together. And there are pictures in the magazine," says Ashlyn.

"I saw those this morning—you two look so cute together," Amanda adds gleefully.

Something is wrong here. *What are they talking about?*

"My sister says they tell lies in those tabloids, but I don't believe her," José says, chiming in on the gossip as he pulls a knot out of my hair. I grimace from the hair pulling and then look at Josie in confusion and panic.

"What pictures?"

"You know—the ones of you and Mr. Steele holding hands outside of a Starbucks." Amanda smiles bashfully while pulling a large makeup brush from her bag and fluffing it against the palm of her hand.

This can't be good. I'm sure Camilla and everyone on staff will have something to say. I fear I'm disqualified.

"I don't know how this happened." I shake my head directly at Josie.

"Honey, you can never be too careful around those paparazzi. They always find you," José says as he separates another knot in my hair.

Josie looks as at me with an I-told-you-so expression.

"No kidding," I say anxiously. I drop my head into my hands.

"No, no, senorita. Keep your head up. I need to finish your hair."

José continues to comb through my tangled hair, putting it into some kind of updo. My mind's racing. My relationship with Nathan is innocent. We've only met a few times off set for coffee, and once we went to the movies. Our conversations have been general and are usually about what's happening on the show. He makes me laugh, and I enjoy his company. Beyond that, I'm not sure where this relationship is going, and now we're splashed all over the magazines. Ben's probably lost all respect for me, not to mention the fact that my reputation is ruined. I'm just waiting for my mother to call. This is not good. I can feel myself starting to hyperventilate.

"Does anyone have a paper bag?" I ask with short, labored breaths.

"Calm down. It'll be fine. Tonight you need to get your head back in place and focus on tonight's competition. We came here to win, okay?" Josie says, trying to snap me back into reality.

Her stern approach works, and for a brief moment, I start to get my mind off the fiasco that is already out of my control. A stagehand walks in and says, "We need all the girls in fifteen."

Josie gives me a hug as Amanda waits to apply my makeup. "I guess that's my cue. Break a leg," she says lightheartedly.

My heart stops. Why do people say that? I mean, I know why, but let's look at my history here. Please never tell a natural-born disaster waiting to happen to break a leg.

"Josie."

"You know what I mean—good luck, sweetie. Don't worry about the other stuff. It will work itself out."

I smile bleakly, a new look of terror appearing on my face. She hurriedly walks away. I'm just one big ball of emotion at the moment.

"Everything okay, senorita?" José says, noticing my anxiety.

"I'm not sure, José, but it's nothing I can't get through with some help from above."

José smiles pleasantly and nods. And I realize putting my faith in God is the only thing that can help me out of this mess.

Chapter 19

No one has a copy of today's tabloid magazines. I've been casually asking around as we wait for the competition to begin. I have to see those pictures. I can't believe this is happening. Nathan and I have been completely casual. I met him last week at Starbucks for coffee because we both happened to be in the neighborhood. He lightly touched my hand as we were leaving that day, and that was it—purely platonic. I made sure of it—I guess not sure enough.

To top it off, we're finishing tonight's competition by modeling designer wedding gowns. I know—the irony. I'm sure this doesn't help to avoid sparking any fancies of romance by onlookers. The gown I'm wearing, a Monique Lhuillier, is exquisite, like something I could only imagine wearing in my best wedding fantasy. The design, traditional with a twist, boasts a hint of soft sophistication with its opaque white Chantilly lace bodice, adorned with a mocha-colored satin sash wrapped around the waist, and its A-line skirt cascading like a waterfall down to the floor. My one accessory is a full bouquet of blushing pink roses.

It's commercial break, and I'm doing the one thing that I'm slowly becoming an expert at: waiting. This will be my second time down the runway tonight. My first catwalk was semisuccessful, as the overall critiques from the judges were positive, with the majority in agreement. But they also said that tonight I'm too stiff and not engaged. Camilla made me more nervous by saying, "We're in the final stretch, ladies. If you want to win this, you have to bring your best game. Katelyn, I'm expecting more from you." I can't deny I'm not giving 100 percent this evening, and the judges couldn't be more spot-on with their observations. Tonight I feel like a robot of sorts, just going through the necessary steps but completely disconnected from everything around me.

De-De is first up to model her wedding-dress ensemble. I watch from behind the stage. She's confident, beautiful, and flawless in her ultrasimple yet elegant Oscar De La Renta pearl-colored silk crepe floor-length gown. Her hair is smoothed back in a side bun, with a purple orchid neatly placed behind her ear; she looks like a Tahitian princess. She dazzles the audience, and applause is generous across the room as De-De nears the end of the runway. The judges give her rave reviews.

I'm next up to walk, and Vivian, who, strangely, has been MIA for the last thirty minutes, is to finish out the top three. I'm starting to feel the pressure. Almost subconsciously, I start to pick up the old nail-biting habit, when Mya suddenly appears, joining me backstage. She mentions that she's thirsty and is standing here waiting on someone to bring her a bottled water. I need to refocus. Here's my opportunity. I'm quickly running out of them. Obviously, I don't have time for a full-on interview, but there must be something I can do. *Hurry, Kate. Think of something clever.* My brain is completely blank.

"Your dress is my favorite, by the way." Mya looks at me as she twists the cap off her water bottle. I take a quick look about, wondering whom she's talking to, and I quickly realize it has to be me. We're the only two standing here, and I'm the only one in a wedding dress.

"It is?" I ask to clarify that Mya's directing the conversation my way.

"It reminds me of my wedding gown." Mya looks right at me, her eyes scanning over my dress.

"Thank you. It's quite stunning, isn't it?" I touch it lightly with my free hand, the other one still holding on to the pink rose bouquet. "I bet you were beautiful in your wedding gown."

She smiles tenderly. "I think every girl looks beautiful in her wedding gown, but you look amazing. You should keep that one in mind for your big day."

I giggle lightly and casually wave the bouquet around. "Oh no! I don't know. Not planning on that anytime soon. You need a fiancé for that, and I don't even have a boyfriend. Not at all! Not even a boyfriend," I say. "Not even a boyfriend."

"Well, that dress really suits you." Mya grins.

"Thank you."

With delicate finesse, Mya lifts up her water bottle, takes a swallow, and sets the bottle down on a chair behind the stage. I know this is my last opportunity. I have to go for it.

"Mya?" I squeak.

"Yes?" she answers softly.

"I'd love to talk with you again. I have some questions for you—one aspiring journalist to another," I say, smiling with a hint of timidity.

Mya kindly returns the smile. "Sure. I'd like that."

She said yes. Great. Okay, what now? I start to stumble over my words. "Uh, well, great. What would be the best way to reach you?"

Mya starts to answer, when a stagehand signals that they're ready for her out front; the commercial break is ending, and the *Runway Star* theme song is playing in the background, cueing us that we're back on air. Just like that, she's gone. Who knows if she'll even remember this conversation? I made the connection, and that's more than I've done in months. There's nothing more I can do. If I go home tonight, I need to update my résumé, because I'm certain I will be out of a job. Louise has given me full warning.

I try to remain calm and pull my bouquet underneath my nose, deeply inhaling the alluring scent. I steal a glance at Nathan on the side of the stage. He has his camera in hand. I wonder if he's seen the magazine. My thoughts start to wander to a far-off place. Will they disqualify me? I realize I've stared too long; Nathan catches my gaze, looks up, and smiles warmly. Out of paranoia, I try desperately not to smile back. I don't know who's watching now and who might snap the next picture. It'll be another headline for tomorrow's gossip: "*Runway Star* Contestant Katelyn Turner Spotted Ogling Her Puppy-Love Photographer Backstage."

"You know, Nathan dated Adrianna for two years."

"Excuse me?" I jump slightly.

I turn to my right, and Vivian is standing there looking at me, eyes full of mischief, the corners of her lips upturned into a sly grin.

"It ended badly, from what I hear. She caught him cheating with some up-and-coming actress."

Viv is wearing what resembles a white wedding gown. Oddly, it looks like a man's white tuxedo but is made out of fine silk and is fastened to a white miniskirt of matching fabric. The top portion of the dress resembles a tapered jacket—short at the waist in the front. The back of the jacket has long tails that extend outward and all the way down to the ground, giving it the illusion of a train but with a feminine, structured elegance. She's wearing a white top hat to boot, with a fluffy white flower and long white goose feathers attached to the side. Her vibrant red hair is flowing down her back. Instead of a traditional bouquet, she's carrying a long white walking stick wrapped in white gardenias. The stick itself doesn't look as if it belongs; it looks as if it's been crafted together by a child. But you can never tell what some of these designers are going to put together.

"No kidding," I reply, doing my best not to act surprised or jealous or show any other emotion.

"Don't worry, sweetie. He's totally smitten by you. I think you may have curbed his short attention span. The tabloids just love the two of you."

"What?"

"Oh, by the way, there's been a slight change to the lineup. They've asked me to go next. They want you to finish the show in the Lhuillier dress," Vivian says, rapidly changing the subject.

She walks away like a cat that has just caught a mouse. I stand there in a daze, still processing Vivian's comments about my relationship with Nathan. Funny, I had always wondered about Nathan and Adrianna. I've never thought to look anything up about the two of them. I don't know why. I guess I really didn't want to know. There's definitely a sense of awkward tension between them. I'm surprised he's never said anything. Then again, why would he? Wait a minute—why would Vivian be sharing this with me anyway unless she knows something and wants to stir up trouble? Why, that little rascal. I wonder if she had something to do with the pictures in the paper. I don't trust her at all. Some people are challenging to even like, even though we're called to love them all. I start to question her before she's out of range, when Mya calls out Vivian's name. Vivian roguishly glances back at me and takes her white flower stick, turning it upside down and dragging it along the ground beside her as she glides out onto the runway.

"Why is she going next? I thought you were second in the lineup," De-De says, confused, now standing beside me. I can smell the sweet scent of the orchid in her hair.

"Huh? Oh, I don't know. She said they changed the rotation and wanted me to go last."

"Who said?"

"I'm not sure. The stage manager, I'm assuming."

"I don't like this, Katelyn. She's up to something. And knowing Vivian, it's not something good. You keep your eye on her."

"I know. I'm starting to think she'd do just about anything to win this competition."

"No kidding. I'm telling you, Kate—watch your back."

"I will. You too."

De-De and I eagerly turn to watch Vivian on the backstage TV monitor as she walks majestically down the runway. The tails of her wedding jacket sweep behind her like a cape as her hips sway from side to side almost as if she's dancing. She stops midway, taps the gardenia-covered cane on the floor, and then continues to drag it along beside her, never picking it up off the ground. The lights sparkle off the glittery silver-jeweled edges of her coattails.

The judges give a peculiar look at the cane and whisper to one another. I look over to De-De. "I wonder what that's all about."

"Who knows? They love her. Camilla just lights up when she talks about Vivian."

"You've got that right. I think Camilla sees lots of dollar signs dancing about her head."

We keep watching curiously as Vivian completes her walk down the runway. Camilla is the first to give her critique.

"Vivian, let me simply say that your walk was magical."

I look at De-De and turn up my nose in disgust. De-De rolls her eyes and nods in agreement.

Camilla takes off her red glasses. "I'm curious, however, where that white cane came from. I don't recognize it as part of the Versace design."

Vivian gives a dramatic look of surprise. "This?" She points to the cane she's holding like a walking stick and says, "It was given to me. I didn't know it didn't go with the dress." She bats her eyes and attempts to innocently look at the audience.

Oh, please—gag me.

"Interesting." Camilla looks at her skeptically but seems to forget the mistaken cane identity. "Even so, I thought it was fantastic. Great job."

The crowd roars in applause. *What's wrong with these people?* Vivian has everyone fooled, right down to the sweet little girl in the front with the pink bow in her hair. *Can't they see how mean and nasty she is?*

Gianni is next to comment, again giving only short but stellar remarks. Adrianna is the only negative judge, saying that she feels Vivian's walk was a bit over the top and too theatrical. She says she felt as if she were watching a Vegas show instead of being drawn in to see the dress and not the model. Vivian's face turns sour at Adrianna but quickly twists into a gracious thank-you as she moves back to leave the stage, still dragging that white cane along the other side of her, making one large circle. I can't help but think of what I would like to do with that cane, and it sure isn't to use it as an aid in walking.

As Vivian leaves the stage, we immediately go to another commercial break, and stagehands scatter over the set. José and Amanda move in quickly to do a final check on my hair and makeup. Amanda has just enough time to brush my lips with a tinted pink gloss. Ashlyn starts to pull on my dress, making sure the ruffles along the bottom are perfectly set.

"Katelyn, are you feeling better? I heard you might have a stomach bug," Ashlyn says as she fluffs out the train extending along the bottom of the dress.

I look at her, confused. "I feel fine."

"Oh, that's good to hear. We were worried. Vivian told us that you said you thought you were coming down with something."

"She did?"

"Yes, so she volunteered to go before you."

I uneasily glance at De-De, and she peers back at me with apprehensive eyes.

"Katelyn, I don't like this. Something's up."

"It does sound a bit fishy, doesn't it? Maybe she wanted to wow the judges before me, thinking it would give her an unfair advantage," I say, mildly concerned, and I shrug.

"Maybe. I have a bad feeling."

"Me too, but what can we do? The show must go on, right?" I swoosh my dress around. Ashlyn's holding the back of the train, following my lead. The runway melody starts to play. "Looks like I'm up."

De-De looks at me with concern. "Good luck."

"Thanks."

"Welcome back, everyone. The pressure is mounting here on *Runway Star*. We're down to our final three contestants. Our final dress of the night will be worn by the girl we've all come to love, our girl next door, Miss Katelyn Turner," Mya says, smiling brightly into the camera, giving my cue.

"Katelyn, you're on," says the stage director as another stagehand gently guides me onto the runway. The light is blinding, as always, as I step out onto the platform. I try to focus on the little girl with the pink bow, who's vaguely in sight. After Vivian's attempts to upstage me, I need to practice extreme concentration. The best way I can think to do this is to breathe in the moment and imagine what it would really feel like to be wearing my wedding gown.

Ashlyn spreads my midlength train out across the platform behind me as I begin to walk. An upbeat remix version of *Pachelbel's Canon* is playing, and suddenly, in my mind, I'm no longer walking on a runway but on a sandy beach leading to a beachside altar. I can almost feel a light breeze blowing against my face and smell the salty ocean. I'm walking barefoot; the sand is gritty and soft beneath my toes. It's like a magical dream unfolding before me. In an instant, the bright light breaks, and I see him. He's handsomer than I've ever imagined; his dark brown hair is richer in hue next to the crisp white linen suit. His deep brown eyes sparkle, and he smiles as I walk to meet him. I'm lost in the moment as, in my vision, Ben is there waiting for me.

The dream continues; he takes my arm, and I feel the earth move beneath me. I always imagined that on my wedding day, I would feel as if I'm walking on air. The dream is so real, as if I can actually feel the earth gliding.

Strangely, the ground moving feels entirely too realistic. Wait a minute—I think it is real. The jostling beneath my feet is not my imagined fantasy; something is moving beneath me. My right foot slips forward, my left foot slips backward, and I'm no longer on a warm, sunny beach. I fearfully look directly to the judges. I see a look of sheer panic on Adrianna's face as she gasps. I'm frantically trying not to fall, my arms flailing and feet sliding underneath me. I wobble to stay upright but quickly slip again in an almost gymnastic split. The surface of the runway is slick, like motor oil. I keep trying to balance myself but to no avail, and I feel myself succumb to my apparent moment of destiny. I hear more gasps and squeals reverberating from the audience. The bouquet I've been gripping for dear life flies out of my hand. I watch but can't stop the torpedoing bouquet, its trajectory taking it straight in the judges' direction. I see the entire catastrophe unfolding as I fall backward with no recovery in sight. The sound of a loud thud ricochets through my ears as the back of my head hits the floor. A cloud of darkness envelops me as my white wedding gown falls down over my head like a parachute.

❀ ❀ ❀

I awake to a throbbing pain in my head and another stabbing pain in my right ankle. A harsh light of a different kind causes me to squint as it penetrates my hypersensitive eyes. I hear the faint sound of rustling paper next to me.

"Oh, thank God, you're awake," says an anxious voice I recognize as Josie's. She quickly closes her magazine and lays it next to me on the bed. I realize I'm not in my bedroom, and this wasn't a bad dream. No, it's a bad reality. I'm in a hospital. I try to sit up, but the rushing pain in my head tells me that's not such a great idea.

"What happened?" I say, confused, and I dizzily lie back down.

"You don't remember? Oh my goodness, do you have amnesia?" Josie's high-pitched voice rises in panic. She firmly grabs my face and looks me square in the eyes. "Do you know my name?" She speaks slowly, dragging out each syllable as if I can't understand her.

"Yes, I know you're name—Jo-C?" I reply in similarly slow, exaggerated syllables, giggling.

"Kate, it's not funny. You took quite a tumble and half scarred everyone in the audience and a few million people in America." Josie sighs heavily while slumping back down into the chair beside me.

"All I remember is being on the beach and walking down the aisle. Ben was waiting for me. He had a red rose on his lapel. He reached for me, and then the world went black."

"You may not have amnesia, but you sure did hit your head." Josie rolls her big amber eyes. "That's definitely not what happened."

So there was no beach, white sand, or ocean breeze blowing against my cheek. And if there was no beach, there was no Ben. I move my head sharply, and a searing pair runs up my right side as the whole nightmare begins racing back to my mind. The last thing I remember seeing is my bouquet of pink roses barreling toward the judges.

"My bouquet. It was heading right for—"

"Yes, your flowers nailed Camilla in the face. It was quite entertaining, actually." Josie grunts. "I mean, despite the fact you fell, of course. It was like watching you on an episode of *The Wipeout Zone*," Josie says, confirming my worst fear.

"I remember stepping out, and the floor was slick. There was nowhere else for me to go but down."

"It was a hot mess—that's for sure."

"Why was the runway slick?"

"They immediately went to commercial when you fell. The runway was covered with vegetable oil."

I shake my head in disbelief. *Really? Vegetable oil? Definitely a sign I should avoid fried foods.*

"It took four people to carry you offstage. They were all slipping and sliding," Josie says, trying not to laugh.

I also try not to laugh; however, the image of the stagehands slipping and sliding while trying to carry me offstage is quite hilarious. I look at Josie, she looks at me, and simultaneously, we both break out into boisterous laughter. A nurse walks in shortly after to see what all the commotion is about. She's carrying a stethoscope.

"Oh my goodness, Miss Turner, you're awake," the young nurse says, surprised. "How are you feeling?"

"Fine except for this terrible headache. And my ankle hurts,"

"You've taken a bad fall, and the X-ray of the ankle showed it's only sprained. It should be better in a few days. It's best that you stay off of it as much as possible."

The nurse reaches down and lightly touches the inside of my wrist. She starts counting. Josie and I try to gain our composure and stop laughing.

"Sounds good. I'll be back in to check on you later. And also"—she looks at me hesitantly—"would it be okay if I get your autograph before you leave? My daughter just loves you."

I'm flattered. This is my first autograph request.

"I can't believe that happened to you on the show. I'm surprised your boyfriend isn't here."

"My boyfriend?" Confused, I look at Josie. She's shaking her head in disapproval.

"The handsome photographer from the show—Nathan Steele. You guys are so cute together," the nurse says giddily.

"I guess the story is out," Josie says, annoyed. She reaches for the magazine on the bed. She holds it up to show me the pictures everyone's been talking about.

My excitement over the autograph request deflates. My head's throbbing. I think my pain meds are wearing off. *Yeah, why isn't Nathan here?* I could be in a coma or on life support, for all he knows. And the man I'm supposedly semidating—or, according to the tabloids, the man I'm in love with—isn't even here by my bedside.

"Well, Nathan and I are good friends. I'm sure he had responsibilities to finish at the show. He knew I was in good hands." I look endearingly at Josie.

She rolls her eyes again; the nurse smiles, seemingly satisfied by my answer, and walks out.

"Katelyn, we need to talk about this Nathan situation."

"Let's not and say we did. Has anyone called my parents? They're probably frantic by now," I quickly say, trying to change the subject.

"I've called your mom every hour since it happened. She's been well informed, and your dad was practically already on a plane. I told them you were resting and would call them as soon as you can."

"Thanks, Josie," I say, relieved.

"Hmmm. Then tell me more about this Ben beach-wedding fantasy." Josie sits comfortably back in the navy-blue faux-leather chair, folds her arms, and looks at me intently.

I don't comment. I was completely in my right mind when I had the image of Ben and me on the beach—it was well before I bounced my noggin on the ground.

"Our dreams can tell us what our heart can't express," Josie says with an introspective tone. Suddenly, we hear light knocking at the door.

"Come in," I call out, welcoming the interruption of Josie's dream interpretation.

De-De peeks around the door and hesitantly enters. She's no longer in the wedding gown but is dressed in casual jeans, a black turtleneck, and large silver hoop earrings.

"Katelyn, are you okay?" De-De asks, noticeably worried.

"Yes, I'm fine, except for this nasty headache and a sprained ankle. No permanent damage done."

"You gave us all a scare."

"Do they know what happened?" Josie asks fretfully.

"They found vegetable oil seeping out of a hole in the bottom of Vivian's cane."

"No! You can't be serious!" I gasp.

De-De nods. "Yep. She denied having anything to do with it. A suspicious bottle of canola oil was found in the ladies' bathroom. They're checking it for prints, and Vivian's being questioned as we speak. I'm just so glad you're okay, Kate."

"I can't believe someone would do something like that," Josie says, stunned.

"No wonder she would never lift the cane off the ground and kept dragging it alongside her. I knew something didn't look right about that flower stick," I say as I untwist the IV tube from around my arm. I'm seriously thinking about pulling this thing out myself. It's unnecessary.

"Katelyn and I have both been suspicious of Viv for a while now. I think it was only matter of time before her little tricks caught up with her," says De-De like a future attorney, pacing around my hospital room. "And if she did do this, her modeling days are over. She'll never work in the industry."

"It's sad. Even though I'm not a fan of her personality, you can't deny that she's very beautiful and talented." I try to muster some sympathy for the girl. "Something has to be missing in her life for her to be so desperate to cheat."

"Some people think cheating is the only way to win, I guess," De-De replies, eyebrows raised.

"You know what this means, don't you, girls?" Josie jumps up from her bedside chair, overly excited, as if she's just won the lottery.

De-De and I look at one another with curiosity.

"You two are in the finals for sure."

"We are?" De-De and I say in unison.

"Absolutely! Katelyn, you did it," Josie says, giddy with happiness.

Maybe by default, I suppose, but I've made it to the finals of *Runway Star*. I'm not complaining in the least. I'll take it.

Chapter 20

This morning, Nathan redeems himself after his absence at the hospital as I awake to four dozen yellow roses delivered to my apartment. After a thorough checkup, the doctor gave me a clean bill of health with the instructions to take it easy and stay off my ankle for a few days. Along with the roses, Nathan includes a note: "Thinking of you. Feel better soon. Love, Nathan."

Love—such a grand word with so many meanings. If Nathan were going for a theme here, I would have expected red roses instead of yellow. I always thought yellow roses meant friendship. Maybe he's trying to tell me something without telling me. Or I'm probably overanalyzing, as usual. If it is love in my heart, then why wasn't Nathan standing at the end of the aisle in my daydream?

The door to my apartment abruptly slams, and I jump, smashing a yellow rose into my nose. The smell now lingers in my nostrils.

"Forget something?"

Josie looks around in awe. "It's like an entire florist shop just took up residence in our apartment. I was in such a hurry I didn't realize there were so many of them," she says, astonished.

"I know. Nathan overdid it a bit."

"I'll say. I can't even find my bedroom."

"So why are you back so soon? Didn't you just leave a few minutes ago?"

"I thought you needed to be warned. There are about thirty paparazzi buzzing around outside, waiting for you."

"What?"

"Oh yes, my dear, they're asking everyone going in and out of the building if they've seen you today and how you're doing. The rumor is that you broke your leg and have amnesia. I heard one girl with a camera say that she heard you were in a coma."

"Didn't know I was so popular." I go to the window to take a quick peek.

They're right outside our building's main entrance with cameras up and ready. Those guys must be hurting for stories if they're all camped out waiting for me. Isn't the Brangelina bunch in town this week?

"Apparently, you are. I wanted to warn you if you decided to go anywhere today, but you shouldn't be doing anything but resting. So please don't go out in your pj's and T-shirt if you have to leave. I don't want you plastered all over TMZ in your SpongeBob SquarePants pajama bottoms."

"Right," I wholeheartedly agree.

"Okay, well, enjoy your day in captivity. You better get used to it. I'm outta here," Josie says on her way out the door.

I walk over once more to the window and carefully sneak another peek. It does appear the paparazzi are holding me captive in my own house. What did she mean by I'd "better get used to it"? I don't know if I want to be followed around like this for the rest of my life. I'm not sure if I'm ready to be a full-on celebrity. I like my anonymity—that's why it took me two years before I decided to join Facebook. If I win *Runway Star*, things really will change. I'm not sure how I feel about that possibility.

I make some coffee, not wanting to go out of the house or get dressed up. I wouldn't want to appear like a slob since there are people now taking pictures of everything I do, not to mention I'm wearing this ugly boot thing on my ankle.

I still have an occasional pain shoot through my head if I move the wrong way. I'm not going to be participating in the show tonight for the final cut before the finale. The authorities proved Vivian was the culprit behind the slick-runway fiasco. Her fingerprints were all over the canola-oil bottle and the white gardenia cane. She finally admitted to making it herself and finagling an actual oil pump inside the cane, which was quite clever, I must say. She also admitted to the blue-toothpaste incident. It's too bad Vivian wasn't using her creative energy on more-productive endeavors. She was immediately disqualified from the show. Josie was right; De-De and I will be announced as the final two. I'm not sure exactly how I should feel—grateful or embarrassed.

On the flip side, no one from the show has said anything to me about the tabloid pictures; the Vivian fiasco has likely overshadowed the faux scandal. Only two pictures of Nathan and me are in the magazine, and neither one shows anything romantic, except Nathan's hand lightly touching mine as we're talking outside of Starbucks. The headline reads, "Runway Love: Photographer Nathan Steele and *Runway Star* Contestant Katelyn Turner Share a Tender Moment over Coffee." I guess you could read more into the photos if you wanted to. Nathan actually tweeted that he's enjoyed getting to know all the contestants on the show and that his relationship with me is purely friendship. At this point, I have to agree.

As luck would have it, this opportunity gives me one more shot to talk to Mya and one last chance to save my current job. My article could still be salvageable; however, the outcome, as it stands, is uncertain at best. I can already see Clive's gloating face as his article makes the January issue, and I might as well be on the chopping block. However strange it might sound, for the first time, I'm not worried about my fate at *Fancy Feline* or my future. I'm coming to understand more and more that there is a greater hand that guides my destiny. Life is more about trusting in that hand rather than figuring it all out myself. No matter what happens, it's time for me to move on from wasting my days writing about something I have no interest in or passion for. I want to start living my life to the fullest and not just being satisfied with the status quo. Now, granted, we all have to pay our dues, so to speak. It's true that for much of life, we're placed in situations that help us grow and mold us into what we're meant to be. It's like that whole refining stuff I've been reading about in my daily devotions. God wants us to shine like silver and gold. He wants us to be a reflection of His love to others. I'm learning that isn't always an easy process. *Fancy Feline* has not been for naught, but I finally feel I have the courage to try something new. Maybe I haven't done it before because I've been afraid of failure. So what if I fail? Failure could be the thing that brings me closer to success.

The day drags on, and the paparazzi slowly drift off, with only one or two faithfully appearing now and again. I spend most of the day napping or immersed in HGTV—I love how the designers fix up those small spaces. My mother has called five times already just to make sure I'm okay. I assure her that I'm going to be fine and convince her not to come to my dire aid, although I do take advantage of her invitation to send me a goody box filled with homemade cookies. Her double-chocolate chocolate-chip cookies send me into a sugar overload every time I indulge—delicious.

Late in the afternoon, out of sheer boredom and solitude, I decide to pull up my Facebook page, curious to see what's going in the world outside these four walls. I click on my profile, and my brain doesn't seem to register the number listed above my friend requests. I have more than five hundred friend requests and countless comments from my confirmed friends posted to my wall. This can't be. I don't know that many people. Who knew that one fall on national television could stir up such popularity?

I sit there stunned and look through the incredible amount of people asking to be my friend; 95 percent of them I've never heard of or seen before in my life. I've been on the show for weeks, but I have never had this response before. As I'm scrolling, my cell phone rings. I answer and start to read a few posts. "Kate, have you seen it?" my sister Kelsey eagerly asks me on the other end.

"Seen what?" I have no idea what she's referring to.

"It's gotten like a million hits."

I love how my sister hasn't even asked how I'm doing after my head- injuring fall.

"Seen what?"

"The video on YouTube! It's gone viral."

"What video?" I ask, intrigued but feeling a little trepidation.

"Someone released the whole thing on video. You slipping, sliding, and falling and then the bouquet smacking right into that Cruella's face."

"You mean Camilla's face?"

"Yes. Cruella, Camilla—whatever. You know what I mean," Kelsey snidely remarks.

Funny—*Cruella* is fitting; Camilla does at times remind me of the villain in the Dalmatian story.

"I'll post it to my Facebook page."

"No! Kelsey, wait," I interrupt.

"Oh Kate, I've got to go. Cory's beeping in." Kelsey giggles and hangs up.

Cory's supposedly the new boyfriend, so I never stood a chance at a full conversation. Scrolling down my home page, I notice someone has already beat Kelsey to it. There it is in all its glory, the "Runway Slip and Slide" YouTube video. A guy who went to high school with me posted it. Big mistake—I'm unfriending him right this second. I'm not feeling so merciful at the moment.

Do I dare watch the video? I've been reliving the scene in my mind all day. The last face I remember is Camilla's, mouth gaping open in shock as my bouquet heads right for her face. I guess I need to see what all the fuss is about. Maybe it's not so bad after all.

Hesitantly, I click the video clip and cover my eyes with my hands. The music starts to play, and I peek through my half-open fingers. In all the time the show has been on the air, I've never watched myself. I'm mesmerized. The girl in the video looks like me, but then again, she doesn't. I'm confident and graceful—not the usual case—until, without warning, the dreadful moment happens.

The slipping and sliding begin, just as I remember from last night. I look like a circus clown. The audience is squealing and gasping until the moment I finally fall. The clip continues, showing the bouquet smacking Camilla in the face. Abruptly, the video ends with Camilla's face frozen in time with the theme to *Star Wars* edited into the background.

My hands now covering my mouth, I sit, astonished. Then something happens that catches me off guard. I start to giggle. I wonder why I'm giggling and not crying. I giggle more until the giggling turns into hysterical laughter, just like with Josie in the hospital last night. This laughing continues for a full five minutes. I can't stop, and I'm giggling so hard that I start to cry in a fit of laughter.

The laughter finally subsides, and I feel better already. Before signing off Facebook, I decide to go ahead and ignore probably 80 percent of my friend requests and then finish by scanning through my wall comments. Near the bottom of the screen, I notice a thumbnail picture that I haven't seen for far too long. I quickly scroll down, skipping several comments, my heart beating quickly.

"I saw the fall. Are you okay?"

So Ben doesn't hate me—definitely a positive sign. I certainly can't tell him of our beachside fantasy wedding at the moment of my tumble. At this point, even if Ben ever had any interest in me, I've lost all hope. Ben and Jessica's babies are probably destined to roam the earth. My heart stings with a hollow ache. *Wonder if I'll get invited to the wedding.*

I gaze longingly at the post and decide to privately e-mail Ben instead of posting on his wall for all his friends to see.

> Thanks for checking on me. No worries. Only minor injuries: a slight concussion, they say, and an ankle sprain. I'm trapped inside my apartment at the moment. Paparazzi all around. It's funny how an embarrassing moment can make you more famous

than ever. Vivian's out of the competition. They want me to press charges, but I'm not interested. I figure she's done enough damage to herself. Hope you're doing well. I pray your mom is doing better. Send her my prayers. Hope to see you soon. Kate

I press the send button and stare helplessly at the screen.

Chapter 21

Josie and I are sitting on the couch, ready to watch this week's episode of *Runway Star*; a mammoth bowl of popcorn and my mom's box of homemade cookies sit between us. I'm absent from the show tonight due to my minor concussion and ankle sprain. Too much liability, they said. The show opens with Mya apologizing to the home audience on behalf of the show for the incident. She explains that I'm doing well and am at home, recovering from my injuries. I will be back next week to compete in the finale. Camilla makes it known that, regrettably, Vivian was the culprit behind the accident and has been disqualified from *Runway Star*. It's evident that she's sincerely embarrassed and repulsed by Vivian's behavior. No one discredits Camilla Sparks and gets away with it, no matter how much talent the person has.

"The look on her face is priceless." Josie points at the TV and covers up with a nearby blanket.

"Camilla's definitely not happy."

"Katelyn, can you believe all this? You're a finalist on *Runway Star*—isn't this insane? And you have me to thank for your future success."

"I do?" I smile hesitantly.

"Yes, you do." She confidently bobs her red curls up and down.

"Okay. I do think you deserve some credit; it's true I couldn't have done it without you."

Josie smiles with satisfaction.

"It's ironic to think that just a few months ago, I just wanted to get past round one. And now here I am, although I still haven't accomplished my mission of interviewing Mya."

"I wouldn't worry. Even if you don't get the interview, your days at *Fancy Feline* are coming to an end. Your exposure alone on this show will look incredible on any résumé. People will be lined up to hire you. I just know it!" She smiles brightly.

"I hope you're right, but I did say I was going to get an interview, and I want to be true to my word."

Josie looks at me endearingly. "If I haven't said it yet, I'm very proud of you. I think you've inspired a lot of young girls out there."

"I hope so."

"Just promise me one thing."

"What's that?"

"Be careful with Nathan."

"Oh Josie." I throw a piece of popcorn her way.

"What? I wouldn't be a good friend if I didn't say it. I think you deserve so much better."

"Thank you. I'll keep that in mind. But wouldn't you miss the at-home florist shop?" I grin and wave my hands at the flowers still encircling our tiny apartment.

"You've got a point there." Josie smiles and lightly throws a couch pillow at me.

I laugh and catch it before it reaches my face as *Runway Star* returns from commercial break. The camera focuses on Mya; she's standing center stage in her simple but elegant black cocktail dress. De-De's standing slightly to Mya's left, wearing a form-fitting purple-and-black dress. Her face looks slightly anxious as she waits for the details of our final challenge. The screen above the stage boasts some of our top pictures from the season so far. I hate that I'm not there to provide more support for De-De.

"Our final two contestants, Deidra and Katelyn, will be encountering a new location for our last *Runway Star* challenge." Mya's smile and eager expression are full of intrigue.

I wonder what this is all about. Judging by De-De's face, she is just as curious.

"We may be cooling down here in New York City, but things will be heating up on our runway. Watch as our girls head down to the sunny Caribbean for a Bahamas beach showdown," Mya says cheerfully. "Who will be our first *Runway Star*? You don't want to miss it."

Did she just say "Bahamas"? The *Runway Star* theme song is playing in the background as I look over at Josie; she's grinning from ear to ear. "Did you hear that?" Josie says gleefully.

"I think so." I look at her, a bit dumbfounded.

"You're going to the Bahamas!"

I should be excited. Fun in the sun; beautiful, sandy beaches; the dream vacation I've been saving up for for months—now completely free. I'll be far away from Louise and article deadlines, but all I can think about is the thing I've been dreading since the beginning of this competition. It's not a word that is in my wardrobe vocabulary: *bikini*.

❀ ❀ ❀

Three days later, our entire *Runway Star* crew arrives in the Bahamas late in the night. I awoke this morning to a crisp blue sky and sparkling aqua ocean clearly visible from our hotel room. I've never seen water that color before; you can almost see right down to the bottom. It's simply amazing. I'm not used to such opulence; we are staying in a brand-new resort hotel that looks like a Mediterranean castle. De-De and I are sharing an oceanfront suite that's as luxurious as the water here. We each have our own room with a king-size bed draped in fancy linens and thousand-count Egyptian-cotton sheets. Our suite also has an incredible bathroom, fully equipped with a Jacuzzi tub and travertine tile floors.

All this fancy resort stuff is great, but I can't seem to fully enjoy it, because I'm utterly terrified to wear a bikini. I know it's

212

inevitable, but I keep hoping I can talk someone into a tankini—totally respectable. As if the bikini isn't scary enough, the scarier part is that I have to wear one with Nathan behind the camera. I get queasy just thinking about it. Since my tumble and the tabloid rumors, Nathan and I have scarcely talked to one another. He did smile politely to me on the plane and purposely grazed my hand on a pass for a bathroom break. I'm still wearing my unattractive oversized boot shoe—doctor's orders after a brief follow-up before leaving for the Caribbean. Another X-ray revealed that I have more of a slight stress fracture than a sprain, which means that this baby's got to stay on for another four to six weeks. The doctor said I could take if off for pictures and graciously decided not to imprison me with a hard cast.

Our first day of shooting begins early, and we're whisked away to a private island beach as the sunrise appears against the distant open sky. With two party-sized boats and a full camera crew on board, we dock beside a serene shore—a white-sand beach glistens against the background of a bright Bahamian blue sky. We've been briefed that this will be a multimedia day involving shooting a commercial for a new cosmetics company as well as posing for our regular photographs. I'm not that nervous about the commercial. I was always good with that sort of thing, and of course, it's been established that I don't have a problem talking, or so I've been told. De-De, on the other hand, has been a nervous wreck all morning. This is not normal for her, with her typically calm and confident demeanor. We received a script last night and practiced late into the night, going over our lines. She still hasn't quite gotten the lines down and keeps repeating them quietly to herself as we get off the boat.

I lightly pat her on the shoulder. "De-De, you're going to do fine."

"I keep forgetting the middle part—something about the powder feeling light as air on my skin," she says, and she looks at me with worry as she gently touches her face as if she's applying the makeup herself.

"Really, it's fine. They'll give you more than one try. No one gets it perfect right out of the gate," I say reassuringly as we step out onto the sandy beach.

"I hope so. I've never been good at memorizing things. I'll never make it in law school like this if I can't even memorize a few commercial lines."

"You'll do great in law school, and you're going to do fine today. So stop worrying." I smile kindly, trying to put her mind at ease.

"Okay, if you say so." De-De sighs and halfheartedly smiles.

"I know so. Now, let's go see what we're wearing today." I give her a little hug as we walk toward the dressing area.

A portable, temporary grass hut of sorts has been set up next to the shooting area, a rather makeshift dressing room. The plan we've heard is that this fragile-looking frame of sticks breaks down quite easily so that they can tote it from location to location over the next few days. From the look of it, however, one good storm could knock it clean over. We lift up the tropical-printed linen drape that serves as our dressing-room door and go inside. I breathe a sigh of relief when I notice that my first outfit of the day consists of a flirty ivory-colored Vivienne Westwood sundress covered in large, bold flowers. I gladly slip it on. It feels like pure silk, light and fluttery. Two days before we left, I spent two hours in the salon with José, adding soft, natural extensions to my own hair. My hair is extralong and wavy, well down my back, mimicking the same soft flow of my dress. My hair and dress move gently in the wind as I run down the beach with Nathan snapping pictures. I've been careful with how I move my body, not wanting to further injure myself; my record is not great. Nathan kindly has been extra patient and gentle when asking me to move in certain poses or while I'm running—or lightly frolicking, I should say. My ankle, not wanting to cooperate, reminds me with every searing pain that it's not fully healed.

Day one of shooting goes well into the afternoon, moving back and forth between snapping photographs and taping for the commercial. My individual portion of the commercial goes pretty successfully, I think, only requiring around five takes for me to deliver my lines. I feel at ease in front of the camera. The producer says I have a knack for acting, which I find completely hilarious. De-De struggles at first, but I stand behind the camera and hold up large note cards to help her with her lines. After an hour, she finally completes a flawless take, and she couldn't have looked more beautiful.

Between lingering traveling and a full workday, by early evening, De-De and I are both exhausted. We decide to do a girls' night in, ordering room service and planting ourselves in front of the television to watch a few movies—chick flicks, of course. I have to try out the Jacuzzi before turning in, expecting a 5:30 a.m. wake-up call. Not the most exciting way to spend my first night on the island, but technically, I'm here for work, not vacation.

Day two of shooting goes a lot easier on the mind and the ankle, possibly because I'm not trying to remember my lines or running along the beach, and the hot bath I soaked in for an hour last night has helped ease the throbbing. I'm standing in a black wet suit with purple stripes down each side, waiting for my turn on the surfboard. De-De is back to her old self, confident and graceful. She looks as if she's been surfing for years; she's perfectly balanced with arms outstretched in a poised position, wearing a white halter-top bikini. She's striking as the bright sunshine bounces off the water droplets already clinging to her oiled ebony skin, the white suit enhancing its glimmer.

Watching De-De on her surfboard reminds me of all the characters we've gotten to play over the course of this competition. Each week, it's been a surprise, although I would really like a redo on the burlap cowgirl dress. It sure is fun playing dress-up in expensive designer clothes. I prepare to take my turn on the surfboard as Ashlyn applies more gloss to my lips and José fluffs out my hair. My injury puts me again at a slight disadvantage because I'm not allowed to stand on any potentially unbalanced surface that could put me in a vulnerable position. This is what I heard the set director telling

Nathan at the beginning of the shoot. Because of my limitations, Nathan has me pretend surfing while on the beach, as if I'm learning the sport. I laugh to myself because isn't that what this whole competition has been—me learning to be a fashion model? I lie on my tummy across the glowing neon-yellow-and-purple surfboard and pose as if I'm learning to paddle. Nathan has me do a few poses sitting on the board and a few balancing on the board while still on the beach. To finish out the morning, Nathan has De-De and me in some shots together. We walk and talk and splash water at each other; that little-girl feeling is returning, as if I'm playing at the beach with my sisters. We wrap up around lunch, and I head back to soak in the sun by the pool.

The long hours have taken a toll on my body, and I'm pretty tired as we reach the last day of the three-day whirlwind modeling extravaganza. De-De and I arrive by boat at the nearby marina where our final photo shoot of the weekend will take place. I'm not sure, but I've somehow managed to avoid wearing anything that comes in two separate pieces and is typically made with sparse fabric. I think that's about to change, as I notice Ashlyn walking into our dressing-room tiki hut with something small and red in her hands.

"Here is your last change of the day," she says, smiling cheerfully.

"Where is it?" I say, as if I haven't noticed whatever she has in her hand.

"Right here." She holds up the red bikini.

"Oh no! That can't be for me!" I start to back away from it as if it's a vile rodent. "You know who would look fabulous wearing that? De-De. She looks great in red."

"I'm sure she does, and so do you," Ashlyn says firmly, not backing down. "I'm afraid, sweetie, this is your last outfit of the day. You didn't think we wouldn't put you in a bikini? You *are* in the Bahamas!"

I frown. "It's just that I haven't worn one of those since, umm, before puberty."

Ashlyn laughs. "Katelyn, you look amazing. You're down, what, four sizes since the beginning of the show? Trust me—you can wear this. You've earned it."

"I don't know," I say skittishly, and I take the two small pieces of red string fabric from her hands. I turn around before reluctantly going into the grass hut. "Did they happen to throw in a sarong perhaps?"

"No such luck, beautiful. Katelyn, now go change." Ashlyn shoos me away with her hands.

Unenthusiastically, I go into the changing room and remove my wet suit. I know it's silly, but I put it back on this morning before leaving the hotel in the hope of avoiding this situation. No such luck, I suppose. I'm growing to like the wet suit because it seems to keep everything well contained, like a Spanx undergarment. This bikini is sure to expose all my flaws. Luckily, however, I am sporting the Insta-Tan. The first day here, I was as white as a ghost, but thanks to few minutes of spray tanning, I'm as golden as Malibu Barbie. It's fabulous!

Delicately, I put on the red suit, as if it might break into pieces, or maybe I'm just hoping it will so that I'll have an excuse not to wear it. Once it's all in place, I hesitantly look at myself in the mirror. Do I know this person? Surely not, but Ashlyn's right. The suit fits me perfectly. Despite the suit's initial miniscule appearance, it's quite tasteful, with appropriate coverage. It feels strange that I'm going to be wearing a bikini in public, much less on national TV and potentially in a magazine. This must be a parallel universe.

I come out all smiles, with the exception of the ankle boot.

"See? What did I tell you?" Ashlyn says triumphantly.

"I know—you were right."

"I told you it was perfect. You've come a long way, Katelyn," Ashlyn says as she untwists a string on the back of the bikini.

"Thanks."

"José and Amanda are waiting for you for in makeup. Have fun."

I walk with a new confidence as I arrive on set, my head held high and shoulders back. Everyone seems a bit surprised to see my attire, including Nathan, who nearly knocks over the lighting tripod he's setting up as I appear. I giggle and turn my head, embarrassed. I've never had that effect on someone before. De-De can walk into the room wearing anything, and mouths drop open. I guess forty-five minutes of cardio three days a week mixed with two days of Pilates, plus a limited allowance of chili cheese fries and those nonfat macchiatos, makes a difference. I believe for the first time that I have earned this body, and I'm going to bask in my moment.

Nathan finishes setting up and leads me over to the front of a snazzy navy-blue ski boat. It's wrapped in cherry wood, sitting atop a sleek white hull accented with a vibrant scarlet stripe extending the entire length of the boat. The red, white, and blue boat is fittingly named *Liberty*, the name printed in gold across the stern. The show has hailed me as the all-American girl from the beginning, and they're playing up this theme for the final shoot.

"Can someone bring me the flag, please?" Nathan says cheerily, our eyes locking. He smiles affectionately.

He takes the large American Stars and Stripes and lets it fall beside me, hanging freely from the side of the boat.

He moves closer. "You look sensational," he whispers, his voice tickling my ear.

"Thank you." I try not to smile too much and touch my ear to stop the vibrating tingle.

It's the first time we've spoken in days, and somehow I'm keenly aware that I haven't missed the conversation or the sound of his voice—not in the way that I hear Ben's voice in my mind all the time.

Nathan finishes attaching the flag to the side of the boat. He reaches around me to grab his camera that is sitting on the seat cushion. His lips almost touch my cheek as he whispers, "Dinner—my room, seven tonight."

Before I can think to say no, I pleasantly nod and smile, trying to avoid drawing any unwanted attention. Nathan continues, completely professional, and proceeds to snap what feels like thousands of pictures of me in various poses on the boat. An hour into shooting, the sun is really beating down. At certain angles, I feel as if my face is on fire, although you would never know with the amount of makeup they have painted on my face today. Amanda said the reason I have so much makeup slathered on is that they want to give me a Marilyn Monroe look, with deep black mascara and ruby-red lips. The makeup feels more like plaster in this heat.

Tired and hot, I'm hoping that we're about to wrap this thing up, when Amanda comes in to wipe a bead of sweat off my forehead. I guess I'm out of luck when she then immediately reapplies a shade of buff powder to my face.

"What do you think, everyone? Should we take this baby for a spin?" I joke to lighten the suddenly serious mood on set, and I lightly pat the side of the boat.

Nathan gives me an eager look followed by a sneaky little grin. Why can't I keep my mouth shut sometimes? My heart starts to speed up, wondering what he's concocting in that eccentric mind of his. The last time Nathan looked at me that way, I found myself with a Smith and Wesson in my hand and angel's wings growing from my back.

After a few minutes of intense chatting with the set producer, Nathan is all smiles. He swaggers over to me, camera in hand. A miniflock of seagulls scatters as he walks down the pier.

Nathan gently places his hand on my shoulder. "Katelyn, you're just full of inspiration."

I look at him as calmly as possible. "Oh, really? What do you mean?"

"I mean that we agree with you. What a great idea for you to take sweet *Liberty* here for a quick spin around the marina."

I laugh. He has to be kidding. Gently, I turn Nathan away from the others. "Nathan, I didn't mean me. I was joking. I don't know how to drive a boat," I softly whisper.

"Only a minor detail, my dear," he says with carefree ease. "Can you drive a car?"

"Yes."

"Okay then, how much more difficult can it be?"

I'm not sure, but for me, it's probably an accident waiting to happen.

I smile skittishly.

"Well, all right then. Let's get you out there." Nathan casually leads me toward the boat.

Don't panic. Let's think about this for a moment. This can't be any more difficult than driving a car. I mean, it's probably easier. I've had no major car accidents in all my driving years—well, except for that one telephone pole that happened to be in the wrong place at the wrong time. I think I'll leave out the fact that I have hardly driven a car in the four years since I moved to the city. One could say I'm out of practice. I just hope they have good boat insurance.

I crank up the boat's engine as Nathan gives a quick directional tutorial of the marina. I'll be following a lead boat, where Nathan will be in the back, taking pictures. He tells me to just be natural and focus on driving the boat. Thank goodness. The engine gives a roar while the dock crew unties the ropes holding the boat securely to the dockside. Slowly, I fumble my way around and manage to safely pull the elegant speedboat out into the open water. You know, it's funny—I think I've done this before, except I was about eight years old, and the boat was much smaller and securely attached to a moving track with no water.

Our speed picks up as I follow the lead boat, which is now pulling ahead. Nathan is positioning himself at the side of the boat and snapping pictures. I try to maintain my composure with a soft smile across my face as the wind blows through my hair. The lead boat starts to do circles around me as Nathan continues to take pictures with his megalens camera. I'm really starting to enjoy driving this boat. I can feel a connection with *Liberty* and enjoy the sound of the water beating up against her frame as we bounce over the trailing wake of the other boats.

The sound of waves and the occasional spray of water hitting my face are lulling me, when I look up to see Nathan yelling something my way. I can't hear him over the boat's engine. Then he starts to wave his hands around in the air. I assume he wants me to mimic the motion for a particular shot. I keep one hand on the steering wheel and wave the other hand in the air, when I hear a loud, blaring horn. I start to cover my ears, but then I realize the horn is for me—a warning to get out of the way.

My eyes start to bulge out of their sockets when I see that the honking boat is directly in my path. Terrified, I abruptly let off the gas, grip the wheel in place, and freeze. *Liberty* comes to a quick stop in the water as a stealthy black-and-blue speedboat quickly swerves to miss my boat. I slump down into the chair, and *Liberty* remains bobbing up down in the water as my heart starts to find its normal rhythm again. Nathan and the other boat quickly turn around and anxiously pull up beside me. The set producer is riding on board, steaming. I guarantee this is the last time you'll see me behind the wheel of a boat on this show.

"My dear, are you all right?" Nathan says, looking at me with a worried, tense expression.

I shake my head, unable to speak.

"What were you thinking?" He heartily laughs as he jumps onto *Liberty*. "This is a very expensive prop you have in your possession."

Dazed and rattled, I don't respond to his apparent cynicism. My goodness, from head trauma to boat crashing, I'm starting to wonder if I need to wear protective gear on a daily basis.

Nathan gently touches my back. "Okay then, let's call it a wrap and get you both safely back to the marina."

I half-smile and lightly nod.

"This time, my dear, I'm driving."

Fine by me. I'm afraid my boat-driving days are done for an undetermined amount of time. Did he forget that I told him I didn't know how to drive a boat? So who's at fault here, really?

"Sure, no problem," I manage to mutter.

Nathan takes his time, and I slowly begin to regain my composure, letting the soft wind blow over my face as the boat glides through the water. We make it safely back to the dock and secure the boat back in her usual spot in the marina. Luckily, there are no scratches on me or any cracks on *Liberty*. I can breathe a huge sigh of relief. I think I'll stick to riding on boats instead of driving them.

Chapter 22

It's promptly seven o'clock, and I'm standing outside Nathan's resort suite. All the executive suites are ground-level, ocean-view rooms with private patios, Jacuzzis, and their own private butlers. A garden oasis of tropical flowers, bubblegum-pink plumeria, and bright purple bougainvillea blossoms usher me toward the front door of the suite.

I'm not sure what I'm doing or how I got in this place. I can't deny that Nathan intrigues me—the good looks, his exciting career, and the lifestyle he offers are incredibly tempting. The glitz and glamour are wonderful things, but none of that changes who I am inside. The question remains: Are Nathan and I a match? I still find myself unsure if I want this. I've yet to bring up the faith question. I have a nagging feeling in my gut, and deep down, I think I already know the answer.

I knock lightly, and Nathan casually opens the door. He looks like a golden angel; his blond hair is glistening brightly as the sun hangs high in the horizon, its rays gleaming through the large open windows. Strangely, his attire reminds me of the way Ben was dressed in my daydream—white casual dress shirt, linen pants, and leather sandals. I feel a sinking feeling in my stomach.

"Hi, glad you could make it," Nathan says eagerly, pointing the way in.

I straighten my baby-blue cotton sundress and glide past him into the grand space.

"Nice room," I remark. His suite is larger than my entire apartment back home. The room is a white canvas with accents of dark island wood in the doors, and the shutter-style windows are open to allow the ocean breeze to freely flow.

He leads me out to the private patio complete with full side bar, grill, and hot tub. There are two rattan chaise lounge chairs, a bistro table already set, and a chilled bottle of wine.

"I noticed you didn't like reds, so I thought you might like a chardonnay."

Nice observation. I can't get over the red wine looking like blood.

"You noticed. Chardonnay is a much better choice. Thank you." I smile kindly and bend down to smell the light pink oleander flower in the glass vase on the small table.

He pulls the bottle out of the ice bucket and twists the corkscrew into the top.

"Katelyn, I must say, you were brilliant today. Absolutely stunning. I really didn't know what to do with myself—you looked so amazing."

I blush. "Thank you. It's getting easier." I push my hair behind my shoulders as he hands me a glass.

"You're a natural. I think you have a very good chance of winning next week. And even if you don't, I believe that you'll have no problem continuing on in the modeling world, if you wish."

"Actually, I've not really thought about much past next week. I never in a million years thought I would make it this far."

"I knew you'd be in the finals. You're the undiscovered beauty, the Cinderella story."

"People keep saying that, but I've never really thought of it that way. I just feel extremely lucky. Who's to say I would even be here if Vivian hadn't pulled such a nasty trick? You could've been taking her pictures out on the *Liberty* today." I take a slow sip of the chardonnay.

"I doubt it. Vivian's talented—I'll give her that much. The difference is that people love you, my dear. They can relate to you in a way they never could to Vivian."

"Yes, but just because they love me doesn't mean I have any talent."

"That's where you're wrong. You do have talent. You need to believe in yourself. Trust me, Katelyn—I've been around a lot of models, and this industry needs more girls like you." He pauses and moves in closer. "I need a girl like you."

I blush again and turn my head. Nathan takes my face in his hands and gently turns me to face him. Slowly, he leans in and kisses me softly on the lips. For the moment, I don't deny him. He takes my glass of wine and sets it on the royal-blue mosaic-tile tabletop.

Like a master of an art, he moves in without allowing me time to resist, pulling me in closer to his chest. He kisses me again with more vigor than the previous soft graze across my mouth. It does feel nice, and my head is spinning a bit. Yet despite the warm, nice sensation, something inside tells me this is wrong. The debate goes on in my mind as his grip becomes tighter around my waist and the kiss becomes more intense. I almost feel my senses losing control, when I see a vision in my mind of Josie behind him, pointing at me with one hand while the other one rests on her hip. She's glaring at me with disappointment. That's all it takes to knock me back into reality. I firmly pull back and push Nathan back to arm's length.

"What's wrong?" Nathan asks, confused.

"I'm sorry, Nathan. This isn't me. I can't do this."

"You can't do what?" he says, still with an air of flirtation, reaching for my arm again.

"This." I wave my hand around the room and pull up the strap of my sundress, which has fallen off my shoulder. "Be alone with a man in his hotel room."

He laughs as he flings himself onto the chaise lounge. "What? Katelyn, you're a grown adult. You can be alone and intimate with a man."

Did he say "intimate"? Another vision pops into my mind: my mother giving me the sex talk. I haven't crawled out from under a rock. I know about sex. I'm twenty-six years old. I'm just waiting. Is that so wrong?

"I'm uncomfortable here. I don't want to do something I'll regret later."

"Something you'll regret? We're just getting to know one another—physically." He laughs casually.

"Nathan, I'm sorry. I'm waiting until I'm married."

"You can't be serious," he says, surprised. His tone registers arrogant condescension.

"Yes, totally serious." I turn around, trying to hide my building irritation.

"I knew you were a bit old-fashioned, but I didn't think you were that old school."

That does it—I whip around to face him. "Old school? This is not about being old school or fuddy-duddy or whatever else you're thinking. This is about a commitment I've made to my faith and what I believe is right!"

Nathan rolls his eyes and lets out a large sigh. "Katelyn, I go to church too, but I don't buy into the whole abstinence-before-marriage bit. I mean, who does that?"

Well, he's just answered the big faith question I've been afraid to ask. I'm not questioning that he has faith; however, I think we're totally at different places in our journey. We're not even standing on the same block.

There's a long, awkward silence between us. Nathan's sitting on the chaise lounge, looking as bewildered as I feel, and I'm scanning the room, trying to find where I put my purse. I'm nauseated, and a sense of shame rolls over me.

"Nathan, I'm sorry, but as wonderful as you are, I think we're at an impasse. The intimacy you want, I'm not able to give."

He stands and starts to interrupt. "Katelyn—"

"No. Let me finish. I'm not perfect, and I don't claim to be. I've broken a lot of promises, but this one I plan to keep."

"I understand." He shakes his head in astonishment. The corner of his mouth curls up slightly as if he's about to laugh, and then he lets out a chuckle.

His lack of respect is annoying me. "You know, it's rude to laugh at someone," I say sternly, my voice getting increasingly angry.

"No. I'm not laughing at you, my dear. I'm laughing at my weakness and the fact that I can't remember the last time I was told no by a woman."

"You can't? I heard Adrianna dumped you."

"Oh, right. Well, I'm just saying I've never been dumped for reasons such as these circumstances."

"Well, aren't you full of yourself?" I say, annoyed.

He looks at me with that coy smile still on his face, as if he's still playing a game.

"Nathan, I'm sure there are plenty of girls waiting in the wings for you."

"Yes, but I'm afraid I'll always wonder about the one who got away," he says as the back of his hand gently grazes my cheek. "Could I change your mind?"

I laugh and roll my eyes at his attempt to woo me. "Always the little devil, aren't you?"

"Maybe. I hate to lose."

"Friends?" I reach out to shake his hand.

"I envy the man who wins your heart." He takes my hand as if to shake it and then tenderly brings it to his lips instead.

"Good night, Nathan."

"You're leaving? Don't you want to stay for dinner?"

"Tempting, but no. I think I need to go for a walk."

❀ ❀ ❀

The air is crisp with a touch of salt as I walk along the beach. Looking out across the horizon, I see the beginning of a brilliant sunset starting to unfold—an array of colors reflect where the ocean meets the sky. I try to disengage my mind and body from the exhilarating and awkward events of the day. It seems my life has moved in directions I never dreamed possible—some favorable and some not so much.

Kicking my feet in the warm water as I walk, in a way, I feel defeated. Nothing significant happened with Nathan—things remained PG, as they say—yet I feel ashamed, probably because there was a brief moment when I felt weak, as if I could've let go of what I believed was right. It would've been easy to forget and let my inhibitions go. It's funny how God works sometimes—the gentle way He protects. I laugh to myself at the image of Josie I had when I was with Nathan. God has such a sense of humor.

I stop for a moment and decide to take a seat on the sandy beach. Briefly, I close my eyes and take in the sounds of the ocean slapping against the shoreline. I say a prayer and thank God for watching over me and allowing me to hear His voice in an unconventional way. Sitting here in silence, eyes closed, listening to the sounds of the ocean, I begin to hear new sounds quickly approaching—the sounds of children laughing. I open my eyes when a little blond-haired boy almost trips over me.

"Preston, watch where you're going, honey," a soft, familiar woman's voice calls out to him.

I quickly notice whom this little boy belongs to. Mya and the rest of the Sasser beauties are walking toward me. *So they really do exist.* I've only seen the rest of the Sassers in pictures or on television. Her husband, Blake, is holding hands with a little version of Mya— her daughter Lexi, all of maybe four years old. Preston, around seven, the oldest, is nearest to me. Mya's holding the newest darling, who looks more like Daddy with a head full of dark hair and exotic deep brown eyes, just the way I imagine Ben and Jessica's child might look like someday.

"It's Katelyn, one of our finalists." Mya recognizes me and turns toward Blake.

"Hi, Mya," I say shyly.

I always get nervous around her. It's silly, really. She's so down to earth and easy to talk to.

"Is everything okay?" she asks with genuine concern.

"Yes, just sitting out here enjoying the beauty," I softly reply.

"There's nothing like it." She smiles and turns her face toward the ocean.

The littlest Sasser begins to cry, and the older girl is tugging at her daddy's pant leg. "Blake, do you mind taking the kids while I chat with Katelyn for minute? Ava's getting fussy," Mya says as she wipes the tears from the baby's face.

"Sure, honey." Blake takes Ava from Mya. The exchange is flawless, as if they've done it a thousand times. "You girls have fun," Blake says happily, and he kisses Mya on the cheek.

"Lexi, Preston, go with Daddy." Mya motions for the rest to follow. Reluctantly, they walk with their father up the beach.

Mya takes off her turquoise-jeweled strappy sandals and sits down beside me, her toenails displaying a French pedi.

"This is the life, isn't it?" She pleasantly sighs and looks out across the ocean.

"Absolutely! You sure have your hands full, don't you?"

"Yes. I do, but they're worth every bit of work." Mya smiles, and her eyes lovingly turn in their direction, watching them disappear into the resort.

"And your husband, Blake—he's gorgeous and such the gentleman."

"He's pretty wonderful, I must admit," Mya says gleefully with a gleam in her eyes, still obviously much in love.

"How did you two meet?"

"In college, if you can believe that. So he's been here from the beginning. We both started out with nothing, so this life we live now we consider a true blessing."

"That's special."

"And the best thing is he loves me for me and has never tried to change who I am."

"Wow. I hope I find someone like that one day."

"You will. Always remember one thing."

"What's that?" I ask.

"Never settle."

I lightly laugh. "I keep hearing that very thing."

She nods in agreement. "It's true." Mya stops, her hazel eyes gazing out again at the incoming waves rolling toward the shore. "I'll give you a tidbit of advice. I've been married a long time, so trust me when I say"—she turns and looks at me intently—"remember, no one's perfect. A relationship is about give and take. And sometimes love happens in the most unexpected places. I met Blake in the cafeteria. He was serving hot dogs."

I laugh, remembering the image I had of myself and my cafeteria wear on a hot-dog line. "Really?"

"Truly," she says, and she laughs with me.

"I'll remember that, Mya. Thank you."

"Anytime, Katelyn. Now, is there anything else I can help you with, my dear?" Another light in heaven has turned on for me. Here is my golden opportunity.

"Well, actually, there is. I was wondering how you feel about cats."

Chapter 23

I t's been a whirlwind since we returned from the Bahamas, with press junkets and interviews nonstop. Kelsey called me this morning, squealing, after De-De and I appeared on the *Today* show. She was disappointed that none of the family could make it for the finale. My nephew, Joshua Turner Stewart, was born yesterday—a whopping nine pounds and five ounces—and he's such a cutie patootie. Kara, however, had a difficult delivery, with sixteen hours of labor followed by an emergency Cesarean. It's understandable why everyone is there helping out. The birth of a child is certainly more important than my being in this competition.

Back in the dressing area, Mya peeks in to wish De-De and me good luck. She winks at me and walks away. Who would've thought my moment with Mya would have come when it did? She's fun to talk with. I consider her a new friend and mentor able to share valuable insight into my future career as a journalist. I told her the whole story about my life at *Fancy Feline* and my writing aspirations. I explained why I ultimately entered the modeling contest and about the article I'm writing about the cats she doesn't have. Surprisingly, she thought the whole thing was hilarious and loved my creativity. We talked about her two dogs, and she said she would take care of the cat for me. Lexi's been bugging them for six months to get a kitten. Mya said the timing was perfect.

Our final *Runway Star* show begins with a bang, glimmering lights, and an opening serenade from Taylor Swift. All of the final twelve contestants, with the exception of Vivian, are back for a reunion of sorts for the night, and each contestant takes another turn down the famous *Runway Star* catwalk. Tonight we all have the privilege of wearing creations from the collection of the newest winner of the SBS's reality show for fashion designers, *A Cut Above*—a convenient double plug for the network. The winner, Felicity Grey, has designed a collection of Caribbean-inspired gowns; each is light and airy, flowing like a parade of exotic butterflies down the runway. It is magical. To top off the evening, there is a surprise catwalk from Adrianna Watts herself. She holds the audience spellbound as she walks in her dazzling, avant-garde strapless black gown by Chanel, with a corseted, gathered bodice adorned with feathers.

The studio is full of people—family, friends, guests, and a sprinkling of celebrities. I'm sure I spotted Carrie Underwood and a few cast members from the *Twilight* movies. Best of all, the fashionista herself, Victoria Beckham, is sitting in the front row, wearing a sci-fi-inspired black leather dress. Rounding out the eclectic audience are lots of reporters from various news stations. The atmosphere feels glitzy, and the room is rumbling with an air of anticipation. Josie once again is representing my family section. She's brought along her entire art class. Philip, Julie, and the girls are also here cheering me on. Chloe and Emma are holding up hand-painted posters: "We Love Kate" and "The Girl Next Door—Our *Runway Star*." I'm touched by their support. Scanning across the audience, I notice one face, however, missing in the crowd—one that my heart fears I might not see again. Somehow, despite the crowds and the glamour and excitement, I feel incomplete.

The events of the night pass by rapidly, with lots of past footage of all the contestants appearing throughout the show. The audience gasps excitedly as a shot appears up on the big screen of Isabel posing in a sleek black bodysuit while doing a bungee jump off a twenty-story building in the middle of Manhattan. *Yeah, no thanks.* I refused, claiming a fear of heights. Everyone has limitations. They did my photos that day in the middle of the rooftop. I prefer a sturdy floor as opposed to flying through the air. More gasps ring out from the audience as the screen features De-De's shot with the boa snake. She's in the snake cage at the New York City Zoo with a twelve-foot snake draped over her as she models a Jean Paul Gautier silk halter dress. De-De, a reptile lover, was in heaven. Again, not my thing—I cringe as they show my underwater shot. It's just as I remember: I look as if a great white shark is about to eat me. A brief shot of Vivian appears; no one tonight has referred to her scheme to sabotage her way to top-model status. No need to dwell on the negative, right?

Moving into the final segment of the night, Mya introduces the next film clip, the cosmetics commercial. I'm excited to see how it turned out. This will be the first time any of the models have seen it. De-De and I wait anxiously backstage as we make our forty-five-second debut. The commercial begins to play, and the brilliant Bahamian sky rolls across the screen.

"Katelyn, look at you. You're a natural on camera. You should really think about acting," De-De says earnestly as we watch ourselves talking about lip gloss.

"I don't know about acting, but I do know one thing is true."

"What's that?"

"After being on this show, I believe anything is possible." I grin.

"I'm so glad you and I made it all the way together. Promise me you won't forget me after this is over," she says, her voice turning slightly melancholy.

"Are you crazy? I couldn't forget about you. I'm afraid you're stuck with me as a friend for life."

De-De beams, her sleek copper-brown hair shining underneath the backstage lights. She's wearing her last garment for the evening, by Michael Kors: a red silk gown attached to an oversized chrome-plated necklace. She looks like a space-age Grecian goddess. I'm finishing out the evening with the ongoing all-American-girl theme, wearing Ralph Lauren. The midnight-blue velvet gown sweeps dramatically to the floor and sits beneath an asymmetrical top; one side is sleeveless, and one side has a gold-embroidered sleeve.

"Girls, we're ready for you," the stage manager says, motioning for us to move onstage. I feel the familiar sensation of adrenaline starting to build inside.

Mya introduces us for the last time in this competition. De-De and I walk in step together to the center of the runway, our gowns glittering in the spotlights. I've grown to love wearing these beautiful pieces of art. Nervous, we wait through numerous commercial breaks before the big moment arrives. All this waiting seems unnecessary, but I guess someone has to pay for this show. After what seems like an eternity, we're finally live on the air, following the final commercial break. The excitement is thick in the room. De-De and I hold hands as Mya announces the winner.

"After twenty-six million at-home votes …" Mya pauses and looks over at the two of us with anticipation. De-De and I smile at one another and tighten the grip on our hands. "The first winner of *Runway Star* is …"

I close my eyes; the spotlight feels even brighter on my face.

"Deidra Douglas."

The applause is loud and thunderous. De-De and I hug. I whisper, "Congratulations," as confetti falls down all around us. It's magical, like colored snow floating down from the sky. I move into the background, and just like that—the anticipation, the work, all the criticism and praise—it's all over. Strangely, I'm not the least bit sad or disappointed that my name wasn't called. The right girl won. I couldn't be happier. The cheers continue to pour in from the audience as all the other model contestants rush in for their chance at hugs and congratulations. We all celebrate the newly crowned queen of the runway.

❀   ❀   ❀

Hours after the announcement of De-De as the first *Runway Star*, we arrive back at our dressing rooms. De-De and I both had scheduled interviews immediately following the show. The repeated question for me from most reporters tended to be "What's next for you?" I could only reply, "I'm not sure, but after all this, the sky is the limit." That's the honest truth.

"Are you sure you don't want to ride with us?" De-De asks me as she starts to leave for the night. "We have a limo." She grins, trying to coerce me with fancy transportation.

"It sounds lovely, but no, thank you. I'll meet you all there. I've got a few things to do here before I head out," I reply as I brush my hair out from the night's updo.

There's a large *Runway Star* after-party congregating at Bistro 77 downtown. I need a few minutes to regroup before the festivities begin again.

"Okay. See ya there. And don't forget those gifts on the dressing table. There were a few things left for you."

"For me? I thought those were for you."

"No, they're for you."

"Thanks. I'll see you at Bistro, Miss *Runway Star*." I grin, and De-De lights up like a firefly as she turns to leave.

I sit down in the chair in front of my dressing table, finally alone with my thoughts. It's relatively quiet, with a few members of the cleaning crew still around. Everyone was mostly gone by the time De-De and I finished with the press. I decide to take it slowly, wanting to relish my time here, which is coming to an end. Josie and the rest of my fan section stopped in for a brief moment earlier, offering their congratulations. Josie was notably disappointed. "I think De-De's great, but I still think you were the real winner. I knew I should've had a call-a-thon set up in the art department."

Quietly, I reflect on the events of the night as I begin to pack my clothes into my purple backpack; a vacuum cleaner is murmuring in a far-off room. I glance over at the designer gowns and garments still hanging neatly on my designated rack. I'm going to miss this place. The energy every week is a bit addicting. This whole experience has changed me in ways I never could have dreamed of. I walked down the runway a girl who was unsure of herself in her own skin and unaware of the talents she possessed inside. I came back a woman with renewed faith and purpose. Divine destiny? I certainly think so.

Packing up the last of my things, I notice the two gifts that De-De was referring to on my dressing table. As I grab the large white envelope, there's a knock on the door behind me. I turn around and am taken aback to see Camilla Sparks standing there in the open doorway.

"Katelyn, good, you're still here," she says, stiff and serious, staying true to her usual demeanor.

"Camilla," I reply, surprised.

What's she doing here? Maybe she's lost an earring or something and needs me to help her find it.

"I don't say this to many girls, so count yourself lucky."

I nod in response. Should I be afraid?

"You have raw, natural talent that's rare in the modeling industry. I was wrong about you. I hope you'll continue in the business. On behalf of Sparks International, I would like to offer you a modeling contract."

My eyes expand in size. I'm confused. I'm pretty sure I just lost.

"But, Camilla, I didn't win."

"It's not about the show. What I'm offering you is not as substantial as De-De, but I see you as a valuable asset to our company. And being the competitive person I am, I don't want anyone else to snatch you up. This is about business, my dear."

"I don't know what to say, but thank you, Camilla." I continue to stand there in shell-shocked silence.

"No. Thank *you*, Miss Turner. I'll have Ariel call you next week with all the details." Her tone is still flat, and she's exhibiting the usual deadpan gaze.

And just like that, she's swiftly out the door. I'm still standing here holding the envelope, mouth gaping. Camilla Sparks just offered me a modeling contract. My heart is racing, and there's no one to share this moment with. This means I'm free. I'm free from *Fancy Feline* for sure. I just traded Louise for Camilla, but I'll think about that later. At least I'll get to wear fabulous clothes and never look at the back of a cat-food bag again. I'm feeling giddy, as if it's Christmas morning. I eagerly open the white envelope. Inside are pictures of Mya and her family holding their new gray-and-white kitten. I grin. Along with the pictures is a note on pretty pink-and-white polka-dot stationery.

> Katelyn, Hope this helps to complete your story.
> Call me anytime.
> 555-715-7899
> —Mya

This is perfect. I can walk away from *Fancy Feline* knowing I completed what I started. Whoever said runner-up was only second best? I'll take it; life is good.

I smile as I move on to the larger gift leaning next to the dresser. This one is wrapped in brown paper and brown twine, with a single red rose attached to it. I take off the flower, smell it, and lay it to the side. My memory flashes back to the recent array of roses in my apartment. I wonder if this gift is from Nathan. *He just won't quit, will he?* I hesitantly open the attached note and quickly realize I'm wrong about the gift giver. Tears prick the back of my eyes when I immediately recognize the handwriting.

> Kate,
> Sorry I haven't been able to help finish the pictures for the article. I hope the ones you have will work. My mother is doing much better. She gave us quite a scare, like someone else I know. Best of luck tonight.
> Your biggest fan, Ben

My heart aches in my chest. I quickly open the large paper-wrapped package. I can do nothing but marvel at what I'm seeing.

It's no less than breathtaking. It's the red-dress moment. Ben's captured it again—not with black-and-white photography but with an artist's brush. The colors are amazing and have a whimsical flare; the portrait is almost abstract, reminiscent of a Van Gogh original. I look again and notice there's something different about this version of the moment. There's someone else in the painting. I look closer. Standing in the background is a faint figure; it's Ben across the room, reflected in the painting's mirror. He's softly smiling, watching me.

Chapter 24

It's Monday morning, and just like that, I'm back to the daily grind of all that is cats, kitties, and everything that has to do with the feline population. The show is over, and I've been reveling in the magnificent painting that is hanging over my bed, my thoughts often drifting to a life with Ben—a life I'm still not sure is possible. I might have ruined my chances forever. I haven't had the guts to call him or Facebook him—or contact him in any way, for that matter. I'm praying for wisdom, and so far, I haven't gotten any confirmation to move forward. So for now, I'm still, and even though my heart aches, there's peace and contentment.

Louise loved the article, but she wasn't exactly thrilled when I also gave her my two-weeks notice. There was something extremely exhilarating about quitting my job. The time has come to move on from the cat race. Camilla's office sent the modeling contract over the weekend, and after thorough examination, I gladly accepted. It's a great opportunity to do some real-world modeling. The contract is small and, as Camilla said, not anything as significant as Deidra's, but it's worth the jump in career. It's a little scary stepping out into something so different from what I've been used to for the past four years. There's a confidence inside me that continues to grow, and I know that with God's help, I can do anything.

While sitting at my desk, scrolling through my e-mails, I hear an exaggerated grunt from behind. I turn slightly, and Clive is leaning against my cubicle wall, arm stretched over the top. He's glaring at me like a predator keenly watching his prey.

He grunts again. "Hey there, Katelyn."

"Clive, is there something I can help you with?" I ask in my most professional manner.

"I heard that you're leaving us." He furrows his brow and pouts his lips.

"Yes, you heard correctly," I confirm, now looking back at my computer screen. I hope he'll take the hint that I'm not interested in a conversation.

"You know, I've always held to my rule of not dating coworkers." He grunts, clearing his throat, and leans in closer. "Now, seeing as how you and I will no longer be working together, I was wondering if we could see each other in a more romantic setting." He finishes with the utmost confidence as the whiff of Stetson aftershave burns underneath my nose.

He didn't just ask me out, did he? I keep staring ahead, trying not to laugh. *What do I say?* Obviously, I would never in a million years say yes. I hate this—it's so awkward. Before I can answer, Clive continues, likely sensing my hesitation at his request.

"I didn't know you had a body like that. Wow! I loved you in that American-girl bikini." He slyly chuckles. "I would love to take you on a ride in my boat, if you know what I mean." He exaggeratedly lifts his eyebrows twice.

I think I might vomit. Mom was right—bikinis are a bad idea.

"Uh, no, thanks!" I emphatically reply.

"Come on, Katelyn. I can show you a real good time," he says, still chuckling, sounding almost like Goofy.

"While the offer may be flattering for some girls, I think I'm going to have to pass."

"Well, when you get lonely out there on the runway, you know who you can call." He points both his thumbs inward toward himself. "This guy." He grins and swaggers ever so slightly away.

"Thanks, I'll remember that."

Why does having any kind of conversation with Clive make me feel as if I need a shower? I return to checking my e-mails and begin to let certain work contacts as well as fellow coworkers know of my plans to leave *Fancy Feline*. On the one hand, it feels refreshing to say those words, as if I've been given a new lease on life. On the other, though, it feels odd. My mind continues to race with different thoughts of jubilation mixed with fear, and then, like a broken record, my thoughts always come back to one loose end.

Ben is always there in the back of my mind, just as he is in the painting, watching over me in a way. Josie casually informed me that Ben's back working at the coffee shop, but only for a short time. He's still planning on leaving for Europe soon. I keep thinking I should at least say thank you for the painting. I mean, that would only be appropriate. I've thought about sending a thank-you note, but that seems insignificant compared to the gift. For now, I've lowered myself to stalker status. I've called the coffee shop every day to see when he's working, but I'm too afraid to go visit. As if that's not bad enough, I've resorted to the office coffee, which is nowhere near the same. I'm equally desperate for a macchiato and a chance to see Ben one more time. I'm not sure what to do or when to do it, so for now, I keep waiting for divine confirmation.

The morning drags on. My stomach is growling from missed breakfast, when I hear a little chiming bell on my phone. I pause in my e-mail responses and take a quick peek at my cell. The message is from Josie: "FYI, Ben flies to Europe 2nite. Last day at coffee shop."

No! He can't be leaving today. He just got back. I haven't had time to say I'm sorry or thank you or whatever it is I'm supposed to say. I feel a pounding in my chest. Is this my sign? I'm not sure. I sit there in silence, holding my breath, waiting for a voice from above to say, "Okay, Kate, go get your man." Well, I guess it doesn't always happen that way. I pray silently to myself: *Lord, I don't know what you want for me exactly. You know my heart, and you know Ben's. If you have a life for us together, I believe you will let us know.* I jump from my chair as my cell chimes again. I read my newest text: "I'm not telling you again, Kate. Follow your heart! Go now!"

I smile to myself. The heart knows what the heart wants. I believe God often works in the natural. I'm not sure if that's my sign, but I'll take it as a yes. I'm quickly realizing I don't need an outward sign for what I feel on the inside, and maybe that's all the confirmation I need. My heart says faith will show me the way.

Quickly, I gather my purse and tell Louise I'm taking an early lunch to run some errands. I'm practically running toward the coffee shop, when halfway there, the sky opens up and begins to pour buckets of rain. *Really?* There was no mention of rain in the forecast today. I'm completely unprepared and have no umbrella or rain jacket. I can't turn back now; Ben's leaving. At the very least, I have to tell him thank you. I'm soaked in a matter of seconds, and I manage to step in the middle of a huge mud puddle. So not only am I soaked from head to toe, but I'm also covered in brown mud. This is definitely not how I imagined I would do this. I could really use a sunny day and a designer original about now.

A sloppy mess, I open the door to Corner Street Coffee Shop, my hair dripping wet, my black dress pants and gray pea coat covered in mud splashes. From a quick glance at myself in the glass window, I see that I have mascara running down my face, and I look like a scene from a horror movie. To my advantage, however, it's a slow part of the day, and only one customer is in the store. That's good—less of an audience to gawk at my disarray. A middle-aged businessman walks past me as I make my way up to the counter. He turns his nose up at my appearance. I smile wearily. "You might need an umbrella, sir. It's raining."

He nods and walks out the door. The bell rings as he leaves.

"You look awful," Shelly says, wiping down the counter.

Way to boost my self-esteem there, Shelly.

"Is Ben here?" I ask, still out of breath from the rush to get over here and out of the rain.

"Actually, you just missed him."

I sigh and hang my head in failure. Wait a minute—if it hasn't been that long, maybe I can chase him down the street. I don't want to seem desperate, but at this point, I'll do anything.

"So how long ago did I miss him? Two minutes? Ten?"

"Uh, I'm not sure. Could be twenty."

I sigh in disappointment. He's long gone.

"Hey, sorry you didn't win. I voted for you, if it's any consolation," Shelly says sympathetically. Maybe this is her way of comforting me in my pain.

"Thanks. I was really hoping to talk with Ben."

"Yeah, today was his last day. I think he had a plane to catch. He had all his gear dumped in the storage room this morning," she says, obviously annoyed.

I stand there unable to move at first. I feel wet, cold, miserable, and utterly defeated. I'm too late. I've missed my chance. Ben's gone, probably forever.

The bell to the door rings again, and I need to go before the customers arrive for the afternoon rush—or before my eyes begin to unleash a fury of tears. I feel as if I can hardly breathe as I turn around to go. A tall figure brushes by me, wearing a pair of chocolate-brown-and-red hiking boots. I don't even bother to lift up my head, as I feel as if I've lost my best friend.

"Katelyn?"

Isn't that funny? I'm already hearing Ben's voice as if in a dream. It's true that you can go crazy from a broken heart.

"Katelyn?" I hear the voice that sounds like Ben again. I'm drawn to it like the soothing sounds of the ocean. When I see the source of the voice, my eyes widen in surprise. No, it can't be. I'm too late. Shelly said I'm too late. I'm startled to see Ben, in the flesh, staring back at me. He has a mammoth backpack in tow.

"Hey," I say hesitantly, still out of breath, my teeth chattering.

"Hey," he cautiously replies.

"I thought you left. I thought I was too late," I say, unable to hide the desperation in my voice.

"I did, but I forgot my guitar." He lightly smiles. "I had to come back for it. Afraid Shelly might try to sell it on EBay."

"I heard that," Shelly fires back from her spot near the counter, "and you're probably right."

I smile, feeling a bit more at ease. The rain is still pouring outside while the silence invades the distance between us. There's so much to say, and I can't find the words to begin.

"You said you thought you were too late?" he asks with a confused stare.

"I had, uh, wanted to thank you for the painting," I say weakly, and then I start to ramble nervously. "I thought about sending you a card, but … It's incredible. Truly amazing." I stop to catch my breath and then quickly begin again. "You didn't have to do that for me. I mean, why did you?" My words continue to spill out in a jumbled mess as I try not to burst into tears.

"What can I say? You're my favorite muse." He shrugs and looks at me tenderly.

I smile bashfully, and then the awkward silence sweeps in again like a drafty house.

"I know you're in a hurry. I don't want to cause you to miss your plane. I probably should go." I glance at the door. I feel faint.

He reaches down to lightly touch my hand. "Wait. I have some time. How about a cup of coffee? You know, for old time's sake."

"Uh, sure, I'd like that." I smile hesitantly. "Sorry, I'm a bit of a wet mess. Mud puddles seem to find me."

He reaches down and touches the tips of my wet hair. "I see that."

Ben's lips begin to curl upward, and his dazzling teeth appear, revealing the smile that I've grown so fond of these past few months—a smile that haunts me in a painting on my wall.

"Where are my manners? You must be freezing." Ben takes off his backpack and pulls out a sweatshirt. "Here, take this and at least get dry."

I nod and take the hooded gray sweatshirt. Shelly hands me a towel on the way to the restroom. I towel dry myself as much

All Dressed Up

as possible, slip into the warm sweatshirt, and pull the hood up around my face. The smell of Ben begins to take over my senses. I feel instantly safe and secure, as if I could stay wrapped up in here forever. After I'm dry and halfway presentable, I go out to find Ben waiting for me at a back table. The coffee shop remains empty except for the two of us and Shelly, who now has retreated to the back.

"Feel better?"

"Yes, very much. Thank you." I sigh in quiet relief. "I would offer to return the sweatshirt soon, but I'm not sure where to ship it."

I have to stop myself from pulling the sweatshirt up to my nose and taking another inviting sniff.

He smiles warmly. "I'll buy another when I get there. Keep it. There's something cute about you wearing my clothes."

My head is spinning, and my cheeks are rosy red, I'm sure.

"Please, sit with me." He politely motions to the empty seat next to him.

I kindly nod and sit down.

"I'm sorry the competition didn't go your way."

"Oh, that's okay. De-De's amazing. It went to the right person."

"You have a good heart, Kate."

"I don't know about all that, but thank you." I grin.

"So what now? I hope they gave you a promotion at the cat gallery."

I giggle and clasp my hands together. "Actually, it's funny how things work out. Camilla offered me a modeling contract. It's smaller, of course, but I accepted it."

"Kate, that's wonderful!" His eyes light up.

"You inspired me, ya know. Remember what you told me that day in the classroom? You said that I had to stop trying to please the world and do things out of my love for God. The rest would follow naturally."

He smiles with his mouth, but a hint of sadness returns to his eyes. "I'm really proud of you. I guess it works out for everyone."

Ben solemnly pauses and glances out the main window. "You'll get to see Nathan more."

"Nathan?" I look at him, confused.

"Well, I assumed you two were together."

I stop to giggle at the absurdity of the thought after the Bahamas. "Oh no." I wave my hands at him and then cover my mouth to stop another escaping giggle.

"I saw the magazines." He looks at me as if he needs an explanation.

"Ben, I'm not with Nathan. I mean, we were sort of," I say, a bit tongue-tied again. "He's just ... I mean ..." I pause and take a deep breath. "Let's just say Nathan and I are not on the same page." I struggle to get the words out. I pause and then continue. "I mean, not like you and Jessica, of course. You make a cute couple."

"Jessica?" He laughs heartily. "You thought Jessica and I are together?"

"Yes. Ben, come on—she was practically camping out at your apartment. I've never seen such a large purse. I mean, it screamed 'overnight bag.' All the phone calls, and always having to leave in the middle of something? Very strange." I roll my eyes.

"Kate." He presses his lips into a smile and attempts to interrupt. I ignore him and continue talking, not only with my mouth but also animatedly with my hands.

"It seemed the only logical conclusion is that Jessica was either your girlfriend—but can I just say she is definitely not your type?—or you are, in fact, a spy."

Ben begins to laugh even harder. I don't know whether to feel irritated or laugh with him. I just stare at him until he's finished.

Ben musses his hair with his hands. "First of all, Kate, my dear, your imagination is priceless. Second, Jessica is not my girlfriend, and third, the option of life as a spy, as thrilling as that might be, isn't for me."

"Okay. Well, who is she then?" I ask, still not satisfied by his sarcasm, folding my arms across my chest.

Ben grins widely and shakes his head. He moves in closer to my face. "Kate, she was just a client—and a very demanding one at that. There was nothing ever going on with Jessica, although she wanted there to be. I wasn't interested. I was only painting her portrait."

Right, he was painting her portrait. I'm so blind.

"Her portrait? Really? That's all?" I ask.

"Yes, that's all. I promise." Ben places his hand over his heart as if he's about to say the Pledge of Allegiance.

I'm so embarrassed that I can't respond. The brightness returns to Ben's eyes the way I remember it that first day here at the coffee shop. The corners of his mouth begin to turn upward into a huge smile. I'm waiting for him to speak, but he just continues to smile. Unexpectedly, he reaches across the table and tenderly takes both my hands in his. His face is inches away from mine, and I feel the slight hint of his minty breath tickle my nose.

"So tell me—is there anyone who you might be on the same page with, Miss Turner?"

I sigh heavily and smile, squeezing his warm, strong hands. I look up into his deep, dark eyes. "Oh, you know, possibly a tall, handsome, guitar-playing, photographer and chef who paints portraits in his spare time."

"He sounds pretty special, this guy," he says, looking at me so lovingly that I think my heart might melt underneath this sweatshirt.

"Oh, I like to think so. He's always been the one." I pause and look tenderly into his inviting brown eyes. "You've always been the one."

Ben lifts up my chin and brings his lips softly to mine. I feel as if I just ate a whole bag of Pop Rocks candy. I can feel the sweet sensation in every muscle in my body. I want to feel this way forever; however, my mind starts to wander, and the bubbly sensation abruptly comes to a halt.

"I knew it. That painting you wouldn't let me see—that was Jessica, wasn't it?"

Ben playfully rolls his eyes. "Yes. It was Jessica."

"Was she nude?"

He signs. "No, but she would've liked that," Ben says sharply, raising his eyebrows. I cross my arms and start to pout. He moves around the table and gently pulls me up into his arms.

"What does that mean?" I look at him sternly.

"That's why she was so demanding. I wouldn't paint her in the nude. It just didn't feel right, and she wasn't happy about it."

"Oh, I see."

I smile. My heart starts to beat faster. I place my hand on my chest, feeling as if I can't catch my breath. "What if some beautiful Italian girl wants you to paint her picture?"

He presses his fingers to my lips. "She'll have to find someone else to paint for her."

I do love this man.

Ben looks over at the counter. "Shelly?"

She peeks around the corner, a box of unopened napkins in her hand, her expression less than perky.

"You bellowed?" she barks back.

"I'd like to order a coffee for the lady, please."

She drops the box onto the counter and huffs loudly, "What does she want?"

He looks at me for approval, and I smile and nod.

"A nonfat macchiato, no whipped cream."

I tenderly touch his shoulder. "Wait. Could you make that with whip, please?" I politely interject.

He squeezes my hands in his. "Now, that's more like it. Shelly, you heard the lady—whipped it is."